Lola grew up in South London and has also lived in Nigeria. She has degrees in Psychology and Psychotherapy and currently works for the NHS as a counsellor. In-between writing and working, Lola likes watching reruns of *Dallas* and *The Sopranos* whilst avidly dipping into a huge tub of ice cream. *By The Time You Read This*, Lola's first novel was published in 2008. She has also written a Quick Read, *Reaching for the Stars*, published for World Book Day 2009.

Find out more about Lola and what she's been up to by visiting www.lolajaye.com

LOLA JAYE

While You Were Dreaming

HARPER

Harper
An imprint of HarperCollins*Publishers*
77–85 Fulham Palace Road,
Hammersmith, London W6 8JB

www.harpercollins.co.uk

A paperback original 2009

1

Copyright © Lola Jaye 2009

Lola Jaye asserts the moral right to
be identified as the author of this work

A catalogue record for this book is
available from the British Library

ISBN 978-0-00-726783-5

Set in Sabon by Palimpsest Book Production Limited,
Grangemouth, Stirlingshire

Printed and bound in Great Britain by
Clays Ltd, St Ives plc

Mixed Sources
Product group from well-managed
forests and other controlled sources
www.fsc.org Cert no. SW-COC-1806
© 1996 Forest Stewardship Council

FSC is a non-profit international organisation established
to promote the responsible management of the world's forests.
Products carrying the FSC label are independently certified
to assure consumers that they come from forests that are managed
to meet the social, economic and ecological needs
of present and future generations.

Find out more about HarperCollins and the environment at
www.harpercollins.co.uk/green

ACKNOWLEDGEMENTS

I'd like to thank God for everything; Mrs Sheila 'Nanno' Graham for always asking – 'how's the book going?' each time we had a natter; Claire 'Tha Editor' Bord AKA 'The Silent Assassin' (She knows which characters have to 'go' and *why*) whose natural calmness to my 'neurotic writer' is a good match!; my mum for being all proud and stuff once she found out my 'little secret'; Judith 'Tha Agent' Murdoch for allowing me the space to be 'me' (see above!) and to Linda 'Aunty Lin' Toogood for being the first 'non publishing citizen' to read WYWD and say 'what a blinding read!'

I also want to send a massive shout out to EVERYONE who has in some way, been a part of the production of this novel; family, friends, ice-cream/brownie/waffle/cheesecake makers, HarperCollins staff and............ (you know who you are, but please pop your name in the space provided!)

Lastly but clearly not least, I'd like to shout a big, heartfelt thank you/eshe/gracias to ALL my readers who have emailed and posted comments on my guestbook. They were read and totally appreciated at a time of my life that has been filled with constant 'pinch me' moments. I am still shocked that people actually *buy* my books!!!??? Wowwwww and Thank You ALL.

If friends are the family you choose –
this one's for my sisters!

PROLOGUE

I tried my best not to puke up my lunch, standing in the doorway, watching the man I was supposed to love having sex with another woman.

A cauldron of emotion sloshed about within me – disbelief, denial, anger – before the inevitable star of the show, Acceptance, finally appeared, letting me know that this was *real* and it was happening. To me. With my boyfriend and with a woman I had trusted.

If only it was possible to teleport back in time, say, to twenty minutes ago, when I was sitting in a cafe across the road, tucking into a giant piece of chocolate cake and daydreaming. Well, in fact I'd been daydreaming most of the day – in between thinking about all the massive things that needed changing in my life. Things I had previously been so scared of discussing but suddenly felt more ready than ever to talk about.

But here I stood, watching my boyfriend's Oscar-winning porn performance, and all those so-called plans began to shatter into miniature shards of hopelessness.

I felt for the notepad and yellow fluffy pen in my back pocket as a shiver sprinted through my entire body; the forgotten half-empty can of ginger beer fell from my hand, its contents spilling out over the hard wood floor. That's when they both stopped, opened their eyes and whipped their heads round, like the girl from *The Exorcist*.

'Lena?' Justin gasped, sounding like a complete stranger and not the man I'd spent the last two years with. I lifted my face up and felt my eyes betray me and begin to moisten. My mouth widened to speak, but nothing came out. I just knew that I had to get out of that flat and as far away as possible. I had never witnessed anything so painful in my entire thirty years on this earth.

Backing out of that door, my knees were ready to buckle. I reached for the banisters to support myself as Justin called out to me in a pathetic, yet desperate-sounding voice. *'Lena!'*

My legs were turning to blancmange. I had to get out of there. To refocus. To think. My mind was jabbering something incoherent and silly, as my body was too damn numb to respond. I was now moving in slow motion, heading for the stairs, placing one foot on the first step in front of me.

I needed to think.

Second step.

I needed to be alone.

Third step.

I needed space.

I suppose, in normal circumstances, I'd have noticed the sparkling sandal that clearly wasn't mine, jutting out from the fourth step and glistening in the sunlight that was pouring in from the window. I'd have kicked it out of the way in rage, or at the very least avoided it. But in my current state I wouldn't have noticed an elephant dressed in a tutu; all I could focus on was the rapid beating of my heart, very runny nose, and the tears that were now coursing down my cheeks. So I'd no chance against that sandal as it attacked my left foot and sent me flying down those stairs. My stomach juices swished about like the inside of a washing machine: porridge, plantain chips, lychees, the giant slab of chocolate cake – all conspiring together to form one big indigestible mass.

My body finally landed in a heap at the bottom of the stairs in a position that would rival any advanced yoga devotee. And then I waited. My mind entering a place where nothing could get to me any more.

I waited for the onset of pain that was sure to come.

I was ready.

Go on, hit me with it. It's not as if the day could get any worse.

My eyes slowly flickered shut like a malfunctioning antique television. I knew it was coming. It was definitely coming . . . Yes . . . it was almost here, now . . .

The pain.

So much pain.

And then. The darkness.

ONE

Cara would always remember where she was and what she was doing the day she found out about Lena.

She was where she'd always been on a Tuesday evening – serving some pig of a customer who this time was insisting she'd incorrectly handed over change for a ten-pound note when he'd actually given her a twenty.

'It was a tenner, I can assure you,' she said plainly, at the same time indulging in a fantasy that involved ramming said ten-pound note down his throat.

'I suggest you check at the till and see the last note you placed inside, Miss,' he said pompously.

Cara rolled her eyes, unable to care if he noticed. Ade was always going on about the customer always being right and, in all honesty, she'd always taken great offence to that line. This was her bar (well, hers and Ade's) and the only person who was right (in this instance especially) was her, and she was about to prove it.

She pressed the button and the till drawer opened.

'Unless it's one of those rare magical and invisible ones, it isn't here and you gave me a tenner. Would you like anything else, *sir*?' she said sharply, hoping this particular customer wouldn't be back. Ever. It wasn't as if the bar needed him. After three long years of hard slog, sleepless nights, and some tense meetings with their teenage bank manager, A&R was finally turning over a profit. Everyone, especially her sister Lena, had warned her that such a move was going to be tough and a high risk. But Cara and Ade had poured their heart and soul as well as blood, sweat, tears, and everything else they had into making it work. Even as the world seemed to be sinking into a global recession, Cara and Ade were still holding their own as East Dulwich fast became a more convenient and cheaper option to the West End. And A&R could compete with the best of the West End bars, with its relaxing and cool décor – low lighting provided by mini-chandeliers, miniature booths with cosy leather sofas, separated by diamante-encrusted muslin curtains. Away, but not too far away in Overhill Road, Cara and Ade lived in her dream flat, which had a beautiful view of what seemed like the whole of London. She was 'sorted', basically. Everything was the way it should be in her life: great boyfriend, beautiful flat, and a thriving business.

Cara ran her fingers through her short crop. She was tired and her feet were starting to ache, which was probably due to a combination of being on them all day without a break and the fact that she was wearing a new pair of satin purple high heels that she'd yet to break in. That was another thing her thriving business afforded her: a pick of shoes. She was on first-name terms with the girls in Kurt Geiger and Bertie, owned a pair of Christian Louboutin's, a pair of Sergio Rossi's and would soon be holding a beautiful pair of five-inch orange and black Gina's. The higher the shoe, the more confident she felt – especially as she was only five foot.

'Cara! Cara!' Ade was calling out to her from across the bar. His voice was urgent, impatient. This wasn't like Ade. He was always the calm to her chaos. The sweetness to her (and she could admit this) abrasiveness. What was going on with him?

'Ade?' They both started heading towards each other, almost as if they were in slow motion. Ade was clutching the cordless phone, his hand placed over the mouthpiece. 'It's for you,' he whispered with a sombre expression.

Her heart began to race. Something was up. All sorts of horrid thoughts ran through her mind. Maybe they weren't as flush as she'd thought. Maybe her business was about to fall victim to the recession after all. She could cope with anything except that. Please, no. 'Who is it?' she whispered, unable to take the phone from him.

'It's Fen Lane Hospital. They . . . they need to . . . to speak to you urgently!' He seemed to be talking in tiny bursts, breathing in short breaths, as if he'd just swum twenty lengths. His eyes were wide and alert.

Cara felt her heart leap into her stomach as she stood rooted to the spot. The Stylistics belted out 'Betcha By Golly Wow' through the state-of-the-art sound system.

'The hospital?' she repeated in a whisper that was drowned out by the music.

'It's . . . its Lena . . .' Ade said.

TWO

Millie was in the middle of what could only be described as a monumental state of bliss as one set of larger-than-average toes jutted out from the end of a very messy bed.

'Wake up sleepy!' she said, the rest of her body emerging from under the duvet. The foot stirred a bit in response and she leaned over to the side table, switching on the tiny pink digital radio. The beginning of a muffled yawn escaped from the snugness of the duvet as the silky voice of the DJ kicked in. 'We're nearing the end of drive time – here's something from back in the day!'

'Millie,' moaned the drowsy voice from inside the duvet, as 'Firestarter' blasted over the airwaves.

'Morning, handsome,' she beamed. She rarely felt this happy and complete: it made a nice change.

'What the . . .?' Rik was still half asleep; he rubbed his eyes frantically.

'It's almost evening, time to get up!' She said brightly, prising the covers away from his head and flashing him a beaming smile. Her untamed shoulder length curls bounced around her oval-shaped face.

'Mmmmm, I'm hungry,' Rik sighed. She'd been seeing

8

him for the past month and she really, really liked him . . . In fact . . . 'Any chance of some food, Mille?' he went on, twirling his hand in the air.

And then there was the way he said her name, the way he scrunched his nose just before he laughed; even his massive feet were cute. She'd fallen for him *hard* and, looking at Rik now, she knew exactly what she needed to say.

'I . . .' she began warily.

Rik leaned over to switch off her tiny pink radio – a twenty-fourth birthday present from Lena only a few months ago that matched Millie's CD player, along with the card inscription: '*To my irresponsible, loving, and beautiful little sister, Millie. Happy Birthday. You're a star. Love, Lena.*

'I'll see what's in the fridge, but it's probably going to be cold pizza from last night. Unless you want me to put together something from Lena's stash. Warning though: it's only going to be healthy stuff like aduki beans and apples. Oh, but I think I know where she keeps her secret store of Toblerone,' Millie said excitedly.

'Actually, don't worry about the food,' Rik said, suddenly changing his mind. He jumped out of bed, sliding his perfect frame into his Diesel jeans.

Her heart leapt. She wanted to say it. She really had to tell him she loved him. And *now*, before it was too late.

'Rik,' she began, realizing her lips had to move fast if she was to get the words out before he left the flat. He hardly called as it was, and they never went out to places (unless you counted the fish-and-chip shop last Saturday), so she didn't know when the next 'perfect' time would come about again. He now had his shirt in his hands, after all, and his trainers had magically slipped onto his feet; she had to work fast or else the moment would be lost.

9

She had to tell him *now*.

Now.

Now! 'I love you.'

And then silence. In fact she couldn't hear anything but the ticking of her Betty Boo alarm clock as they stood facing one another as though they were in some type of face-off, his belt unbuckled, muscular six-pack tantalizingly naked.

She bit her bottom lip nervously and waited.

Rik merely sighed and then averted his gaze to his jacket – hooked on the edge of the wardrobe door, which was itself hanging off its hinges. He slipped into his shirt, still saying nothing, and Millie grabbed the duvet, hugging it close to her as she suddenly felt quite cold.

'Aren't you going to say anything, Rik?' she asked hopefully.

'Millie, I do like you . . . But . . .'

And there it began. A jumble of words that, once strung together, all amounted to the same thing.

He. Didn't. Want. Her.

'I think we need time apart,' he muttered finally.

She pretended not to hear him, desperate to shut out the words she'd been hearing for as long as she could remember. From guys, mainly. Ex's who clearly weren't as perfect for her as Rik. And he was perfect for her. Rik, who spelt his name without a 'c'. Rik, who made her feel a lot less lonely. Rik, who looked out for her. Of course she had Lena and sometimes Cara (very rarely, Cara), but it was so nice to have someone like Rik around and she needed to remind him of just why they were so, so, so, so perfect for one another. She loved him. He was the one for her and she for him.

She needed him – didn't that count for anything?

10

So, what Millie did next came naturally.

'No, stop it Millie,' he murmured, pulling away from her tight kiss. This was futile, of course, as she was clinging onto him oh-so-desperately. Her hands digging into his arms as he attempted to extract himself from her grip and possibly from her life forever. And she couldn't have that. Not this time and not again. She didn't know if her heart could cope with yet another crack.

He gripped her shoulders firmly. 'I said no, Millie!' His voice was strong, firm, like a father telling her off, she suspected.

The mixture of pity and coldness she clearly recognized, though.

'Don't,' he said, as he gently moved her face away from him. 'Don't do this, Millie.'

A huge feeling of rejection washed over her, threatening to devour every one of her senses if she didn't begin some sort of damage limitation.

'I get it, you're knackered, I shouldn't have woken you up! Go home, get some rest and I'll see you later?' she said breathlessly, but he returned a look she couldn't quite read – or didn't want to.

'No, I don't think it's a good idea, seeing as though—'

'No! Don't say it!' she snapped, jumping off the bed and leaving the bed shaking in her wake.

'It has to be said because you clearly weren't listening earlier, Millie,' he replied gently.

She silently begged him not to say the words again. Yes, she'd heard *something* in the early hours of the morning after a lovely evening together but, as usual, her natural refusal to absorb or process any of the hurtful words had kicked in.

'It's over,' he said.

11

She placed her hands over her ears, wanting to switch the radio back on, needing to block out what he was saying to her.

'*We* are over. I thought I made myself clear before.'

She threw her hands back down. 'But, I thought—'

'You thought that if you managed to get me into bed again, have a few drinks, everything would be all right. Well, it isn't, Millie. I wanted to make sure you were all right, you know. . . . You said you wanted me to hold you, so I did and then we . . . I'm sorry. I really am.'

'So, if you're sorry, then don't do it. Please don't leave me!' Millie didn't care how desperate she sounded; she didn't want him to leave. She didn't want to get dumped *again*.

But Rik's eyed were darting frantically around her room; taking in the stained mugs, half-read magazines and lip-gloss-covered towel. Millie's mind attempted to separate and communicate the whirl of questions, answers, protestations, and pleadings that were rushing around in her head like an out-of-control carousel. 'So . . . so, are you really going?'

Rik now had his jacket on and was picking his way through the clutter of boxes that Millie had not yet unpacked since her move from the Bow bedsit, three months ago.

'This room is in such a state,' he said as he scanned his eyes over two fat bags of washing that still hadn't made it to the launderette.

'Thanks.'

'I've lost my watch, ' he said circling his left wrist. 'If you find it, can you let me know, please?'

She was glad that the place was a mess, that he'd misplaced his beloved, stupid watch. That way at least she had something of his to hold onto and he'd have to come back for it sometime. And perhaps when he did come back, she'd answer the door in that New Look chiffon minidress she'd bought a few months ago. She'd also pile on that new Rimmel mascara her mate Nikki was always going on about and, if she could afford it, she'd splash out on a trip to Monique's to get her hair straightened. Actually, on second thoughts, Rik liked her soft curls: he'd told her that once.

'So, you're really going then?' she asked, her voice breaking.

'Yes, Millie. I'm sorry. I mean, you're a great girl and everything but nothing's changed since last night. I'm sorry, Millie,' he replied, buttoning up his jacket.

And with that, he slipped out of her bedroom, quickly. And although she had pretty much used up any last scrap of dignity, all she could do now was listen as he hurried down the stairs, each step he took feeling like one more chip away at her heart.

She shut her bedroom door and sank down onto her bed. Men broke up with her all the time, but she hadn't a clue why. She was attentive, respectful, loving, sexy, and could usually pass off one of Lena's delicious dinners as her own. What was wrong with her?

She took a deep breath, wanting to pull herself together, but knowing she couldn't yet. Yes, she was twenty-four. A big girl now. And she was used to this; but, nevertheless, she was no less tired of it all. Just over two months ago, Olu informed her it couldn't, 'wouldn't work', and a month before that, Kenny stopped returning her calls. She wiped her eyes just as her mobile phone belted out a rubbish version of the theme tune to *The Simpson's*. She stood up quickly, her little toe banging against the edge of the bed.

'Owwww!' she cried as the pain shot through her body. The phone stopped ringing and she threw herself onto her bed as the tears came freely. She wasn't crying because of her toe (though that had bloody hurt!) but she sobbed for the loss of Rik and every other man she'd longed to have a relationship with.

What was wrong with her?

Both her sisters had great relationships.

Why did this only ever happen to her?

Ten minutes later, she was still crying when the phone rang again. This time she answered it.

It was her sister Cara, who normally texted her short, sharp messages – when she wasn't nagging or shouting at her, that was. Lena was the sister that always tried to keep them from decking one another. Always wanting them to 'be close'.

Being the youngest meant that Millie grew up bearing the brunt of Cara's 'jokes' when she was irritated or just bored. Like the invention of Spiralicious the sea monster, which was ready to eat her at any moment if she didn't do as Cara said. At five she'd believed ten-year-old Cara as she regularly threatened her with 'it', frightening her into doing extra chores and basically scaring the shit out of her. She'd regularly go and hide, usually under the stairs, and it was always Lena who would find her and try and convince her that Spiralicious didn't actually exist.

In fact, it was always Lena who would come to her rescue and pick up the pieces. Soothing her, comforting her, and promising her that bar of Toblerone she'd always keep under her bed.

'Hi Cara,' Millie sighed, ready to be told off for something or other.

'Are you sitting down?' said Cara, her voice uncharacteristically gentle and quiet. It sounded as if she'd been crying. Actually, she'd never heard or seen Cara cry before.

'What is it?' Millie asked, sitting up straight, suddenly terrified.

As Cara spoke, Millie gripped the phone tightly to her,

14

her chest heaving with loud, frightened sobs. She knew that by answering that call, her life had just taken a startling turn. In fact, she felt she'd do *anything* to go back in time to her childhood, find a corner and just hide, until someone told her that this new state of horror didn't actually exist.

THREE

One Week Earlier . . .

'You're my Prince Charming, dear!' Enthused, the silver-haired old lady thanking him as he handed her the last of the coins that had toppled out of her purse and onto the pavement.

'Don't worry about it, you just take care,' he said with a straight smile. Now that was a first, he thought. Prince Charming. Women usually made references to his 'lovely bushy eyebrows' (that he hated), long girly eyelashes, (which he detested) and the chiselled (chiselled?) jawline, but he'd never once been described as Prince Charming before. This was definitely a first. He rubbed his stomach consciously. A diet of greasy takeaways and fizzy drinks had meant he was beginning to develop a slight gut, but somehow he'd not plucked up the courage to take a leaflet from one of those muscly types who stood outside the station handing out 'free gym trials', probably because he just wasn't that motivated to do anything that involved leg lifts, sweat and pushy instructors. What energies he did have were reserved for trying to improve his financial situation and well, his future. He had plans and was going to stick to them. Of course he hadn't always been a 'miserable git' as his sister Charlotte sometimes liked to call him. He liked to think he had his 'moments.'

But for now he was on his way to the job he detested, where he spent the bulk of his time regularly checking sales figures on products he just didn't care about, and every 4.5 minutes checking his computer clock, which only told him he had too long to go until he was allowed back into the flat he also hated, next door to a bunch of neighbours – the noisiest neighbours in the world – that he hated almost as much as his job. So, as Michael headed towards the bus stop with a million things on his mind and, again, with a complete lack of motivation to start tackling them, he did so with a heavy heart. Of course, at thirty-one he knew he couldn't continue feeling the way he did about . . . everything. Feeling half the man he wanted to be. Feeling that anything great, any major accomplishment, seemed to be easily within the reach of others but way out of his. Everyone in his life – family, boss, mates – seemed to expect him to act like a performing seal, when all he really wanted to do was go away and get things done, his way. Not that he begrudged his family anything at all. He actually felt useful when he did odd jobs for his mother and fixed things for his sister and the kids – he just wanted a bit of a rest from some of the bad *feeling* sometimes. Just so he could focus on all the plans he had. But then his sister Charlotte would often say he had *too* much time on his hands and why didn't he go out more?

As usual, he made his way up on to the double-decker bus with his Oyster card, a part of him hoping to catch a glimpse of the girl he'd noticed just the other day.

He'd never really noticed her before. His head was normally glued to the back pages of *Metro* as he made his way to the stairs – a good tactic for blocking out the madness around him. But that day, he didn't have a paper, and when he reached the stairs, he glanced up to notice a stunning girl with the plumpest lips he'd ever seen, smiling in his direction from the back of the bus. When he smiled back, she bent her head in embarrassment. He'd noticed her eyes too. Green. But not just any green. Totally 'out there' green. They were striking against her exotic complexion, and he could tell that she was curvy rather than skin and bones. She was dressed quirkily, a multicoloured hair band holding back her big unruly hair.

It was probably a good job she'd turned away, because suddenly any grain of confidence he might have had left dissipated and he slowly lifted himself up the stairs, away from the green-eyed girl. He wanted to kick himself, but he just didn't have the courage to talk to her. She wouldn't be interested in him. He was plain old Michael Johns who lived in a rented council flat on Dog Kennel Hill Estate and who hadn't driven a car in a year. Women were supposed to love money, power, and confidence, yet Michael was all too aware that he possessed none of the above. But he did have bushy eyebrows though. And for reasons unknown to him, he'd never had much trouble attracting the ladies.

Take Jen.

Beautiful and sexy Jen. Lovely flowing hair and gorgeous shapely thighs you could die for. He'd met Jen outside Tesco's where a large (large in the muscley sense) bloke seemed to be hassling her for her number. She was rolling her eyes and checking her watch as the man seemed to reel off a 101 reasons why she should hand over her phone number to him. Michael without even thinking blurted out a loud 'Babe, there you are! Hurry up love, the kids are in the Merc causing major havoc!' as he proffered his hand. She took his hand, a plastic smile on her face, perhaps not knowing if he indeed was going to be worse than the guy she was currently trying to get away from. But taking the chance on him nevertheless.

'You saved me,' she'd said that night as they had dinner and she joked about how their fictional car had been a Merc and not a Mondeo. They'd started out as friends but then one night things went beyond the realms of purely platonic. Part of Michael wished that their friendship has stayed at just that, especially when Jen started dropping hints that she was ready for a proper relationship. And for a while, he allowed his ego to sing at the thought of this beautiful girl wanting him, but soon fear began to take him over. Their 'relationship' could never go further anytime soon. For a start, what could he offer her?

Now, sitting on the bus, Michael decided to make a little detour into Camberwell and pay Jen a visit. Perhaps the green-eyed girl had stirred him up a bit because it was very rare for him to call Jen from work and say, 'Can I come over, tonight?' It was usually Jen calling him up and telling him how much she needed him.

He buzzed the intercom and, as always, Jen was ready and waiting at the door for him as soon as he reached the top of the communal staircase. But instead of appearing in the silky black and gold pyjamas she normally changed straight into as soon as she got home, she was still in her work clothes, a sharp-looking trouser-and-waistcoat combo.

'Hi,' she said. She smelt delicious. He reached over to kiss her, but she shifted her head slightly.

'You look nice. And you smell good too. All peachy.'

'Papaya, actually.'

Jen didn't say much as she disappeared into the kitchen and emerged with two plates on which sat an 'M&S special', accompanied by a tub of hummus, even though she knew he hated the stuff.

Michael began to eat, feeling her eyes boring into him. It would have felt unnerving if he hadn't been so hungry.

They hardly spoke during the meal, and no sooner had he finished his last mouthful than she reached over to clear his plate. He attempted to circle her waist with his hands but she removed them slowly.

'We need to talk, Michael.'

He shifted uncomfortably in his chair.

'This is serious.'

She dragged her chair closer to his. 'Where are we going?' she asked, forcing him to make eye contact.

'I'm not sure what you mean.'

'You know what I mean.'

He knew all too well. They'd been here once before, yes, he remembered now – about a year ago.

'You said six months.'

'I know . . .'

'That was two years ago, Michael.'

Two years? 'Are you sure?'

'I'm sure,' she replied sharply. 'I've known you for three years now.'

He hadn't realized it had been that long.

'"Just give me another six months or so to sort myself out," you said. "Then we can be a couple."'

Michael felt utterly and totally in a bind. At the time he was sure he'd meant it. Hoping to have improved his living/job/financial status somewhat, but, as that had yet to materialize, well . . .

'Well?' she folded her arms, and Michael swallowed. 'I need to know we are going somewhere. That this . . . this *relationship*, if you can call it that, is leading us to something bigger . . .'

'I just need time,' he said.

'Yeah, another few months,' said Jen, clasping her arms even tighter.

'What's wrong with that?'

'Because when is it ever going to be the right time? You seem to think we have all the time in the world! That when *you* decide you are ready, things will just snap into place!'

Sounded feasible to him.

'I think I need to wake up and realize that I'm not it, am I?' she said quietly, her voice trembling slightly. Michael hoped she wasn't about to cry. He couldn't handle that.

'What aren't you?'

'I'm not The One. If I was, you wouldn't need to make all these excuses, we'd just be together. It shouldn't be this hard, Michael.' She sighed heavily.

'You know I don't believe in all that "The One" stuff, Jen. Come on . . .' He extended his arm in a warm gesture, but she just looked at him blankly.

'Just think about what I'm saying, Michael.'

He looked at Jen and knew that if he began to explain, she just wouldn't understand.

'Michael, I am not getting any younger – neither of us are. And I'm sick of waiting. For some reason you seem to think we have all the time in the world. Newsflash: We don't!'

'Jen—'

'I'm sick of you coming round here when you please, without a thought for me. I don't even have a toothbrush at your flat! You don't even like me coming over!'

Because, he wanted to reply, my flat could double up as a rubbish tip and I'd much rather you didn't see it. Especially as you own your own flat, drive a decent car *and* buy your hair stuff from Selfridges! Whilst I don't have anything to give you really. Nothing of value. Not at the moment anyway, but someday. Soon. Definitely.

Yes, when he got his act together, things would be different and only then would he begin to live the life he'd always craved – now he just had to tell Jen that, knowing that he'd probably sound like a commitment-phobe.

She continued. 'And I've only met your family twice. Both times in the supermarket. By accident!'

'Well it's not as if we're in a proper re—'

The expression on her face switched to frightened anguish . . . and so he shut up.

'What did you say?' Her eyes squinted and then widened just as quickly. 'What am I doing?' she said to herself with a hint of resolution.

She ran her hands through her hair as if to physically get her head straight.

'What *am* I doing?' she reiterated.

'Jen . . .'

'Michael, please leave,' she then said, her demeanour suddenly composed.

'Jen, I'm sorry,' he said, meaning it. Making her all upset was never part of the plan; he still cared about her after all.

'No, I'm sorry. It's over, Michael.'

As he walked the short walk from the bus stop to his flat, he realized that, whilst he'd hated hurting Jen, he couldn't shake off the huge feeling of relief he'd felt ever since she'd said; 'It's over,' just over thirty minutes ago. They'd hugged, she'd stuffed a couple of gifts he'd given her into his pocket, and they'd said their goodbyes like the civilized human beings they were. It felt right. And if it felt right, then it must be . . . right. Jen was a nice enough girl and he really hoped she would find someone else. A bloke who would appreciate her more and be able to give her what she needed. And she would, he was sure of that. In fact, he had to believe that, otherwise he'd feel like the biggest bastard ever to have walked the streets of South-East London.

So, he was free to focus on what really counted at the moment: getting a promotion, moving out of the flat and into his own home; oh, and mustering up the motivation to put those wheels into some type of credible motion.

And he would find it.

Somewhere.

He hoped.

FOUR

Two and a half weeks later . . .

'She just looks asleep to me,' said Ade.

'Peaceful,' said the nurse.

'Do you think so?'

'Serene even,' she added.

'I've never seen her look so beautiful.'

'Oh, give me a break! She looks far from beautiful hooked up to a tube and I'd much prefer it if you stopped talking about her like she's dead! She's just been asleep for a while, that's all!' Eleven days, actually. 'And she's not going to be here much longer, either. Doesn't anybody get that?' Now Cara was feeling irritated. Again. In fact her moods switched from hopeful, to hopeless, to frightened, to angry, and all the way through to irritated. She was beginning to forget who she was.

'No, you're right,' said Ade awkwardly as the nurse with the northern accent shifted nervously on her feet, as if to say, 'who are you trying to kid? The longer this girl stays like this, the worse it will be for her when she finally comes round.'

24

But Cara knew different. She knew that Lena would soon be out of that manky bed and safely following her round a branch of Kurt Geiger ready to spell out the disadvantages of spending £150 on a pair of killer heels when half of that money could be used to buy a couple of goats for a third world village. Then they'd go to Lena's favourite cheapo noodle bar off Old Compton Street where Millie would show up late with no money and Cara would turn her nose up at every limp and greasy dish, wishing she was in her favourite local Thai restaurant instead, with its nicely dressed waitresses and dishes that sounded like islands. They'd eat, then chat for a bit, before each rushing off to start their night shifts: Cara at the bar, Millie off out with her mates (along with a loan from Lena), and Lena to the kids' telephone helpline where she had worked for the past four years. Funny, the last time the three of them had managed to get together at the Noodle Bar was just before the accident.

Cara turned her gaze away from her sister lying on that bed, hair in a multicoloured Alice band, and gazed around the hospital room. She hated hospitals, she decided. Luckily she hadn't had much to do with them over the years, apart from the obligatory visit when one of her friends had a kid. She'd rush in, armed with flowers and a teddy bear (which Ade had bought), counting the minutes until she could leave.

This time, though, she was going nowhere.

She'd been in every day for almost two weeks now and was getting used to the sight of people rushing about armed with flowers, their faces painted with worry, fresh-faced junior doctors with spiky hair studying charts, consultants swanning about with an air of self-assured arrogance. She was a part of that now, and not just some bystander who'd happened to tune into a rerun of ER. This was real life. This was her life. For now.

Thankfully, her sister's hospital room was away from everything and looked clean at least. But it was bland and lifeless. There was a small window and a tiny side-cabinet on which stood a small vase containing a less-than-fresh arrangement of flowers, lemongrass oil moisturizer for Lena's hair, Vaseline for her lips, cocoa butter, a plastic comb, and a box of pink and yellow tissues.

The walls were a beigy neutral colour and a faded picture of a Victorian bloke with a huge nose hung on one of the walls – an attempt to bring some cheeriness into the room.

'We need to stay positive, yes. We *have* to.' Ade's voice interrupted her thoughts. She hated that he didn't sound convinced. Was she the only one who knew her sister would soon wake up? The doctors were hopeful. Lena was breathing for herself. Things had improved. Okay, stayed the same – but *she* was hopeful, and she didn't need anybody telling her different or she wouldn't be responsible for her actions. People needed to stay positive. For Lena. For her . . .

Time at the hospital involved sitting by the bed, willing Lena to wake up, and trying to work out how this had all happened. Why her sister was asleep on an alien bed underneath a picture of some bloke they didn't even know the name of. Why, why, why? She knew it was doing no good asking such questions, but it just felt easier to turn her thoughts into anger and then direct them at a certain person. Justin. Lena's boyfriend, who was, as far as she knew, the last person to see her *awake*. She swallowed hard, and tried to push him from her mind. He'd keep.

Instead, she thought about the bar and when she could put in a shift. This was important for two reasons: 1. She would probably go mad with all the things festering in her mind as she sat by the bed every moment of every day, thinking about the whys and the what-ifs; 2. The barmaid Eliza (Doolittle), currently left in charge with Ade, would probably bring them one step closer to bankruptcy, what with the amount of glasses she got through in a day. So, no, going back to work by no means meant she was giving up on Lena, no matter what that tiny voice in her head kept on saying. She'd do a few shifts, whilst still coming to the hospital every single day to see her sister.

Cara ran a beautifully manicured hand through her short crop and wondered where on earth her other sister – Millie – had got to. She was meant to be here by now and was late.

'I thought your sister was supposed to be here?' Nurse Gratten remarked, as if reading her thoughts. Cara ignored her and peered at her watch again, wondering where indeed her irresponsible little sister had got to. Or rather, into whose bed she'd climbed.

'Cara . . .' began Ade in a 'I want to chastise you like a little kid for ignoring the lovely nurse, but we're in a public place and oh, I should know better than to try that, if I *ever* want to share a bed with you again' voice.

'Ade', Cara interrupted him, 'this is the third time she's been late. Doesn't she get it? Lena's stuck in here and yet that doesn't seem like a big enough disaster to force her to get her act together. She's such a kid!'

'Don't upset yourself.'

'I can't get any more upset! We've a bar to run and she can't just swan in when she feels like it!' she snapped. She was aware she was taking her feelings out on the wrong person, but she also knew Ade could take it. They'd been together for over ten years; he knew her ways. And he knew how much she loved him.

'She'll be here,' whispered Ade into her ear, his taut, strong arms enveloping her in a hug. At well over six foot tall, Ade was strong enough to hold onto her, whether she resisted or not. But it was as if she needed to resist in order to fully appreciate what he was offering: love, protection, safety.

27

He held onto her before she managed to pull away from him and turn her gaze back to Lena and the situation as a whole.

Actually, the whole situation was ridiculous. Lena, the most careful person in the whole world – she wrote lists, for Pete's sake! – tripping over a shoe, indeed (a bloody shoe?)! Falling down the stairs. Ending up in this hospital bed. Hard to believe, yet it was all so very, very real. The doctors had tried everything they could but nothing seemed to be working with Lena. And, as each day passed, she could see the doctor with the bad teeth becoming ever more doubtful as her sister remained in that deep sleep, fed by a nasogastric tube, the odd reflex action reminding family and friends gathered around that she was actually still alive.

'Damn it. Damn all of it. That shoe. Justin, for being a crap boyfriend and not looking out for her! What was he thinking?' she said hoarsely.

'Let's all just calm down a bit,' said Nurse Gratten, as Cara made a mental note to put in a complaint about her as soon as Lena was discharged from this dump of a hospital. About what, she wasn't yet sure, but someone had to pay for this. Of course she knew she was sounding irrational, but nothing felt rational any more.

'There's a lot of research that says Lena can hear everything you're saying, so try and keep it . . .' She looked towards them, and perhaps remembering her place, relaxed a bit. 'Let's all stay calm, for Lena. She needs us all to be strong.'

Friends and colleagues of Lena had trickled in to the hospital in the first week to see her, but Cara had found it difficult to converse with the unfamiliar faces. Eventually, they stopped coming. Who could blame them, though? They had their lives to lead. The only people Lena needed were her two sisters and Ade – everyone else (and that included the handful of aunties that resided in Southampton) were mere acquaintances. So nowadays, in Lena's room, all she could expect was the sound of her own voice as she muttered words of encouragement to her sister or the clicking tap-tap of shoes travelling up and down the corridor outside the room. Whenever she, Ade, and Millie sat together, none of them really knew what to say. No one really wanting to look at Lena because to look at her would make it all seem real.

Ade rushed off to get her a coffee whilst Nurse Gratten muttered something about seeing to the other patients – and at last Cara was alone with her beloved sister in that room.

Just the way she preferred it.

Cara clutched her hand. Lena's nails were uneven and cracked. A stark contrast to her own manicured fingers. She wasn't going to cry – no, she'd never do that, but that didn't stop her fantasizing about what it would be like to just lose herself into a dark, dark place, away from the hospital, where she'd be free to just release a plethora of emotion, and perhaps even let a few tears flow. But she wasn't sure what that would look like, how it would feel . . . and she'd learnt a long time ago that showing weakness and emotion was never product-ive. She had to keep it together. For Lena's sake and for her own.

'How are you, sis?' she said. She often spoke to Lena when no one was around. She wasn't quite sure why, but she figured if Nurse Gratten was right about the research then Lena could perhaps hear and if she could . . . well, she might want to hear her sister Cara's voice.

Cara racked her brain and wondered what she should talk about. She'd long since run out of 'niceties' days ago – and she now longed to tell Lena all about her worries and her fears. But if she did that then she'd be waiting for Lena to solve everything – something she'd always done in the past. Petty things like small rows with Ade, bar stuff, or that 'crisis' she'd had when she'd forgotten her car keys and Lena had

had to leave work to drop the spare set off at the bar. At the time, such issues seemed like the most important thing in the world and now . . . they were nothing.

She sighed deeply, recalling the day she'd just picked up her new souped-up coffee-coloured Mini from Kentish Town, complete with black leather seats, alloy wheels and built-in sat nav. It had to be one of the last times she'd seen Lena. Cara had picked her up for a trip to Tesco's but her main motivation had been to show the car off to her sister. Yet predictably, Lena wasn't that impressed (commenting on how the twenty grand she'd paid for it could have fed a million people, or something). Lena was going on about some bloke she'd met on the bus into work, talking about the possibility of changing her route because of him. Yet, Cara couldn't recall if the man was harassing her or what. She just couldn't remember much about that time, more concerned with bragging about her new car and latest pair of killer heels. Things that just didn't matter now. She squeezed her eyes shut, willing herself to remember in more detail what they had spoken about that day. The man. What Lena had wanted to eat that night – anything that could make her feel more connected to Lena; because, at that moment, she'd never felt more alone.

She wracked her brain, but all she could recall was Lena buying a birthday card and then guiltily she heard her own voice, complaining about the bar, talking about herself and not listening at all to Lena.

Surely it hadn't been that way?

Cara squeezed her sister's hand. Typical Lena Curtis, always thinking of others. Every time someone's birthday came around (and they seemed to be on a continual loop), or a kid popped into the world, Lena was always the first with a card, a gift, and a kind word. She never forgot anything or anyone. She seemed to live by her lists. Always planning stuff and scribbling away in her beloved notebook. On numerous occasions,

Cara had pointed out the existence of a diary and memo function on her phone, but no, Lena insisted on writing things down. She hated to forget anything.

Bet *this* wasn't on the list, big sis, thought Cara sadly as she gazed towards Lena. Her Corkscrew high-lighted curls were still radiant in the light. Once as a teenager, Lena had dyed bits of her hair blue. Her cheeky sense of fun was totally at odds with her sensible self. Yes, Lena was the sensible one, whilst Cara took risks. Millie however . . . well Millie was just Millie.

Ade returned with the coffee. 'I just got a call back from that hotel in Brazil.'

'Oh right,' she replied with a yawn.

'Your mother's already moved on from there and gone elsewhere.'

'Where to?'

'I don't know. Maybe she's gone to stay with a friend? Does she know any one in Rio de Janeiro? São Paulo?'

'How should I know? I mean, how hard is it to find one pensioner?'

'Brazil's a big place, babe.'

She knew what Ade was thinking. In his head, he was imagining his own close-knit 'can't fart without the other knowing' family. They regularly got together, phoned each other, and knew exactly what everyone was doing. This felt alien to Cara. If one of Ade's family was ever in trouble, the whole clan would gather immediately to sort things out. She knew he found it difficult to comprehend how she could not have taken down the address of her mother's hotels as she gallivanted around Brazil. But the truth was, the only person who would have bothered would have been Lena.

'I hope she gets back soon. She'll be devastated to know Lena's been like this for almost two weeks without her knowing,' he sighed.

'Don't bank on it. This is just typical behaviour for her, putting herself first. Even when her daughter's in hospital, she just can't be bothered,' Cara burst out, then immediately felt guilty. Lena didn't need to hear that.

'We'll find her okay?' assured Ade, gently rubbing her tense shoulder.

But Cara turned back to look at her sister and felt more than a little bit hopeless.

FIVE

'MILLIE!!!'

'Huh? Cara?' said Millie into her mobile phone as she switched off the vacuum cleaner.

'I've been calling you for the last half an hour!'

'I was hoovering.'

'Now I know you're lying!'

'I *was!*' protested Millie.

'I don't care! Just get your skinny arse over to the hospital, right NOW!'

'Has something happened?' She froze.

'We've been waiting for you for ages and Ade and I have to get to the bar!'

'Oh that.' She wondered why the poxy bar couldn't just wait. Surely Lena was more important?

'I'm sorry, Cara, I forgot,'

'That your sister's in hospital?'

'No! Of course not!' Millie really wished she could stand up to Cara, just this once.

'Get down here, Millie!'

Her heart sank at the thought of another 'shift' at the

hospital. It wasn't that she resented going, it was so much more than that.

She packed the vacuum cleaner away and pushed a pile of magazines under her bed. She'd tidied up her room the best she could and made a slight dent on the lounge, which in Lena's absence had begun to resemble a pigsty. Cara was right about one thing – she didn't do cleaning. But with all that was going on, it really helped to keep busy – especially as she still didn't have a job. Besides. Lena would need a clean house to come home to. So, perhaps in a day or two, she'd even tackle the bathroom, spare room, and maybe even the kitchen. Lena's room would remain the same, though, just as she'd left it. In fact, Millie hadn't been in that room since Lena's accident.

She freshened up and slid into a pair of skinny jeans, running a tube of lip gloss over her full lips. She looked good. Presentable. Sexy even. And her arse was far from skinny – more shapely and firm, apparently, judging from the reaction of the builders renovating the house a few doors down. Millie grabbed her handbag off the floor and glanced round proudly at her almost tidy bedroom. The place definitely needed a dust – now if she could only find out where Lena kept that huge green feather duster she used every Sunday as she listened to her MP3 player, singing at the top of her voice. Millie giggled, picturing the image in her head – Lena wasn't the greatest singer!

As she turned to leave, Millie caught the glimmer of something shimmery on top of the television and spotted Rik's watch. He'd have to come back now, she thought, with a lurch of excitement.

Millie blocked out Cara's whingeing as she placed a finger softy onto Lena's cheek. It wasn't cold. She always expected it to be.

'Are you even listening to me, Millie?' questioned Cara. She'd been moaning about her lateness and how she needed to be at the bar, blah, blah, blah. Millie could never win with Cara.

'I am listening,' she replied with a sigh. Actually, Millie had been trying to remember the last telephone conversation she'd had with Lena, but she couldn't. Had it been after her shopping spree at the pound shop, when Lena had called to see if she was all right because she'd been stood up by Rik the night before? No . . . it was some time after that in the form of a text. Yes, that was it. Lena had done a load of shifts at Kidzline, one after the other, whilst Millie had been spending quite a bit of time at Rik's. Their paths weren't crossing much, even though they lived in the same house, but Millie remembered Lena sending a text one day just before the accident. She'd read and deleted it straight away, though, because her phone was running out of memory space, which had been taken up with all the texts she'd kept of Rik's. Now, she felt her throat constrict as she remembered with absolute clarity what it had said: *I miss you, little sis. Lets have breakfast sometime!*

She suddenly began to recall all the times she'd ignore her sister's calls and texts when she'd decided to go AWOL because of some guy. Yet, when she got kicked out of her bedsit, Lena had been the first one there for her whilst Cara had just berated her for being so irresponsible. And when each and every boyfriend dumped her, Lena was the one to hold her, smooth down her soft curls, wet with tears, and tell her that everything was going to be all right. Just like when they were kids.

'I just wish this hadn't happened,' Millie said helplessly. She waited for a dig from Cara, who actually surprised her for once.

'Don't we all,' she said wearily as they both stared at Lena, as if the joint force of their stare could magically force her eyes open and they would once again see those beautiful emeraldy-green sparklers. To think, as a child, Millie believed they made her older sister look like an alien.

'Hurry up and get out of this . . . Please. I – we – need you, Lena.' She placed a hand on her sister's arm but, instead of being overcome with the usual sadness, Millie was gripped by a new but just as powerful emotion that swished about inside of her; holding on so possessively, she missed a few breaths.

Guilt.

What Cara felt, she didn't know, but for her, it was definitely guilt.

The sprawling four-bedroomed house on Underhill Road was where they had grown up and spent their entire childhoods. It had a wooden gate at the front of a small garden that matched most of the other houses on the street. Now though, it seemed to stand out more, as the Curtis household was one of the few that had retained the original layout, as most of the others had been converted into flats.

Now, without Lena, the house felt incredibly lonely. Admittedly, since moving in again, it had only been the two of them – once the lodger Meg had moved on – but Lena had this ability to make it seem like the house was full again. She was like a huge rainbow of light, with flashes of stars sprinkling all around whenever she walked into a room. Not just because of her eyes, but the mad hair, often bunched into a hairband or up in a ponytail (which Millie hated). She always seemed to be in that suede gilet with the fur trim, multicoloured scarf, jeans skirt or bootcut jeans and those massive Uggs she seemed to live in; not because they were fashionable, but because they were comfy. How Millie hated those boots! Millie scrolled down to 'Lena' on her mobile, and called the number for the third time, waiting to hear her sister's answerphone message.

'Hi, it's Lena. Leave a short message and I will get back to you. Thanks for calling. Bur bye!'

She dialled again.

'Hi, it's Lena. Leave a short message and I will get back to you. Thanks for calling. Bur bye!'

And again.

'Hi, it's Lena. Leave a short message and I will get back to you. Thanks for calling. Bur bye!'

She'd called the number every day for the past week, hoping that Lena might actually answer with a noisy laugh, claiming a well-deserved victory in the biggest wind-up ever, admitting that the last two weeks had been a joke.

Millie scrolled down to 'S' on her phone. No, she wouldn't. Not yet. In fact, she was going to do everything in her limited power NOT to do THAT this time. So what if her sister was in a deep sleep? Or that she was alone, jobless and without a boyfriend? She was not going 'there'.

She glanced around her room, which was now neat enough after the overdue trip to the launderette, the rest of her clothes now packed into her wardrobe and out of the suitcases they'd lived in ever since she'd got thrown out. That hadn't been *her* fault, though – she'd defaulted on a couple of months' rent because her benefit had stopped when she'd found a job. No one had bothered to tell her she'd have to start paying full rent *immediately*, had they? Lena had bailed her out of that mess by letting her stay after the lodger had left. As always, Lena had been there for her. And, as usual, she'd repaid her by not helping out around the house or even attempting to cook a meal with which to present Lena after one of her long and demanding shifts at Kidzline. Sometimes she didn't get home until 11 p.m.

Millie smiled bitterly, knowing that she would actually give everything she owned just to have Lena back here, nagging at her to do the washing-up or clean the hair out

37

of the plughole in the bath. She missed her sister furiously scribbling away in that little notebook of hers. She missed the way that they could never walk past a charity shop without Lena wanting to wander in and look at a rusty old mirror or a Victorian tea set whilst Millie would much rather drop into Peacock's or New Look.

She missed everything about her big sister and, lying in her bed alone in the house, Millie had never felt more lonely in her entire life.

Cara on the other hand was currently experiencing the luxury of 'forgetting' – albeit temporarily, as she rushed about the bar, in chef/barmaid/boss mode. Mixing June bugs, Mojitos and Caipirinhas; making sure table six got their bar-food platter and keeping one eye on Eliza. So not until the end of her first full shift back, when the bar was locked up for the night and she drove the short distance home, did she begin to think about Lena. She felt a little guilty at this, as she flashed her security pass and the gate opened to let the car through. Shouldn't she be thinking of Lena 24/7?

Ade was home and, judging by the smell, had prepared something delicious. She slipped out of her 'bar clothes' and changed into the pretty silk pyjamas that Ade had bought her two Valentines ago. She hoped he wouldn't see this as a signal for any midnight loving – she was knackered. Her body had got used to the lack of pace and she needed time to readjust.

'Have you spoken to Justin, lately?' asked Ade as they settled on their huge comfy sofa.

'No, I haven't. Why should I?'

'Because he's Lena's boyfriend. We should be supporting him.'

'Don't start, Ade, I've had a long day.'

'I'm just saying. We should be there for him.'

'Why? You've never got on with him,' she said, tucking her tiny feet under her.

'Of course I do!'

'Only when you found out he was into basketball. How many men in this country are? You had no choice.'

'He's Lena's boyfriend, Cara.'

'You think I'm going to forget that? Luckily, he is such a coward, I hardly ever see him at the hospital.'

'That's just his way of dealing with it.'

'Ade, I really hate the way he treated Lena. He always took her for granted, for a start. Lena mentioned a couple of times that it was really getting her down.'

'What did she say?'

Cara cast her mind backwards, finding it funny that she could not remember any recent stuff but incidents from months before – that was easy . . .

It had been a particularly busy night at A&R. Some blokes had decided to start their stag night there, which meant all hands on deck, especially as Ade was at his mum's doing some errand. Lena had bounced in, all smiles, asking for her usual ginger beer, ice and a slice of lemon.

'Hold on a sec, sis, just need to serve that table these beers. Give me one second,' said Cara, expertly placing four bottles of beers between her fingers.

'Come on, darling, give us a dance!' leered one of the blokes.

'You're in the wrong place, mate. But I'm sure Spearmint Rhino can oblige,' she replied as politely as she could.

'I like my girls tiny and sweet, like you!' he replied, which was fine, save for the hand on her thigh.

She moved her face close to his and whispered in his ear as the crowd seemed to erupt in 'wey – heys' and guffaws. 'If you don't take your manky little hand off my thigh, the heel of my stiletto will connect nicely with your tiny little balls. Understand?' she smiled as he pulled away and his hand quickly retreated from her thigh. 'Right, anything else boys?'

Lena was still seated on one of the stools and had finished the ginger beer.

'Want another?'

'No thanks. I would like some advice though.'

'On . . .?'

'Relationships . . . And keeping them alive,' added Lena.

'Well, I just tell Ade what to do and he does it.' Cara said playfully.

'I'm serious, Cara! Me and Justin have been drifting apart lately. It's like he doesn't even notice I'm in the room sometimes. He's always working and I know I can be just as bad . . . but I wish he'd just talk to me . . .'

Eliza appeared with a worried look. 'Someone's been sick in the Gents',' she announced.

'Then clean it up! Isn't that what I pay you for?' Cara said irritably.

'Erm, I tried but . . .'

'I'll do it! Look Lena, can we finish this conversation later?'

'But I'm planning a special dinner for Justin later. I just wanted a few pointers, you know, on being extra romantic.'

'You'll be fine. Listen can I call you later? Sorry sis.'

'He was always taking her for granted,' said Cara angrily, deep down knowing that maybe she was no better. 'And she didn't deserve that. Now if you don't mind, I don't want to talk about that loser on my night off.'

'All right.'

She knew it wasn't 'all right', but Ade knew better than to contradict her on the subject of Lena's boyfriend. She just didn't like him. And no sweet words from Ade would change that. In fact, knowing just how bad Justin had been as a boyfriend made her appreciate Ade more. Ade was gorgeous. Well, certainly the most gorgeous man *she'd* ever seen. Perfection inside and out and she loved him with everything she had, knowing she'd have sunk without a murmur over the last two weeks, if it hadn't been for him. He was a part of her family, well, what was left of it. Both her parents were now enjoying new lives that didn't seem to involve her, Millie, or Lena. Their father had moved to America about ten years ago, as soon as the ink was dry on the divorce papers, and was now living it up with his new family. Millie and Lena had maintained a bit of contact in the beginning, but that all stopped eventually – he just didn't want to know. As for their mother – there was still no word from her as she currently gallivanted around Brazil. Ever since she'd moved to Southampton five years ago, it was as if she'd rediscovered her youth, jetting off all over the world. Of course remortgaging her house and leaving poor Lena to pay the ensuing bills allowed her to do that.

Cara got up and padded into their bathroom, a beige and cream marble affair that she'd insisted should look identical to the one in the show house they had seen. The only thing missing was the His 'n' Hers washbasin. She peered at herself in the large mirror. Her hair would soon need trimming, but it still looked okay; her eyebrows were a perfect arch shape. To the outside world she was the Boss Lady Cara – not to be messed with and always able to deal with whatever life threw at her.

When she returned to the living room, Ade was lying patiently on the couch and she curled up in his arms and twisted her head round to look up at his smile. She loved him so much and thought back over the last few days to how spiteful she'd been to him. She'd taken out her hurt and anger on Ade and suddenly Cara felt bad about that.

Her mind drifted back to a few weeks ago; she was sitting

on the very same couch waiting for her dinner to cook, thinking how lucky she was to have almost everything she'd ever desired.

Now, though there was a great big gaping hole in her life. A space that could only be filled by Lena.

SIX

The sun was shining over the inhabitants of Dog Kennel Hill Estate and for a moment, Michael let the warmth of it spread across his face, cheering him momentarily before he realized how heavy-headed he felt due to yet another broken night of sleep.

In the past, Michael had found a strange type of reassurance in knowing how his day would start, proceed, and end, and he'd no reason to believe today would be any different (unless of course he saw the girl on the bus again). Basically his working day would be as follows; arrive at the building with just over eight minutes to spare, pass the elderly security guard, catch the lift to the second floor, ignore the receptionist's plastic smile, and be at his desk on time and ready to be part of the (at times mundane) working day. For the most part, he would do as he was told and give the minimum standard of service. This wasn't to say he was a bad worker – more average. Working to rule and not going beyond any calls of duty. If a problem arose, he'd deal with it efficiently and with a smile, pretending the sales figures in front of him were the most important thing in his life. At one o'clock sharp, he could be found eating lunch in one of the overpriced cafes across the road. He'd perhaps buy a tabloid if he'd finished with the *Metro* on the way in and then get annoyed at the story of yet another overpaid 'celebrity' flaunting their wealth. The remainder of work time was spent clock-watching, working and peeking a look at holiday websites. Back home at his flat, after he had picked up a take-away, he would doze in front of the television, remote control in hand, knowing he wouldn't be getting a good night's sleep that night's whilst trying not to worry about it.

The one saving grace in his life seemed to be his sister Charlotte and her two kids, but at times even *she* would make him feel on a downer. Of course it wasn't her fault. It was just that when he saw how hard she struggled to bring up two kids on her own, it irked him massively that he couldn't put his hand in his pocket and really help her out. Bung her some cash to pay the latest set of bills or give her a few hundred pounds to go away with the kids for a break. He was a totally useless brother and seeing Charlotte and the kids just seemed to amplify his inadequacies. However, he'd promised to fix the light switch in George's bedroom and he was sure he could do that much.

'Glad you came over; the kids miss you!' his sister said warmly as soon as he entered the house.

'How are the little ankle-biters anyway?'

'My beloved children are great. Actually George has been playing up lately and I kind of hoped . . .'

Michael hated it when Charlotte expected him to act as disciplinarian to her four-year-old son George.

'What's the matter?' he asked, hoping it didn't sound too much like a whine.

'The matter is, when he's with his father, he's as good as gold. But when he gets back home to me, he's a complete sod.'

'I'll have a word with him.' Or perhaps just buy him a packet of chocolate buttons, Michael said to himself. He didn't want to 'discipline' the little man any more than he desired a teeth extraction. What the kid really needed was his dad around – even Michael could see that or even just a male to look up to . . . Once things got better for Michael, he'd take George every other weekend and they could have a boy's night in, hitch up a tent in front of the telly and pretend to hunt dinosaurs. But for now, he never wanted George setting foot in his dingy flat in Dog Kennel Hill. He'd have to wait until he bought a house. Perhaps one with a garden and they could go camping for real. He couldn't wait for that!

For the time being, Michael did manage to mumble a few things to George that sounded mildly stern, confining him to his room as punishment, satisfied with his work until he remembered that said room contained a box full of toys and possibly a bag of Haribos.

Uncle duty done, Michael headed back to Charlotte and Serena in the lounge.

'Did you sort him out?'

'Yes, I did,' he replied, sitting on the sofa and absently sorting through the pile of magazines on the side table. Charlotte was forever reading self-help books, magazines, basic tosh.

'So, you've finished with Jen then?'

'Yes,' he replied, as his eyes glanced over a couple of psychology magazines.

'So, you're a commitment-phobe?'

'No, Charl.' Michael picked up a day-old newspaper from the sideboard, revealing a stack of papers and leaflets beneath it including some money-off coupons for Tesco and an Argos catalogue followed.

'You were together with Jen all that time and I didn't even meet her! Oh I take that back – I saw her in the supermarket once!'

'It wasn't anything personal,' he insisted, to no avail. He knew Charlotte had already made up her mind. He was used to Charlotte analysing him every time he came to visit.

'Mumma!' wailed fourteen-month-old Serena again and again, repeating it in blocks of ten, effectively drowning out Charlotte's voice.

'Yes, I know it's your new word, but I'm trying to speak to your uncle!' laughed Charlotte. 'I can't believe she now calls me Mumma instead of just Dadda. Result!'

'It is,' said Michael, genuinely touched by his niece.

'And you, my love, have a stinky nappy,' she said, lifting Serena's bottom in the air and sniffing it. Charlotte headed out of the room, her daughter tucked under her arm.

The silence did not last long. 'Hello, Uncle Mike, Mummy says I can come back,' said George, walking in, looking remarkably composed after his 'telling off'. 'You dropped this,' he added as he bent to pick up a small card.

'Must have slipped out from one of the magazines. Your mum has loads of them.'

'She said when Dr Phil comes back on, she won't read lots. What's Dr Phil?'

Michael shrugged as he took the card from George.

'Your sister's asleep in her cot, so keep the noise down,' said Charlotte when she returned. 'Knocked out by her own pong, that one. Now where were we?'

Michael was busy studying the orange card – for Kidzline, a children's charity – and felt a pang of familiarity as he flipped over the card and studied the caption: '*Only a phonecall away*'.

SEVEN

Cara sat on a bench, overlooking the entrance to the hospital.

Ade had given Cara the warning that her mother was on her way. He'd even predicted how long it would take the taxi to arrive from the airport – and he'd been almost spot-on. The black cab pulled up outside Fen Lane Hospital and Cara watched as a woman, just a bit taller than herself, stepped elegantly out of the vehicle like a movie star at a premiere. But instead of the paparazzi flashes, the sky lit up with small bolts of lightning. Instead of the roar of an adoring crowd, there was the wailing of an ambulance siren getting louder and louder as it approached Accident and Emergency. The woman was in her sixties, but looked at least fifteen years younger, complete with a sassy walk of someone half her age.

'Keep the change, darling,' she said to the taxi driver in a fake posh accent, smoothing down her bobbed hair.

From the bench Cara was sitting on, she could tell the cabbie was delighted as he placed the shiny silver case and black weekend bag onto the pavement with a cheeky wink.

'Thanks, luv,' he said.

The woman pulled out a mirror and lipstick from a tiny

silvery handbag and applied a fresh coat. She then looked down at her flat black shoes and grimaced; perhaps missing the feel of a good pair of stilettos against her feet, the way they automatically shaped calves into something sexy and alluring. Possibly the one thing Cara would ever agree on with her.

The woman wiggled slowly towards the reception, her case making a loud, annoying squeak as its wheels rolled along the ground. Cara was tempted to stay put outside, a break from the bleak hospital room, but the sky was darkening as the cracks of thunder grew louder and she knew she'd have to go in and face her mother.

'Hello, Kitty,' said Cara, acknowledging how ridiculous it sounded, but determined never to call her mother anything but Kitty.

'Cara?' She turned away from the lift and faced her, palm flying across her chest dramatically. In times like this, her mother really reminded her of Millie.

'Darling, I just got a flight in from Rio. How are you?'

Cara winced at the term 'darling'.

'Fine.' She cleared her throat and made no attempt to embrace her mother.

'It's so good to see yer!' Kitty said, suddenly switching into the not so posh accent Cara was more used to. Kitty opened her arms for an embrace but, as Cara wasn't moving, the older woman enveloped her in a stiff hug.

'Are you sure you're okay?' asked Kitty.

'I said I'm fine. It's Lena we have to worry about.' She was definitely fine, even if her tummy was in the middle of some type of semi-spasm. 'Where have you been?' she asked curtly.

'I was in Brazil.'

'Lena's been in here for over two weeks.'

'I only got the message about twenty-four hours ago. Hortense had heard from Ade. Luckily, I was just about to leave the hotel and move on to . . . well, that doesn't matter . . . I'm here now and I just want to see my daughter.'

They had reached Lena's hospital room now, and as Cara pointed to the door, Kitty slowly opened it, with Cara following slowly behind her. A good position it would seem, as she was the one to catch her as Kitty's whole body collapsed towards the freshly cleaned hospital floor.

'Are you okay? Let me get a doctor,' said Ade. Kitty had been 'out' for about three minutes and, after the initial moment of panic, they had managed to move her onto one of the chairs in Lena's room. Cara was soon wondering what she'd been playing at. Fainting indeed! Any excuse to upstage Lena!

'Oh . . . I . . . I just wasn't prepared to see my baby girl laid out in the hospital bed like the dearly departed. That's all,' she said breathlessly, that posh voice returning.

'Of course not,' said Ade, sympathetically.

'I told you she'd be all right,' said Cara, who had retreated to the other side of the room in sceptical mode.

'I'm all right, no need for a doctor,' insisted Kitty, straightening her hair which Cara now realised with mild horror, was actuallly a wig.

'I'll get us all some tea,' said Ade.

'I don't want tea. I just . . . I just want to see my child.' Kitty attempted to get up, wobbled a bit, then sat back down dramatically as soon as she clocked Lena again.

'Take it easy, Mum, please,' said Ade. Cara tried really hard not to snort at the word 'Mum'. 'Let me get you something.'

'There is something you can do for me, son.'

'Anything,' he said, brushing her arm.

'Just call me Kitty. I know you liked calling me Mum when I used to live here, but, well, you know . . .'

'I thought, well I know me and Cara aren't married yet. I just thought—'

'Put a sock in it, Ade. Even I call her by her name and I'm her real daughter! It's what she prefers.' Cara said briskly.

'And you have never complained about it before,' chipped in Kitty.

'I'll get those drinks.' Ade sighed, not sure what to do with himself. 'Now, are you sure you don't want me to get a doctor?' he asked Kitty.

'I'm in the best place if something were to happen. I just want to be with Lena.' Kitty slowly stood up and moved over to Lena's bed. And Cara heard a quick gasp as Kitty slid into the chair and placed her hand on her daughter's forehead, slowly running her fingers across her skin. With her other hand, she stroked Lena's frizzy curls and ran a finger across the Alice band that held the strands back from her face.

'Oh my little sweetheart, what happened?' She sighed as a single tear plopped onto Lena's pillow. Cara turned to Ade, who seemed to be taken in by this display, as he looked close to tears himself. Cara didn't quite know what to say to her mother, who had disappeared for weeks without even bothering to phone or send a postcode. She suddenly felt claustrophobic, and longed for the frenzied normality of A&R.

Ade finally went for the teas as the two women sat in silence, both staring at Lena, Kitty holding onto Lena's hand.

'I am so sorry I didn't get here sooner.'

'Nothing much else you could have done. We have it covered.' Cara said curtly.

'Even now, your mouth is spiteful. Why can't you be nice, just this once? Your sister is lying here after all!' Kitty cried out.

Cara wasn't sure how to answer that, as she was all too

aware that she couldn't think of anything nice to say to Kitty. Some things were best left unsaid.

'Maybe me being here will help her,' Kitty added hopefully. 'What do you think?'

Again, Cara tried to bite her tongue, for Lena's sake. Because if she did open her mouth she feared she would tell her mother that her presence would probably *not* help rouse Lena out of the sleep. Why would it? Kitty had hardly ever been around the last few years. And, in fact, even when they were growing up, her presence and input had been minimal.

'You know where I can find the toilet?' asked Kitty.

'Turn right, straight down, first left.'

'You know your way around here.'

'I'm here every day,' she replied, her tone accusing. She wanted to throw missiles at Kitty and she wanted them to hurt.

'I don't want to argue with you, Cara.'

'She's been here for almost two weeks!'

'I didn't get the message! I told you that!'

'What were you doing, anyway? Gallivanting around Brazil? I thought you'd just got back from Las Vegas a few months ago!'

'I don't have to check in with you, Cara.'

'Of course not, because that would be changing a habit of a lifetime, Kitty!'

'I got on a flight as soon as I could, with no sleep, and at my age it's no joke,' they locked eyes and Cara knew she'd won that round.

'This is silly. I haven't got the strength to fight with you, Cara. Please save it for another day.'

Kitty sounded defeated and this put Cara off guard. She was ready to have it out with her, more than ready. It was as if seeing her mother again had bought all the long-since-buried 'stuff' to the surface.

* * *

51

Millie on the other hand, arrived at the hospital dressed in her 'interview gear' (skirt and blouse). She was finding it increasingly hard to contain her excitement at the arrival of her mother Kitty. She hadn't seen her in ages – well not for six months at least, when Lena had insisted that Millie and herself make the trip up to Southampton to see her. She'd gone and spent the day with her mother and Lena and had enjoyed it. The only missing piece of the puzzle, as usual, was Cara.

Millie was glad Kitty was back and they could sort of be a family for a while. The four of them together for the first time in well . . . ages. However, as Cara was not talking to Kitty and Lena was unable to talk to anyone it didn't exactly feel like the perfect reunion.

Millie cleared her throat. 'I wish Dad was around.'

'What, so we could all be one big happy family?' replied Cara.

'He may be a useless excuse for a man, but he has a right to know,' said Kitty. Even though she was probably right, and even though he'd never made any effort to get in touch over the years, Millie had felt that comment hard, wishing and still hoping after all these years that it wasn't true. That he wasn't 'useless' and most of all, he still loved them. Loved *her*.

'Maybe Lena has his new number,' offered Cara as she moved a stray curl away from Lena's closed eyes.

'In the notebook? But no one's seen it,' said Millie.

'No, in her phone.'

'Has anyone checked?' added Kitty, fixing some dangly earrings into her ears.

'If he gave a damn about anyone but himself, he'd have phoned at some point and we could have told him. Fact is, he just isn't interested in us. Never has been. Face it,' said Cara.

Millie felt as though she'd been punched in the face. So what if she wanted her whole family around Lena's bedside, talking together and being together? Was that so bad? Millie had wanted to call her father as soon as they'd all found out about Lena, but he'd left the country and their lives ten years ago and had not made much contact since. She was only fourteen at the time and on the cusp of womanhood, trying to discover the nature of boys and desperate to leave the confusion of adolescence behind. It had been totally bad timing.

But walking in and seeing her mother had been a nice shock. She'd embraced her tentatively at first, not sure what to say really, but instantly familiarizing herself with Kitty's usual smell of jasmine. Kitty's face, as always, was defying the years, but she wore a little more make-up than she really needed.

She was still Kitty, though. Her mum, who for as long as she could remember never really wanted to be called Mum. On the acting circuit she was known as just Kitty and she insisted her kids called her the same. Not that Millie minded, because at school, before the breasts and shapely thighs, Millie's popularity was through having an actress mum. She wasn't on the telly, but she'd done a few plays, and once appeared in the background of an orange juice advert. Kitty often flounced into parents' evening wearing a long dress and frilly hat and talking about auditions and name dropping famous actors who had helped her with her lines. It had all seemed cool at the time, but as Millie grew up, a lot of things including calling her Kitty just felt more and more alienating and maybe just a bit cold.

But none of that mattered now. Kitty was home.

She glanced at her watch, knowing she had missed the interview for the job at Dorothy Perkins and felt a mixture of guilt and relief wash over her. It's not that she didn't want a job – she just knew that retail wasn't for her.

'So how have you been, Mills?' asked Kitty.

Her mother had always called her Mills as a little girl and Millie was touched that she was calling her that now.

'Apart from . . . you know, everything that's happened with Lena, I've been okay. It has been hard, though.'

In fact, Millie's life had been more about getting to and from work and trying to keep up with the rent on her bedsit, getting kicked out of said bedsit, getting sacked (again) and moving in with Lena. But Kitty didn't need to hear all that.

Cara took out a copy of *Pride* magazine and buried her head in it as Millie updated Kitty on what her life had become – minus the *really* crappy bits.

As soon as they got back to the house, Kitty went to sleep, jetlag, sadness, and age having taken hold. Millie threw herself onto her bed, strangely yearning for the atmosphere of togetherness that she'd felt in Lena's hospital room. They were messed up, but they were still a family, she thought as she looked up to the cracked ceiling. Since Lena's accident, and even before it, the nights had been the worst. With too much time to think, she often wondered whether anyone would ever be capable of loving *her*.

Or perhaps she was just unlovable.

Perhaps that was it. Her parents had kind of proved that theory a long ago when they'd both upped and left. First their father, Donald Curtis. A towering six-foot-three chunk of a man who never seemed to show them any affection when they were growing up. In fact, Millie had thought their lives quite normal, until one day she'd managed to blag an 'excellent' grade for her spelling test whilst her friend Margo only got a 'satisfactory'. The way Margot's dad almost hugged the life out of her outside the school gates was a scene Millie would never forget. Especially as when she'd handed over her own certificate to Donald that evening, he'd smiled awkwardly and said 'Good job' before going back to his newspaper. At the time, those two words had meant everything to the eleven-year-old Millie and she'd treasured that sky blue certificate as evidence that she could actually please her dad. But three years later, when he divorced the family, those words meant nothing.

It was all right for the other two, they were adults and living away from home, plus, judging from their reactions, they hadn't seemed that surprised at the split. But to Millie it had been a complete and utter shock. She'd returned home from doing a mock exam to see her father packing his things clumsily into a holdall, driving away in the family Volvo, and promising to call her.

She had felt Donald's absence hugely – it was a pain that never went away. Kitty on the other hand seemed to be energized by divorce, strutting her stuff around the world before finally escaping to Southampton to 'find herself', no doubt. But who was looking out for *Millie*?

Who would find *her*?

She turned her gaze to a group shot of her and her mates larking about at a club wearing orange feather boas and bright lipstick. Nikki and Tosin were her friends and they loved her, didn't they? Or was it all about getting drunk and falling out of nightclubs on the arms of various guys? Lena loved her. But Lena wasn't here. Not really. And not for the first time in her life, Millie felt incredible pangs of loneliness as she pulled out her mobile and slowly punched in the number, which, unfortunately, she'd come to learn off by heart.

Two rings later. 'Can I come over?'

'You can always come over,' replied the deep voice.

She wiped her face and applied a fresh coat of lip gloss. She'd remain in the clothes she'd worn to the hospital, all too aware that dressing up would be pointless. Stewart would provide her with the company she needed. Make her feel loved, wanted and whole – if only for the night. And she would deal with the revulsion in the morning. She wrote a note for Kitty and pinned it onto the fridge door with the orange Kidzline magnet.

Gone out. Back tomorrow morning.
Mills x

EIGHT

The next morning, Millie walked into the house to the sound of a singing Kitty crouched on all fours.

'I wanted to make myself some breakfast this morning, went to the fridge, and was almost knocked out by the smell!' she said, head deep into the fridge.

'It's not that bad!' said Millie, placing her handbag onto the wooden table.

'It is!' replied Kitty as she stood up and clocked Millie.

'You look worse than me and I'm jetlagged. Partying, were we?'

'Of course not!' replied Millie, a little offended as to why Kitty would think she'd be partying whilst Lena was still in hospital.

'Millie, surely you're not so lazy that you can't clean the fridge?'

Millie stared at the batch of sweet potatoes and the thick ashy mould congregating on them. The garlic and apples were still okay, but the potatoes were definitely on the turn. Kitty grabbed the sponge again and got to work, as Millie remained rooted to the spot. Kitty assumed Millie must have got very slack over the years. But to Millie, these were some of the last things that Lena had bought before going to sleep. She'd picked them out, paid for them, and loaded them into the fridge with her very own hands. Chucking them away would be like chucking out something that Lena had been a part of.

Millie knew it probably wouldn't make sense to anyone but her, but it was simple; she hadn't been ready to take that step. Just as she didn't want to go into Lena's room.

As Kitty tied up the large bin bag containing the rotting groceries, Millie thought her heart would break. 'Can you take this downstairs to the wheelie bins?' Kitty asked her.

Outside, Millie heaved the 'rubbish' into the big green bin and slowly shut the lid. It was a sunny day and a car whizzed by with its bass line blasting out. A neighbour two doors down was loading glass bottles into the recycling bin. Life was ticking along as it always did but for Lena, it was as if everything had frozen in time.

If Millie had done a superficial clean of the house, Kitty had made it sparkle. They spent the day together and went food shopping.

'Lets cook up something lovely for dinner. Cara could come over, too. Would be like old times, us all eating together!'

Millie cast her mind back to their childhood, and remembered the umpteen TV dinners that Lena would dish up whilst their mother went to another audition or just shut herself away in her room. She was too polite now to taint her mother's rose–tinted memory and didn't want to spoil what had been a really nice day together.

Millie called Cara, who said she didn't want any dinner but would need to come over later anyway.

Kitty was packing away the last of the dishes as Cara walked in.

'I saved you some chicken,' said Kitty.

'I'd better not thanks though. Ade's cooking later. I just came to check things like the bills and bank statements. I'm not even sure if there's enough money in her account to pay for everything and keep things ticking over while she's . . . away.'

'She's still getting paid, so there should be,' added Kitty rather carelessly.

'Well I'd better check through everything, see if there are any policies to be renewed. Like insurance policies might need to be renewed,' said Cara as she parked herself on the cosy sofa that had cost twenty pounds in a car-boot sale. 'You know what Lena was like – is like. She would have everything listed somewhere.'

'The sensible one of my girls,' said Kitty, which Cara took instant offence to. 'Do you know, she has a list of everything that gets paid when, just so she can double-check with the bank? I found it in the drawer in the kitchen. I'll go and get it.'

'Where is Millie, by the way?' Cara asked.

'She's having a bath. Got in this morning!' she said with a wink, which Cara found almost as distasteful as Millie shagging her way around South London whilst Lena was in hospital. She made a mental note to have it out with her when she had a suitable moment.

'It's probably best we all go in to look for the documents,' suggested Cara, who suddenly started to feel uncomfortable at the thought of entering Lena's room.

'I know what you mean. Three pairs of eyes are better than two.'

'Exactly.'

'It's only a room, though, isn't it?'

'Yes,' replied Cara, looking towards the carpeted floor. But of course it wasn't 'only' a room. It was Lena's room, and the thought of invading her sister's private sanctuary suddenly filled her with dread. 'We'll need to get papers, accounts, outgoings. Especially as no one can find her notebook. I need to check that things are in order. I know she had insurance – you know, in case she couldn't work.'

'I understand,' said Kitty. She sat on the small sofa opposite and folded her hands.

'I like what you've done with your hair; it suits you. I'll have to rely on wigs until I go back to Southampton. I only trust Marina with my hair. Yes, it really does suit you short,' Kitty said softly.

Cara tucked a loose strand of hair behind her ear self-consciously and muttered, 'Thanks.' Feeling shy all of a sudden and, maybe, just a tad pleased her mother had noticed, she glanced at the clock again, cleared her thoughts and lifted herself out from the squishy sofa. 'I'm going to make a coffee whilst we wait for Millie. Would you like one?'

'Yes, please.'

Cara tried to remember how Kitty took her coffee and failed.

'No sugar please. My figure ain't what it was. Used to be small and slender like yourself. You remind me of me at your age, you know.'

That comment alone induced a wave of dread within Cara and she wasn't quite sure why it felt so strong. But she decided to ignore it as she stood on her tiptoes to reach the top cupboard. The kitchen smelt of bleach and, for a second, reminded her of the hospital. She wondered if she'd ever forget the smell of the hospital ever again or if it was something that lingered forever. She rooted around and spotted Lena's mug. A huge black-and-white polka-dotted thing. The last time she'd peered into this very cupboard, before fixing herself 'a brew', she'd no idea the next time would be with Kitty sitting next door and Lena . . . She moved to the sink and hunched over it. Fix up, fix up, she thought. She had to be strong. To cope with Kitty. The bar. To cope with anything that was about to be thrown at her.

She placed the coffees onto the tray, as Millie appeared in a pair of jeans, hair hanging limp and wet around her face. She had to hand it to her, she looked gorgeous even fresh out of the shower without a scrap of makeup on. Which probably explained why she was never without a man.

'Are you both ready, then?' asked Kitty after her final sip of coffee. Actually, Cara was not remotely ready to open the door to Lena's room – not today, tomorrow, or next week – and could definitely hear the sound of her own heartbeat. She'd been dreading the day she would have to invade her sister's personal space, rifling through her things like a thief in the night. But it had to be done, she kept telling herself. It had to be done.

Millie was not ready. This was the first time she'd gazed at the door for more than a second – choosing instead to flee past it every day. That had been easier. What they were about to do felt bloody hard.

Kitty's phone rang, but by the time she'd found it in her handbag, it had stopped.

Kitty placed her hand onto the door handle and slowly turned it. As soon as the door opened, a faint smell of lemongrass hit them. One side of the wall was a warm cream, the other wallpapered in chocolate and florals. A picture of a dreadlocked child in a mahogany frame on the wall hung over Lena's large bed, which had brass bedknobs decorated with red fairy lights, and massive Indian silk pillows propped up against them. The throw that her boss Andy had brought back for her from Madagascar took pride of place on the bed, along with a pretty striped bra that Lena had probably considered wearing that fateful morning. Millie picked up one of the pillows and held it close to her nose, inhaling deeply. At once she smelt the scent of lemongrass lanolin-free herbal moisturizer, and she felt oddly soothed, as if Lena was right there next to her.

On the old-fashioned dressing table stood a white marble hand draped in costume jewellery – rings, necklaces and colourful bangles – and, beside it, a really cheesy photo of Lena and Justin sitting in a red love-heart frame. A bright pink posty note that read 'What About Me?' written in hasty felt-tip was slapped against the dressing-table mirror. Millie did not allow herself to digest those words as her mind remained transfixed on finding Lena's notebook, which she'd insisted on keeping every year since they were kids. The note-book sometimes doubled up as a diary and changed in size and colour every year. The current Smythson one was Lena's favourite – mainly because she'd bought it for two pounds at a car-boot sale that Lena had dragged her along to. The seller had been an angry-looking women bent on revenge since the Smythson had belonged to her cheating 'son of a biatch' ex-husband.

Millie smiled as she recalled the moment she'd discovered one of Lena's notebooks when she was seventeen – a red and black book with bouncing moon shapes dancing out from the words, *Lena's Diary*. She was excited to have finally discovered it, only to be bitterly disappointed at its contents, which comprised of lists of 'things to do', and boring day-to-day stuff. Millie had called her a saddo at the time – to her face. And she could remember the hurt in her sister's eyes. Lena had bailed her out so many times, like paying her rent when she couldn't and offering her a room when she messed up yet again. She really had been a sister in a million – it had just taken some-thing so horrific to make Millie see this. Perhaps during her next visit to the hospital, she could tell her she was sorry.

Beside the dressing table, a pair of platform trainers and a used ball of cotton wool that had missed the target of the small plastic bin sat beside the freestanding full-length mirror she and Lena had bartered for in Peckham High Street.

'Here it is!' said Cara. Millie had forgotten she wasn't alone.

'You've found what you need?' asked Millie.

'The bank statements, yes,' she replied, popping a folder marked 'bank stuff' into her large shoulder bag. Millie was glad that Cara had a head for such things, as she wouldn't have known where to start.

Millie scanned the room for any glimpse of her sister's notebook, which the hospital hadn't uncovered, even though Lena carried it everywhere with her. She had to find it. She was determined to find it. And no, it wasn't about finding out clues to their father's whereabouts, it was so much more than that. It was about Lena not being around to tell her how she was feeling. Therefore, she could at least find out what was going on in her mind before the accident – considering she'd never once bothered to ask her.

For Cara, going into Lena's room felt like one big fat, betrayal.

She ran a finger across the dressing-table mirror, gathering a film of dust as she did so. She noticed the chip in the side and remembered the day Lena had first spotted it in the second-hand shop.

'I love it, love it, love it!' Lena had enthused.

'It's a manky old dressing table, Lena!'

'You sound like Justin. It's beautiful. Think of the history. All the places it's been.'

'I'd rather not!' said Cara as she brushed an imaginary piece of fluff from her coat. 'It needs to go in the bin!'

'Fifty quid!' said the dirty-looking shopkeeper who'd been licking his lips ever since they'd walked into the flea-infested 'shop'. Cara had to be in the bar in an hour and really didn't have the time to be bartering over manky furniture.

'Forty?' asked Lena sweetly.

'Do I really need to be here?' asked Cara, glancing at her watch.

'You've got at least an hour until your shift!' protested Lena, as the shopkeeper smiled repulsively at Cara. Uggh!

'I know, but I have some paperwork to be getting on with.'

Lena sighed. 'Okay, I'll be quick. How about forty-five quid?' she said, returning to the man.

He nodded his head in agreement. 'Because of your eyes!'

Cara smiled at the memory of their usual debate regarding modern versus classic. Lena just loved old stuff. So much so that Cara often envisioned her walking in hand in hand with some old wrinkly. Then again, anyone was better than Justin. The moment Lena had introduced him to her she'd taken an instant dislike to him. He was always talking about his precious job. It was all he ever seemed to talked about. Cara could never work out what it was that Lena saw in him. But she'd never really bothered to find out.

On the dressing table was a half-empty perfume pump spray – those old-fashioned ones you squeezed at the bottom, pink with tassels. There was a jewellery box decorated with shells, a tacky little thing Lena had actually bought from an antique shop in Church Street. Cara couldn't bring herself to open it. It felt wrong, without Lena there.

Cara glanced at Kitty, who was on her knees reaching into Lena's wardrobe. Millie was sitting on the bed, just staring at the pillows. Everyone was quiet. Cara sat down and carefully opened up the top drawer of the dressing table and pulled out a plastic sheath with a white sticker and CURRENT IMPORTANT STUFF written on it. There were papers inside as well as a dried-out mascara brush. No doubt Lena was recycling it – for what, she'd no clue. She took out the papers, carefully. A couple of bills, an old newspaper with printed tokens for a trip to Thorpe Park offering dates that had just passed. She opened a folded piece of paper that had been torn out of a pad.

Deciding that was a bit weird, she carried on rifling through the papers, feeling ever more determined to find what she was looking for.

And then she found it.

Lena's latest bank statement.

£6.99 Hampton Cards (Lena never missed a birthday)

£1.99 Steve's Organic (she loved their organic chocolate brownie, even though Lena knew deep down that it was a rip off)

The odd hole-in-the-wall withdrawals. All very proper. And then, after the mortgage and bills were taken out, the end of the statement read £3,600 OD.

Cara had to sit down for this.

Overdrawn?

She peered into the folder marked BANK STUFF for previous months, March, April, May, June, July, August – all had ended in a massive overdraft and never seemed to be in credit. The interest was vast. In some months, Lena had actually been going *over* the overdraft. Cara felt a wave of shame wash over her, as she wondered why Lena had not come to her. She could have lent her some money. The remortgage on the flat had come through a couple of years back and she could have done so then. Instead, they'd ploughed most of the money into A&R, which paid for a new sound system and a set of luxurious muslin curtains! Hadn't Cara and Lena once talked about travelling to Africa one day? Cara could actually have taken some of the money and just said to Lena, 'Come on, I'll pay your debts and still have money left over to go on a trip'. But no, a set of poxy muslin curtains had taken priority!

She stuffed the papers back into her bag, suddenly

feeling her resentment towards Kitty rising. Because it was Kitty who'd landed Lena in all this mess in the first place.

Then just as she was about to get up, she spotted a crumpled page, torn out of a magazine or a book poking out from the pile of papers.

Child Psychology

Course Description. This course will focus on children and their development from birth into adolescence. Major theories will be explored, such as child development, social and cognitive development, and language acquisition.

This module will be of interest to many, particularly those who work or wish to work with children. This course provides a foundation for those wishing to study at degree level.

The page was worn. As if Lena had flicked through it a hundred times before. But Lena had never mentioned anything about wanting to study child psychology. Or had she? Perhaps Cara had been so caught up in her own stuff that she hadn't listened. Think! Think! She clutched the paper tightly and tried to think of a time Lena would have mentioned wanting to study. She looked up to the lemon and white coloured clock shaped like a giant daisy and then she remembered.

'What's in the bag?' Cara had asked as she served a dry Martini for a customer and Lena jumped on to one of the bar stools awkwardly. Her hair was even more frizzy than usual. It was a Wednesday night and the customers were slowly edging inside.

'Do you actually ever comb your hair, Lena?'

Lena stifled a yawn. 'Lemons.'

'What are you talking about?'

'I need some lemons because I'm baking a cake for one of the advisers at work. Haven't you got loads?'

'Why don't you just go into Marks and Sparks and grab a cake?'

'Might be a bit pricy – besides, I have all the ingredients except the lemons. And it's more personal this way.'

'Or you could just not bother! That's two pounds fifty in total,' she said, turning to the customer. It had been steadily busy all night and this was pleasing, especially as it was still only midweek.

'Cara, I've been thinking about something.'

'What?' she replied, mildly irritated. She hoped her sister wasn't after some heart-to-heart; she was short-staffed and had been working since one o'clock.

'I've been thinking of going back to studying.'

'Why? That's three fifty please. Cheers,' she said to the second customer.

'I'm getting a little fed up with just getting a call from a child in trouble and having to pass them onto an agency with more qualified people. I want to BE that qualified person. I want to BE the person who can help those kids. I mean really help them!'

'Oh right.' The door opened and in walked a horde of eager looking young men ready for a raucous night of drinking.

'Lena, can we talk about this later?'

'Okay.' Sighed Lena.

'In about an hour, on my break.' Cara replied.

'I'll have to go and start on the cake, soon.'

'Actually, you couldn't stay and help me out. I'm really short-staffed.'

'But Cara, I did a hectic shift today at Kidzline!'

'Pretty please? I'll pay you AND we can have that talk. Promise.'

'What, minimum wage for one hour?'

'Plus all the lemons for your cake?'

'You know I'll be doing this just for you and not the cash,' she said as Cara handed her a beer glass.

They never did 'talk' that night. Lena ended up working for three whole hours, and even forgot to take the lemons.

Worst of all, Cara hadn't even kept her side of the promise.

Cara closed her eyes in shame and didn't notice a small white card as it flew out of the pile of papers.

'What's that?' asked Millie, reaching for the card. Kitty remained on the floor and seemed to be looking through the bottom of Lena's wardrobe, pulling out multicoloured socks, a battered empty purse, a leather belt with a silver loveheart buckle; staring aimlessly at each and every item.

Millie handed the card to Cara as Kitty, clutching the belt, used the edge of the bed to help herself up.

'Since reaching fifty, I've started to feel all these aches and pains in my bones. Bloody 'ell,' She mumbled.

'It's a card,' whispered Millie.

'I can see that,' replied Cara as she flicked the card round.

Michael Johns. Sales Manager. *Call me*.

And a phone number.

NINE

The shrill of his office phone startled him.

'Hello?'

'Hello,' said the female voice.

'Michael, Michael can you come to the hospital?'

'Charlotte? Oh no, what's wrong?'

'Don't panic. It's George, he's had an accident – cut himself in the garden. It's nothing serious though. I just need you for the company really. Especially as his dad's in Spain with his skinny and intellectually challenged fancy piece. I need someone to vent my feelings of inadequacy at.'

'I'll be right over. What hospital?'

'Fen Lane.'

'You can head off, it's going to be a wait,' said Charlotte nearly two hours later, as she cradled her sleepy son in her arms. Michael had refused to go anywhere, but he had to admit, he was bored stiff. Like his nephew, he needed some form of stimulation but, unlike George, was too old to just curl up in his mother's arms and full asleep once he'd given up trying to find it.

'I'm just going for a walk,' said Michael.

'Okay. If you come back and we're gone, just come and find us in one of the cubicles.'

Outside, the cool night air made him catch his breath, as did the heel of a tiny little woman who had literally bumped into him as it pierced his foot.

'Ouch!' he complained.

'Watch it!' she said gruffly. How rude, Michael thought, not glancing to look up as she stomped off.

Cara waited for the lift and bent down to inspect the scuff on her green suede slingbacks. Bloody idiot was lucky she didn't present him with a bill for her scuffed shoes. Green suede and dirty trainers never made a good combination. Anyway, she had more important things on her mind, like this Michael Johns character. Who was he, and why was his card in a pile marked 'Important Stuff'? By now Cara had worked out that she hadn't listened to Lena as much as she perhaps should have, but if she'd told her about having another man on the scene, her ears definitely would have pricked up. No, Lena wasn't the affair type. Millie, yes. Lena, no.

She walked into Lena's hospital room as Kitty sat combing Lena's hair, the smell of lemongrass oil moisturizer lingering in the air.

'What's going on?' asked Cara with a shot of alarm.

'Just doing your sister's hair. I wanted to do something nice for her.'

'But that's my job!' Cara cried, instantly regretting it after the words left her mouth.

Kitty put the comb down and shook her head. 'Sorry darling, I just thought . . .'

'Never mind,' Cara said. It seemed churlish to be moaning over who combed Lena's hair. It was just that she too needed

70

to feel useful around Lena. 'Have you seen Millie? I need to speak to her.'

'She's at the Job Centre. Said she'd come here on her way back. Anything I can help with?'

Cara looked at her mother and opened her mouth to speak. To tell her about this Michael Johns, ask her if it was okay to trust a man who had a surname that could also be a used as a firstname (although Curtis could also be used as a first-name, but that was different!). To discuss why Lena would even have his card in her 'Important Stuff' file to begin with. To ask her whether she thought she should ring this guy and tell him about the accident?

But of course, Cara just stuck with a curt; 'No, it's okay' instead.

Millie headed back from the Job Centre, she was feeling more and more dejected. The whole process had been a nightmare. As usual, full of posts with low pay, plus a sarky little boy telling her it was time she 'got a job'. That much she already knew; she just wasn't sure what type of job she'd like to do. Something in fashion perhaps, but not in retail. Something that was current, fun but with less than demanding hours maybe. Bugger it, maybe she was one of those people who never knew what they wanted to do. She wasn't like her sisters – Lena loved helping children and Cara liked bossing people about. Besides, these days there weren't any jobs to choose from.

She passed a gang of locals congregating by the bins, ignored their wolf whistles and smiled at the old lady who always walked on Under Hill Road dressed in a pristine two-piece suit with two tiny dogs. She soon approached the familiar large Victorian house that had been her home since childhood. But as she rummaged around for her keys, she noticed a red Micra parked beside a clamped car, the familiar number plate making her heart skip a beat or two.

She peered through the window, not wanting to believe her eyes, wishing she'd worn something a lot more sexier to the Job Centre that afternoon.

'Kenny?'

Inside, and bobbing his head to the latest Jay-Z CD sat Kenny, her ex-boyfriend, who had broken up with her before Rik. He was looking as gorgeous as ever.

'Hi, Millie,' he said, unhooking the seatbelt and making moves to get out.

She absently-mindedly placed her hand to her chest in joyful surprise, unable to hide the new grin etched onto her beautiful face.

Kenny and Millie had spent two blissful months together earlier that year, her toothbrush even finding a home in his bathroom cabinet. They'd discussed moving in together (well, she'd asked him to think about it), but they had split up not long after that very conversation. The split had been rather sudden and without warning; he'd never fully explained the reason for it, only that he needed 'time to grow', whatever that meant. But seeing him in his little Micra again produced a rush of nostalgic love, desperate to regain its place in her heart again.

Kenny stood to his full height of six foot two, towering over her and making her feel safe. Inside the house, he politely asked after her sisters (even though he'd never met them), and she was polite enough not to mention what had happened to Lena. When the door swung open, she was eager to slip out of her 'looking for work' attire and into something sexier.

'I'm not staying, Millie!' he said as she led him to her room. He was instantly fixated on a couple of pictures lying on her dressing table. One of Rik.

'It's not what you think,' she said, desperate to dismiss the photo.

Kenny turned to face her. 'It doesn't matter, Millie, I just came for a couple of box sets I left behind. Do you still have them?'

She felt the weight of her heart plummet to the depths of her heels.

He'd only come for the DVDs.

She composed herself. 'Oh, of course. I'll get them for you.'

Millie searched the bedroom as Kenny turned his gaze to the wall with an impatient whistle. Under the bed she searched, as well as inside her giant laundry bag packed to the rim with dirty clothes and an electric hairdryer, then in the drawers. Then she remembered that beautiful feeling of release she'd felt just after stamping each DVD to death in a fit of rage.

'Actually, I think I lent them to my sister,' she said quickly.

'Which one?' he asked with that mixture of anger and irritation.

'Lena,' she lied.

'So, can we go to her room now and get them? They are really expensive. I'd forgotten about them until my cousin asked to watch them with me.'

'I'm sorry, we can't.'

'Why?' He looked even more irritated.

'Because . . .'

'Because? What does that mean?'

'Because my sister's in hospital, that's why.'

He scrunched his eyebrows in apparent disbelief. 'Is she bad?'

'As bad as it can get. So I don't think now's the time to, you know . . . ?'

He scratched his head. 'No, sure. I'm sorry, really. Are you okay?'

The look of concern etched onto his handsome features shocked but pleased her. Maybe he did care about her, after all.

'Some days are better than others.' Technically, she was telling him the truth, but she would be lying to herself if she didn't acknowledge the fact that she was pleased at his sudden switch in attention. Perhaps he would give her a hug next.

He moved over to her and placed his palm on her shoulder.

'I hope your sister gets better.'

'Thanks, Don't you want to stay – for a drink?'

'I'd better not,' he replied abruptly before appearing to think better of it. 'Okay. Just one then.'

Millie slipped into her favourite skinny jeans in the bathroom and they talked over old times, favourite television shows, new music, and why they'd split up in the first place. It would seem that one drink had loosened Kenny's tongue just enough to trample on any hopes of a hug or a cosy night in.

'You were just too clingy,' he said.

'How do you mean?'

'I mean, you wanted me to move in after a few weeks and you were . . . Look, this isn't going to get either of us anywhere,' he said, standing up. 'I should go. Thanks. I'll expect the stuff in the post, when you can. Hope your sister gets well soon.'

Millie drained off her glass.

'Wait. Please, don't leave me alone. My sister . . .' She was fully aware of how pathetic she sounded. Kenny gazed at her for a moment with *that* look. The look that had the power to melt her whole body into a slushy mess, as he'd done so many times before. Only this time it didn't speak of lust or wanting, only pity.

'Don't do this, Millie.'

'All right, all right,' she sniffed, turning away from him too sad to even feel slightly embarrassed.

That evening, the hours drifted away along with the remaining alcohol. She was supposed to be at the hospital hours ago, but she just couldn't face it. Millie hated the trips to the hospital anyway. Everyone expected her to behave in a certain way and she hated the pressure of it all. Just like at the bloody Job Centre.

She drained the glass. All she wanted, all Millie really wanted, was time alone with Lena where she could just be herself. Because, to be honest, Lena was the only person she had ever truly been herself with. Men expected her to live up to the sexy image her long legs, slim waist, and sexy walk all seemed to convey. Whilst her family? They were even worse. But with Lena, it had always been different. Lena seemed to see something in Millie she'd yet to see in herself.

'You're a work in progress, Millie. This isn't the whole sum of you. You'll get there. One day.' She'd used to say.

Or there was that time Lena had cradled Millie in her arms, mascara running down her face, as she cried and cried and cried after being dumped via text.

'One day you will meet someone who sees what I see,' Lena had said softly, kissing her forehead like she used to do when they were younger.

Millie thought about giving her mate Nikki a call and have a long overdue girlie chat over some drinks. Tosin would be up for it too. Perhaps they could be like those groups of women in those girly films and novels; always armed with a bottle of white wine, chocolates, and a sharp tongue to tell you what was what. But they were just mates, not proper friends. She had no real deep bond with them. Not like she did with Lena. She'd always got on better with boys anyway, as girls seemed to think she was ready and waiting to steal their boyfriends. Lena once told her, women probably found Millie intimidating because of her looks but Millie had brushed Lena's comments off as silly. Yet all her so called friends had disappeared since school and college. And all the men she knew in her life had really just been a string of ex-boyfriends.

She opened a cupboard in the kitchen and reached for the bottle of Jack Daniels. He would keep her company tonight.

'WAKE UP!' shouted a voice as Millie opened her eyes to Cara's angry little face.

'Don't shout, Cara!' managed Millie as she acknowledged the full force of her banging head and a mouth which tasted like the bottom of a gerbil's cage.

'Where were you yesterday? I waited for you at the hospital.'

'I—'

'Actually don't answer that, I've just seen the bottle. What's his name this time?'

She pulled herself up in the bed. 'It's not what you think.'

'In fact, I don't care. What I do care about is this Michael Johns character. Who is he and what was Lena doing putting his card in her Important Stuff folder?' She placed the card in Millie's hand.

'Why not just call and ask him?' Millie's head hurt too much to think.

'Yes, well, I was thinking the same, but I wanted to talk to you about it first.'

'Talk to *me*?' Millie wasn't sure if she was still drunk, but Cara had just said something about asking *her* for advice. An absolute first in the history of their sisterly relationship. This pleased Millie and she wished she wasn't suffering from a hangover so she could truly savour the moment.

'Wow, Cara asking ME for advice!'

'Don't push it, sis!'

'Hold on while I get my phone to record this.'

'I said don't push it!' said Cara, stilling a smile. Cara turned over the card in Millie's hand, displaying the 'Call me' request scrawled in blue.

'I think you should definitely call him, Cara. Today.'

TEN

Michael wasn't beyond ignoring his work phone when it rang. Work had recently installed one of those fancy Cisco phones, which had caller display so he could ring the person back anyway. Besides, he was busy alternating between the sales figures and a bookmarked page on the Internet.

Why not try Sri Lanka? With over a thousand miles of palm-fringed, sugar-white sands, it looks just like a post-card! You can enjoy plenty of snorkeling and scuba diving opportunities. As for eating, Sri Lanka's sizzling and exotic cuisine is made from homegrown ingredients, including freshly picked spices and vegetables such as cinnamon, nutmeg, turmeric, and chillies. Sri Lanka has it all! It has everything and it's waiting for YOU! You CAN have your dream holiday here, whatever your requirements. Go now and beat the crowds. Prices start at £649 per person. What are you waiting for?

Michael would at times find himself dreaming about basking on a beach, riding elephants, and doing all the fun things that people told him they did on holiday when he hadn't even asked them to. Wondering what it would be like to just hop on a plane and wake up in another country. So, as usual before a particularly boring sales meeting, he dreamed of the possibilities, before dismissing it as a silly fantasy that he'd no chance of fulfilling *yet*.

The phone rang again and he clicked off the website. He glanced over at the number, noticing it was withheld. He'd have to answer it.

'Hello, Michael John speaking' he said in his profession work voice.

There was a short silence before a soft female voice stuttered. 'I-I . . .'

'Give it here!' he heard from a second person. Michael scrunched his eyebrows in suspicion and took a sharp intake of breath. The boring sales meeting was in five minutes.

'Can I help you?' he asked.

'Maybe,' came the more confident voice. A lot sharper. 'I think you know a relative of mine. A woman. Do you know someone called Lena?'

Just then, the boss peeped his head around the door. 'Michael, we're meeting in boardroom six today. Apparently five had a flood.'

'Yes, okay,' Michael said. 'I'll be with you soon. Boardroom six you say?'

'Heeellooo?' said the impatient voice on the line as the boss left.

'Sorry about that. You were talking about a woman called . . . what was the name again?'

'Yes . . .' Suddenly she didn't sound that confident any more and then, just as quickly, the first voice was back.

'Sorry to have bothered you, mate. Goodbye.' And they were gone.

Michael replaced the receiver, literally scratching his head with the other hand.

What had just happened there?

It was just a phone call, but something deep inside was telling him it was important. And who was this girl they were asking about, and why?

Who was she, and why were random strangers ringing him up? He didn't owe anyone any money. Must have been a wrong number, he thought as he headed towards the boardroom. But, as he sat on one of the leather chairs and fake-smiled at his colleagues, he knew that that call was going to mean something. He just wasn't sure what, exactly.

As he slumped in front of the telly that evening, with a cuppa watching the news, he couldn't stop thinking about the phone call.

His doorbell went. He shot up, disturbing the pile of magazines and bits and bobs making an unsightly mess on the arm of his sofa. Michael hardly ever had visitors – by choice, as he remained ashamed of his surroundings.

'Who is it?' he said through the intercom.

'Your sister. The ex- is back from Spain and has the kids, so I'm free for the night and we're having a few drinks. So let me in!'

As he put the kettle on, he could hear Charlotte rifling through his things in the lounge.

'This is a nice flat, just needs a bit of a tidy,' she said as usual. 'Get rid of all these papers for a start. You're just like Mum, a hoarder.'

'And just a bit like you?'

'Yes, okay!'

The kettle had just boiled as Charlotte entered the

kitchen with a bewildered look on her face. 'What are you doing?'

'Fixing us some hot chocolate.'

'Are you serious? I get one night off in a zillion years and you want us to stay in and have cocoa? We're going out!'

'But it's gone nine o'clock on a work night!'

'What are you, ninety? Come on, just one drink, please? We'll go local, take a walk up to East Dulwich. It's pretty swish down there. Come on!' she beckoned, almost shoving him out of the front door.

They settled on an overpriced bar he'd never have chosen. Frilly drapes with studs separated one booth from the next, and glass chandeliers hung from the ceiling. It was a bit posh for Michael's taste but he tried to be enthusiastic for Charlotte.

He perched on a bar stool while he ordered drinks. A Mojito (for him) and a beer for Charlotte. One of the good things about cutting most of your friends off was not having to take the ribbing that ordering a cocktail would usually bring. Yes, he enjoyed the odd beer like the next man, but the sweet-and-sour blend of a Mojito (when mixed right) couldn't be beaten.

'You girl!' ribbed Charlotte anyway as she took a swig of her beer.

He opened his wallet for the money as Charlotte shook her head. 'Nope, it's on me.'

They talked a lot about the kids (so much for Charlotte having the night off!) and he was tempted to mention the call he'd received earlier that day. Michael insisted on paying for but, realizing he'd no real cash on him, rummaged around for his credit card instead. As he handed over the card to the barwoman, an orange card poked out from beneath it.

That night, as Charlotte slept in his bed and he took the sofa, he pulled out the orange card and looked at it, really stared at it, as if seeing it for the very first time.

'*Only a phonecall away*' was written in computerized kiddie scrawl. On the other side the printed 'Kidzline' logo was clear to see.

ELEVEN

Several weeks earlier . . .

He'd been disappointed to see the girl's seat occupied by a fat bloke digging his finger into his ear, but Michael had grudgingly made his way up the stairs anyway and towards his usual seat near the back and closer to the annoying school kids and their tinny mobile-phone music. Someone had had the audacity to sit in his usual spot by the window, whilst the kids messed about in the back.

But then he noticed a mass of corkscrew curls with bright highlights, currently peering into one of those huge Many Poppins bags that women seem to carry their entire lives in. Hers was a shiny patent blue, with yellow beads hanging off one of the straps. And as his bum hit the space next to her, her face climbed out of the bag with two white wires dripping from her ears as she sang along (really badly) to whatever she was listening to.

It was the girl with the green eyes and the gorgeous smile. Abso-lute-ly stunning.

'Sorry about the noise,' she said, sweetly.

He didn't want to sound like an old fart, but couldn't help it. 'No . . . it's okay . . .' he said his tongue all in knots.

'Lena,' she said quickly. 'My name's Lena.'

She took out the tiny pink MP3 player and rolled the Off switch.

'Hello, Lena. I'm Michael.' He sounded like a prat, that much he knew.

'Sorry, if it was a bit loud. I love that song.'

'What's it called?' He asked although he was just too busy trying not to stare at those eyes.

'"Why Don't We Fall in Love?"'

'Huh?' he said, startled, feeling himself blushing like a school boy.

'That's what the song's called.' She said laughing.

He felt an idiot. 'Well it wasn't as loud as that lot back there.' He said nodding his head in the direction of the school kids.

'They're just expressing themselves.'

'That's true I guess . . .'

'I usually sit downstairs and I've seen you get on this bus quite a lot.' She covered her mouth in embarrassment, which made him smile.

'Lena's an unusual name,' he said to break the tension.

'Named after Lena Horne.'

'Oh right. I've heard of her. Great singer.' That was a fib. Michael had never heard of her.

'She is.'

And then she mentioned her sisters.

'One of them is called Millie, after Millie Small. You know?'

'"My Boy Lollipop"?'

'Yes!' she said enthusiastically and he noticed the glow of her green-studded earrings, complementing the sparkle of her eyes. She wore an unusual chain around her neck with a wooden Nefertiti hanging from it.

'I bet you can't guess who my sister Cara was named after?'

'Are we sticking with the musical women theme here?'

'Yes.'

'Cara . . .?'

'Actually its really her middle name because her first name is Irene, but she's always hated it. Says it makes her sound ancient. There I've given it away now!'

'Have you?'

'Yes! Think of the kids from Fame?'

'Nope, sorry, you've lost me.'

'"I Wanna Live Forever"?'

'Do you?'

'Do I what?'

'Want to live forever?'

'I would if I could. There's so much I want to do – but there's just so little time . . .' She seemed to trail off and she peered out of the window, as if deep in thought, before turning back to him as he caught his breath – the girl was unbelievably beautiful.

'Cara, my sister was named after Irene Cara, who sang the Fame song,' she said more seriously.

They were only on the bus together for a short while but Michael felt like he'd known Lena forever. There was something about her . . . and he'd hoped he would see her again on the bus.

Suddenly it all fell into place. The call – it was about Lena. It had to be. Because of that, because of everything, he now couldn't get her out of his mind. On the way into work, at work, at lunch, on his computer screen (instead of sales figures), he only saw her face. The image becoming more vivid each time. Like a mirage turning into a screensaver. Her lips, her hair, those beautiful green eyes with flecks of gold that shone like emeralds in the dark.

What a prat!

But, to him, her absence on the bus was now so blatantly obvious during each journey. His eyes would scan the entire bus hopefully, for just a glimpse, straining his neck and gazing through the window to see if she was getting on at each of the stops. He knew it was irrational, it was silly, and it was so not him. But, despite his logical side trying to dismiss these feelings, deep down he knew it was imperative that he should see this woman again, and he wasn't quite sure why. Charlotte's theory was that he was depressed and scared and focusing on this stranger was just another way of not dealing with his life. Yeah right!

He leafed through his wallet for the card he had found at Charlotte's – identical to the one Lena had given him – whilst the original remained in his wallet. He'd already decided to call the printed freephone number and find out if she still worked there. How hard would that be? He would definitely be calling. After work. So, that morning, Michael felt he had something to look forward to as he passed the aged security guard reading a paper by the lifts in his office building, walked by Moira the receptionist and began his daily ritual of switching on the computer, reading various emails that were mostly from his boss quoting monthly reports and things he wanted Michael to do and other nonsense. But thinking about Lena now broke up his day a bit. As he wondered what had happened to her. And who those voices on the phone had been. Was she in trouble? Was someone after her? His imagination was in overdrive. He had to pluck up the courage and phone her.

Michael took a detour to Charlotte's.

'So, what are you going to do about the mystery woman?'

'I told you, I'm going to call her workplace.'

'And say what? I'm a psycho stalker and you must tell me if Lena works here?'

Now it didn't sound like such a hot idea. 'What do you suggest, then?'

'Leave it well alone?'

'I don't want to.'

'Maybe it's for the best that you do, Michael. The way you treat girls and everything.'

Michael felt stung. 'I'm not a bad person, you know,' he said defensively.

'No. You're a wonderful person – just a shit boyfriend.'

'You don't understand, Charl.'

'Yes I do. I understand that any woman you've got close to since your last real relationship ended *five years ago*, you've treated badly.'

'I don't . . . mean to. It's just that they always want more than I can give.'

'Like?'

'All of my time. Things—'

'It's called a *relationship*. What is wrong with men these days? The going gets tough and they get going. Look at George and Serena's dad.'

Michael knew that his sister's anger was really directed at her ex-husband and not him.

'Let it go. It's a little pointless, don't you think? As you always say, you need to sort yourself out first,' she said in total big sister mode.

'Yeah. I know.' He replied glumly.

'I can see I'm making you miserable. Let's ditch the tea and open a bottle of wine.'

After several glasses he started to feel a little better. 'Another one?'

'I shouldn't not with my babies upstairs. You go ahead, though. It's enough fun watching you!' Charlotte giggled.

Charlotte reached for the phone. 'You remember when we were kids and we used to play knock-down ginger?'

'Yesh.'

'Let's play, I dunno, knock-down phone!'

They began to giggle uncontrollably, until Michael said, slightly nervously, 'Let's call Kidzline!'

'Let's!' she replied, the warm fuzzy effect of the wine melting away Charlotte's sensible head.

'No, we couldn't, could we?' said Michael excitedly.

'Yes we could.' Charlotte said.

He pulled out the orange card from his trouser pocket.

Michael was drunk enough not to care that his sister was dialling Kidzline in the middle of the night to ask for a girl he'd only ever spoken to for seven minutes or so. And if he had drunk less wine, he'd have had the strength to stop his sister regressing to childhood and punching in the number for Kidzline.

'Is that Kidzline?' she said.

'Don't!' he cried weakly. 'If she'd wanted me to call her, she'd have given me a proper number, not the national one!'

Charlotte waved him away. 'I have two kids and I'm really worried about the . . . the best school to enrol them in . . . that's it! And I need to speak to Lena about it.'

Charlotte and Michael both tried to suppress giggles. She then blinked a couple of times, said 'thank you', and hung up the phone.

'What happened?'

Charlotte sat beside him, hands on her lap. 'She said advisers never normally give out their real names. But anyway, Lena was off.'

'Okay, so she's probably gone on a long holiday. At least she hasn't left.'

'I don't think so.' Suddenly, Charlotte looked serious.

'Why d'you say that?'

'Because if she was on holiday, then why did that woman on the phone just burst into tears?'

TWELVE

Although they'd totally ballsed up calling Michael Johns, Cara had to admit that it had been fun. It was the first time in ages that Millie and Cara had done something together. As kids they weren't the closest, with Cara seeing her little sister as more of a nuisance than anything else. Lena was the one who always seemed to be the glue binding them together, encouraging them all to meet up. But lately it hadn't felt quite so forced. Millie was good fun, and perhaps more sensible than Cara ever given her credit for.

With Millie's encouragement, she'd felt strong enough to look through Lena's phone. Of course Cara would never admit it, but the thought of having Millie there was what enabled her to handle the whole thing. Lena's phone wasn't one of those fancy ones likes Ade's that seemed to do everything except wax the car. Although unlike hers, it was attached to a ridiculous faux leather chain with L.E.N.A. spelt out in beads.

'Switch it on then,' Millie had said.

'Just wait!' she'd snapped. Cara switched on the phone and watched it flicker into life. It was clearly running out of battery, even though it had been inactive for weeks, so she needed to work fast in order to get what she needed. She scrolled down through the menu until she reached the inbox and Lena's saved text messages.

'It feels weird going through her phone, like were snooping,' said Millie weakly, but who was she trying to kid? They both wanted to know more about their sister. They both wanted to find a way of communicating with her, even though they couldn't really. Most of all, they were desperate to know what had been going on in her life in the weeks leading up to the fall – because they really hadn't been paying much attention at the time.

Sorry, cant make dinner with you and Millie. Next month?

That was from her.

Sorry didn't get bak 2 u as promised. You free tomm?

Millie.

Pick up a bottle of wine on your way to mine & pringles? Love you. J

Justin, The Prick.

Sorry cant make it

Cara.

Can't u ask 1 of yr sisters??

Justin.

I need you to do a shift for me. 2nite. Pleeeeaaase??

Cara again.

I know I didn't show up 4 yr birthday meal. But doesn't
mean I don't love u. J

Cara had seen enough so, eager to shut the phone down, she
inadvertently pressed a button that displayed all of Lena's
current and unopened text messages, which mostly seemed
to be from someone called DT:

Where R U? Call me bak.
Y U nt callin? Bell me asap
Getting mad worried. Call me bak

Cara attempted to retrieve the DT's number, just as the phone
gave up and finally switched itself off. They'd both sat in
silence, praying, hoping, and wishing that Lena would never,
ever do the same.

Millie had reached out and held her hand and for once,
Cara let her.

Something inside Cara had melted. Suddenly all the anger
and pent up frustration she'd been carrying on her shoulders
disappeared and she realised in that moment how much she
and Millie needed each other.

'I am ready to start my shift!' sang Millie in a faux American
accent as she flounced into the bar, swaying her hips and
wearing bright pink lipstick and the shortest jean skirt Cara
had ever seen.

'What? I'm on time, aren't I?' said Millie as she winked
at an old man ogling her behind a muslin curtain.

'I should hope so, considering it's a five p.m. shift, Millie!'

Millie walked around to the other side of the bar and
started rummaging around.

'What are you doing?' asked Cara, wondering if this was such a good idea.

'Trying to look busy. There aren't many customers yet.'

'No problem, you can look busy by giving the loos a once-over.'

Millie dropped her bottom lip. 'Are you serious?'

'The cleaning stuff is out back and you might want to change your shoes,' she said with a smile as Millie's eyes widened in absolute horror.

Of course she hadn't meant to give Millie quite such a horrid job on her first shift but she did want her sister to understand what a good day's graft was really like. But Millie surprised Cara. Not least when she finished cleaning both the gents' and the ladies' and (with a beaming smile) washed up, then had begun serving the customers efficiently and quickly as the bar filled up. The short skirt hadn't gone un-noticed with the randier regulars, which meant she also cleaned up on the tips front.

'I'm knackered!' said Millie as she slid into her faux leather bomber jacket at the end of her shift. It was almost midnight.

'Welcome to my world. You did a good job.' Cara said, really meaning it.

'That's a first!'

'What, you doing a good job?'

'No! You, actually saying so!'

After a short walk home, Millie let herself into the house, which was filled with the delicious aroma of a fish curry. For a second it felt like old times. When she'd roll in famished after a hard night's partying with Nikki and Tosin, and Lena would always leave her a plate in the oven with a note that read 'You dirty stop-out'. Kitty was on the sofa.

'Kitty, you're still up!'

'Just about. I left you some food in the oven.'

'Thank you,' it smells yummy!' Millie smiled. Although

she'd worked harder than she'd ever done in her life, she also realized she hadn't felt so good in a long time. 'What are you reading?' she said.

'It's just a leaflet I picked up.'

'Lena doesn't need surgery, does she?' Millie was confused.

'No, it's for me, silly!'

'You need surgery?'

'No. Yes. But not in the medical sense! It's about plastic surgery.'

'Why would you want to read about that?'

'You really want me to answer?'

'You're lovely!' said Millie, totally surprised that her mother would even consider such a thing.

'A lot of women seem to go for it. You'd be surprised at how many have things done. Anyway, I'm going to heat up your food. Go and clean up, Mills.'

Millie padded into the bathroom, stifling a yawn. Kitty's things were dotted about the place; a long, straight wig draped around the tap, dripping with water after a shampoo and set no doubt; dermatological body cream; Ladyshave, Vicks VapoRub. She loved having her mother back at the house and was trying not to think about the moment when she'd inevitably leave again.

After freshening up, Millie sat down to eat. She was ravenous and finished the plate quickly. Although Kitty had never been the typical mumsy mum, she could cook a mean roast.

'Remember Sunday nights and how you girls would always fight over which bit of the chicken you got. You all loved the wing, but of course you all decided to forget that a bird only has two of them!'

'Lena would sometimes let me have hers.' Millie said sadly.

'And your greedy father would always insist on having a leg and a thigh. That should have given me an inkling about what he was like.' Kitty chuckled.

It felt good talking to Kitty. Perhaps they could repair their relationship after all, but who knew how long Kitty would be staying around this time? It could be weeks. Months. Then Millie suddenly thought with horror that how long Kitty stayed depended on how long Lena remained asleep. And she wanted Lena awake and out of that hospital as soon as! Of course!

'You don't talk much about Dad. I know he really hurt you . . . I mean he hurt all of us . . .' Millie was treading carefully. She didn't want to upset her mum but they'd never really spoken about their father or the fact that his walking out on them ten years ago had splintered their family into tiny little pieces.

'Yes he did. The bastard messed up everything we had. Whatever that was.'

'What do you mean?'

'Well . . .' Kitty began, her eyes distant. 'You know. Everything I believed in. Marriage, babies. I thought I was going to live this fairy tale – like the ones I used to read as a little girl. I thought I'd meet my prince, get married, and live happily ever after – oh, and become a famous actress in between!'

'So what happened?'

'Everything just wore me down. And he didn't help.'

Suddenly Kitty turned to Millie and laid her hand gently over hers. 'It's late and I need as much beauty sleep as I can get these days. Have you seen my bags?'

'You're gorgeous, Kitty.'

'Why thank you, Mills. But I really have to go to bed. I was only waiting up for you.'

Millie wanted to carry on this conversation, but Kitty was right, it was late.

'Just promise me one thing, Mills.'

She nodded her head.

'You won't ever let any man treat you badly.'

THIRTEEN

'Lena. I'd like to speak to Lena, please,' reiterated Michael impatiently.

The operator's voice, previously laden with the joys of spring, suddenly went mute.

'Hello, are you still there?' asked Michael.

'Y . . . yes . . . I am.'

'Can I speak to Lena, please?'

'She's not here at the moment. Can I . . . can I . . .? I'll put you through to someone else who may be able to help you with your . . . your enquiry.'

Michael didn't quite know what to make of that, but at least she wasn't crying like the woman on the helpline the other day. Now *that* had been weird and totally unexpected. Michael's stomach clenched painfully as he thought: what if something really bad had happened? But if that were so, why had he received that strange phone call? Michael waited with dread as a wannabee Celine Dion warbled unwelcome into his ears.

'May I help you?' said a woman's voice, finally.

'Lena? Is that you?' he asked, hopefully. People always sounded different on the phone, not that he could actually remember what Lena sounded like with all the bus noise, just those lovely piercing green eyes . . .

'No, this isn't Lena, but can I help you?'

'I'd much rather speak to Lena.'

'Was it something specific you wanted to speak to her about?'

'No, I'm a friend and I haven't been able to get hold of her for some time.'

'Oh, I see.' The voice faltered. Followed by silence.

'Are you still there?'

'Yes, of course.' She cleared her throat. 'When . . . when was the last time you spoke to Lena?'

'A good few weeks ago.' His voice faltered. What was going on?

'So you wouldn't have heard?'

'Heard what?'

'I'm sorry, I . . .'

A pause as Michael began to fear the worst again. 'What's happened?'

'I've already said too much. We have confidentiality procedures in place that must be followed. I don't even know who you are.'

'I'm a friend . . .'

'Then I suggest you contact her family.'

Michael was sure he was being tested. For all this woman knew, he could be the resident psycho and if he was the friend he claimed, surely he'd know her address or at the very least have another number for Lena.

'Please . . .' he pleaded.

'We're all so . . . so devastated here,' said the woman, her voice faltering. Any minute the woman was going to break down, he could feel it.

'Devastated? About what? Please, please, I'm desperate.' In more ways than one, he thought.

'Look, she's in hospital and that's all I can tell you. Please, I've said enough. Have . . . have a good evening.' And then the line went dead.

So that was it. Lena, the girl on the bus, was in hospital.

But what did that mean? Was she seriously hurt? Was that why he hadn't seen her for weeks? Who had called him and why? Michael's head throbbed with all the questions. He had to know what had happened to Lena.

He immediately made a list of the hospitals that were close to the bus route: King's College, St Thomas, and Fen Lane.

At work, he'd made the decision to visit each and every one of those hospitals. But then he'd begun to think how pathetic that was, considering he didn't know what ward she was in, or anything much about her condition. On the bus home he began to feel a bit hopeless about finding Lena, and decided to drop in to the bar he and Charlotte had been to the other night.

'Can I have a Mojito please?' he asked the barwoman.

'That will be five pounds sixty, please.'

'But it's happy hour!' he protested.

'That finished five minutes ago,' she said in a 'do I give a rat's bum?' voice.

Michael sighed at the injustice of it all and handed over the money. There was something strungely familiar about this woman.

'Okay,' she relented. 'You look like you've had a worse day than me. And in honour of that, you can have it half price.'

'Thanks.'

'I'm feeling generous. It'll never happen again.'

'Sounds like you need one as well,' Michael said.

'Don't let's get all cliché now and start swapping sad stories over the bar.'

'Point taken,' smiled Michael as she prepared the mint for

his drink. He sipped his Mojito, his thoughts consumed by the girl with the green eyes.

By now, Michael was on his third drink and it wasn't even happy hour. The drink tasted so much better than the first time he'd bought a Mojito there, which probably had a lot to do with the tiny woman, who made the best Venezuelan Mojitos he'd ever tasted.

'I met her on a bus,' Michael suddenly blurted out.

'A bus. Romantic!' The woman smiled.

'We've only spoken once.'

'You need to get a life.'

'Maybe.'

She handed another Mojito to him.

'We have spoken, though. Just once.'

'You said that already. Is she nice? Hold on a sec. Yes, what can I get you?' She said, turning to another customer. Michael was finding it strangely comforting talking to a stranger about Lena.

'Okay, carry on with the story,' she enthused.

'We've spoken yes, but only for a few minutes and just once. She has these really nice—' Michael felt himself blushing.

'Careful there.'

'Eyes! She had really nice eyes. And she was so warm and friendly to me.'

'You've got to speak up, mate!' she shouted, because some idiot had just turned up the music and it was deafening.

'I'd better go home,' he said, losing his nerve yet again. Same boring, silly story. He didn't need to bombard this woman with it all.

He hopped off the stool, feeling a sharp rush to his head as the alcohol he'd consumed started to make him feel quite woozy. He was just about to leave, when the tiny woman who'd served him patted him on the shoulder.

'Off already?'

'Getting late.'

'Sorry about before. The music and that. My sister mistook the bar for a disco just because she'd finished her shift. What was it you were saying?'

'You really want to know?' he asked, surprised but pleased.

'Not really. But something happened to me recently and, if anything, it's made me think about . . . I don't know . . . listening more to people. So don't for a minute think I give a damn,' she grinned. 'It's just the guilt talking. Besides, have to keep you sweet, you're a paying customer and you do like to down those Mojitos at an alarming rate.'

They headed back to the bar area and Michael slid onto a stool.

'On the house,' she said as she began chopping the lime. 'Get on with it then. The girl.'

From what he'd seen of her in the bar, this woman was a fiery little thing who could definitely hold her own. She wasn't afraid to speak her mind, which she did – but not in a way that made him feel like a loser. So he continued this time more slowly and more clearly. And it looked as if she was listening, even if she did serve a dozen customers in the meantime. He was rather tipsy, that much he knew, so he wasn't quite sure if he'd offended her as suddenly her face took on a strange pallour. And especially when, without warning, she turned her back and calmly walked away – returning a few moments later and slid a photograph across the counter towards him.

'This her?'

FOURTEEN

Michael stood outside Fen Lane Hospital feeling a bit of an idiot.

He was wearing the smartest clothes he owned and was clutching a massive bunch of red roses as he tried to ignore the fluttering in his tummy and the mix of excitement and dread that had followed him about all morning.

Last night had been a monumental, colossal moment of surprise. Everything had seemed to come together in the space of a few minutes.

And yet he still couldn't believe it.

He blew out an exaggerated puff of air, his arm aching with the awkward way he held the roses, which on retrospect were probably a bit much. And they were red. What did *that* say?

He'd been shocked but pleased when Cara (the one named after Irene Cara! Of course!) had asked him to visit and said it might help Lena. But he began to wonder what he'd say once he got there. He'd only spoken to Lena once. He didn't really known her like her family and *real* friends. But Cara was aware of this; she had admitted calling him that night and yet had still felt comfortable enough to invite him along.

Was she insane?

Was *he* insane to agree?

What would he say once he got there? 'Err hello, remember me? I'm the idiot on the bus who was complaining about the teenagers.' Of course she wouldn't remember, even if she hadn't been asleep for almost five weeks. This was beyond silly. They'd hardly ever spoken. A woman as lovely as Lena was probably used to all sorts of desperados chatting her up.

No, visiting a virtual stranger in hospital was not how he'd planned to spend his day off. No way.

But he was going in.

He had to go.

So, Michael greeted Cara warmly as she met him outside the sign: ICU to the right. Antenatal Outpatients to the left.

'You came!'

'I don't think this is a good idea,' he said with a slight shiver. It was a cold October day, but he had to admit that the trembling was more down to nerves than the temperature.

'It is a good idea, trust me. Millie thinks so too, and we never agree on anything!' she said.

'Millie. Named after Millie Small.'

'How do you know that?'

'Lena told me. On the bus.'

Cara smiled warmly. He suspected she didn't smile much.

'Anyway, Cara how is Lena going to feel?' Michael was still not sure. 'You bringing a stranger in there to see her? I don't think she'll thank you for it later.'

'You never know, it might help. A different voice. Especially one she went on about!'

'She did?' This surprised Michael, and he felt a flutter of pleasure at this disclosure. 'She spoke about me a lot then?'

'Well, to be honest, I'm not sure. She mentioned you at least once.'

'Once or more than once?' Michael was intrigued.

'I don't know, do I? You see, I had this knack of not listening to her.' Cara replied quietly.

It wasn't long before he was following Cara into the hospital, up the stairs and outside the ICU ward.

He peered in through the open doors to the department. The ward was lit by dull lighting. Nurses tended to patients and machines beeped, while a doctor scribbled down notes suddenly Michael wasn't sure what he was doing there. He felt disrespectful, like a voyeur, as he stood beside Cara who was wearing the highest heels he'd ever seen.

'Lena's not in there, she's in Primrose Ward.'

His short sigh signalled his relief and they went on through to Lena's ward, stopping outside her door.

'Michael, just trust me on this one,' she said before they went in. 'You are meant to be here. I didn't find your card amongst Lena's things by accident, and you didn't just walk into my bar for no reason. You're meant to be here. Just trust me.'

And then Cara opened the door.

It was her. He recognized her instantly.

Granted, the last time he'd seen her she'd been awake, eyes open, vibrant, singing really badly about falling in love on a smelly and noisy bus, and not lying on a hospital bed. But this was – unmistakably and without a shadow of a doubt – Lena.

Cara explained again about the accident. How Lena had fallen down a flight of stairs at her boyfriend's house. The deep sleep. The lack of change in her condition. But while Cara spoke, her voice began to almost float away as Michael's whole body remained transfixed on the girl with the beautiful eyes that right now, were closed shut.

'I can't believe it,' he whispered.

'We couldn't either. But it happened.'

He couldn't believe that he had found her. That the girl

he'd first seen on that noisy bus, was right there in front of him. Asleep.

She was just as beautiful, even asleep. And he couldn't take his eyes off her. Her hair, was just as wild as he remembered, even though it was tied up in a band. She also smelled of something lemony and sweet. It suited her. He wondered if her skin was warm but didn't dare touch. The sheets on the bed were clean and white. Crisp, even, just the way his mum's sheets always looked. He wondered what she was thinking. Feeling. And was she actually thinking, feeling, and dreaming? He hoped she was dreaming.

'I'm glad you came, Michael.'

He jumped upon hearing Cara's voice because, for those few moments, he'd thought it had just been him and Lena.

An older lady came in, introducing herself as Kitty, Lena's mother, and Michael was instantly aware of the tension between Kitty and Cara.

'I haven't seen you before. You a friend of Lena's?' she said, holding out her hand.

'Erm . . .' he began as he took her hand and glanced at Cara, who nodded her head as confirmation to continue. 'Yes, I'm a friend,' he agreed, certain that Lena's mother would work out he was an impostor. He sat back down onto the chair as she arranged the flowers he'd bought.

'Red roses. Nice. I used to get those on opening night.'

'You're an actress?' He asked, still unable to take his eyes off Lena.

'She did some amateur dramatics a few decades ago,' Cara grumbled.

'I thought the roses looked nice in the shop,' he said nervously changing the subject.

'Expensive. And romantic.' Kitty gushed.

'No . . . it's not like that!' he added, quickly.

'I'm only joking. Ignore me. I just need to make a joke

from time to time – otherwise,' she pulled in closer to him and whispered, 'it can get a bit serious around here.'

'The flowers are fine,' said Cara.

'I know, but for next time, perhaps get some daisies. Lena loves daisies – that much I remember.'

'I'll get some next time.'

'So you will come again?' asked Cara, almost telling him as opposed to asking.

'Yes,' he said, sounding more sure than he actually felt.

'It's good to see you here. A few of her work colleagues have come. Where do you know my Lena from, then?'

Michael didn't want to sound stupid, but guessed he would whatever he said. 'We ride the same bus into work.'

'Oh, okay,' said the mother.

He glanced over at Lena, then to Cara, then back to the mother. The obvious animosity between Cara and her mother was a bit stifling, coupled with the whole crazy scenario he now found himself in.

And then the final piece of this crazy puzzle arrived.

Millie.

She was clutching a huge Argos carrier bag and dressed in a pair of black shorts and sheer tights. She was good looking in a 'sexy vamp' type of way. And certainly not his type.

'Hi all . . .' she said, stopping in her tracks as she set eyes on him and smiled warmly.

'What's in the bag, Mills?' asked Kitty.

'Oh just some shopping.'

She opened up the plastic bag and box, to reveal an oval-shaped pink radio/CD player. 'This is for Lena. I just bought it. I thought playing some of her favourite tracks might . . . I dunno, help bring her round? Oh, I don't know, I just used to see it happen on the telly sometimes.'

'No, you're right. Anything could help. It must have been pretty expensive, though,' said Kitty.

'Not really. Just sixty quid.'

'You've only just started at the bar and it's only for two weeks! Couldn't you have just bought your one in?' added Cara.

'It's tip money, okay?' she said, sounding mildly hurt. Not surprising, thought Michael, considering she had done a good deed and was getting questioned about it. What was with this family? And why did these girls call their mother Kitty?

'What CDs do you have there?' asked Kitty.

'Just two at the moment. Amerie's *All I Have* and Oasis's *What's The Story?* She was always listening to them on her MP3.'

'I've heard of Oasis,' said Kitty. 'Those brothers. Who's the other one?'

'Amerie's an American singer,' cut in Cara as she inspected the CD player.

'I'm more into Ella, Aretha, and some Gladys, me. Amerie? Don't they know how to name their kids?' Kitty tutted.

'You named us after singers, Kitty!' said Millie.

'That's true!'

The four of them giggled and suddenly the tension in the room evaporated.

Kitty excused herself and headed out for a walk around the grounds as Cara pushed the play button on the pink CD player. It was on low, faint, but loud enough for Michael to catch the beat. The voice of the singer was smooth and silky.

'Lena was very secretive about you,' said Cara.

'In what way?' Michael wasn't sure what she really knew or what Lena had told her about him, but he was curious.

'Well, as I said before, maybe I wasn't really listening . . .' She trailed off as if deep in thought and Michael felt a bit sorry for her. 'But when I saw your business card in her "Important Stuff" folder, I knew you must have meant something.'

He was in her 'Important Stuff' folder!

'Lena has a boyfriend right . . . Jason?'

'Justin. Who hardly visits and who I don't really want to waste time talking about if that's okay with you.'

'Sure.' Michael sensed an overload of animosity towards this bloke and decided he wouldn't probe any further.

'But if I know Lena, she must have been thinking of you on some level, even though she'd never have cheated on Justin. You must have made her think . . . enough to want to call you one day . . . Oh, I don't know . . .'

'And the notebook no one can find,' added Millie.

'There were occasions she tried to speak to me about loads of stuff really, and I, well let's just say I had my own things going on and didn't give her much of my time,' continued Cara.

'Me too,' added Millie quietly.

Michael could see the pain in both their eyes, especially Cara's. Of course *he* wasn't going to embrace her, but figured a hug was what they both needed. Perhaps from one another – and he wondered why they weren't doing that.

'Don't beat yourself up about it,' he said.

'You don't understand,' Cara's voice was harsh, self-critical. 'With me it was always: Lena, shall I buy a bar? Shall I buy a flat? Can you do a shift at the bar for me?'

Michael didn't need to be a shrink to grasp that this weird family seemed to be missing key ingredients. But at that moment, he was more interested in what Lena had said about *him*.

'I wish we could have spent more time together. As friends . . . well . . . She seemed fun.' Michael said cheerily.

'She was . . . is,' added Millie.

They were all suddenly lost in their own personal memories of Lena until Cara's face launched into a smile and, for a second, she looked a lot less severe. 'I still can't believe you're here. If I wasn't such a cynic, I'd have called this fate.'

'Maybe it is fate!' protested Millie, whom Michael suspected had to be the 'softer' of the two, with Lena somewhere in between. Lena had to be tough to do the kind of job she did, but when it came to matters of the heart, he suspected she was a big softy.

'Can you play track one again?' asked Michael, pointing to the CD player.

'And you both like Amerie. Spooky,' said Millie, as she flipped back to the first track.

'I'd never heard of this singer until now.'

'You will again, don't worry. That's if you come again . . . I mean it's your choice, after all. We could just give you a call when she wakes up if you'd prefer? Which she will soon. Very soon,' said Cara determinedly.

There was just something about this girl with the pretty eyes, named Lena Curtis that he was so desperate to know more about. To be able to do that, he would have to visit her regularly, and spend time with her. Of course he would be coming back. It was a no-brainer.

As the electric doors of Fen Lane Hospital slid open that night, he took a deep breath and wondered why he couldn't feel the usual presence of a cloud that seemed to follow him around most days. In fact, as he jumped off the bus and made his way to his flat, what he felt was a bit alien and something he couldn't quite articulate at that very moment. All he knew was that when he opened his front door and immediately sat on his sofa, he wasn't feeling the usual stabs of negativity and hopelessness he'd become accustomed to.

Something else was going on for him and it felt very, very weird.

And really, really, really good.

FIFTEEN

Cara loaded the dishwasher as she listened to Ade voice his concerns.

'Just what do you know about this Michael bloke?'

'I know that Lena mentioned him once or twice.' Cara shrugged.

'Did she like him?'

'Are you suggesting my sister was about to have an affair?'

'Of course not!'

'Just kidding, babes. Gosh, you're easy!' she said, reaching up to tickle his chin playfully. 'Course, I wouldn't blame her if she did. I mean, look at Justin, he was hardly there for her when she needed him, those text messages prove that.' Of course she wasn't going to mention her own messages that Lena had saved.

'Even now, when she needs him the most, he's isn't there for her. I've hardly seen him at the hospital.'

'I don't know what's going on in his mind, but I know that if anything happened to you I don't know what I'd do,' he said, running his hand through her hair gently.

'Anyway, I just know that Lena's going to be okay. And meeting Michael, I mean, that just tells me something . . .'

'What does it tell you?'

'I don't know, Ade, something. Maybe I'll never know. But it's like he might just be the breath of fresh air that could help her.'

'I just want you to be careful,' he said, scooping her into his arms again.

'I will be. Don't you worry about me.'

Michael was in a mood so upbeat that it could almost match the pulsating beats coming from Warren J's Muzic Yard, as he pushed open the shop door.

'We're about to close, mate!' said the man with the large Mohican behind the wooden counter. All around, posters advertising upcoming concerts, new CDs, music week-enders, singers, rappers, and a couple of bands he hardly recognized, adorned the walls. He suddenly felt a thousand years old.

'I'll come back.' Michael turned to walk out.

'Oh alright just a quick browse, then,' beckoned the man, as he carried on putting up a poster advertising an event at a local bar.

Michael hesitated, feeling a bit of a wally before making his way to the counter. 'Do you have someone called Anna Marie?' he asked the man, who had blue and green high-lights in a neatly cut goatee.

'Anna Marie? Nah, haven't heard of her. Sorry, mate.'

Michael touched his own chin absently. 'Oh right. She sings love songs.' As soon as he said it, he knew how stupid he must have sounded.

'Sorry, mate. Tell you what, if you know the name of one of her songs, that would be a start.'

Michael scratched his head trying to remember the name of the song Lena had mentioned on the bus.

'I think it's called, "I Want to Fall in Love with You"?'

It felt totally wrong saying something like this to another bloke. Michael looked around him quickly, but luckily no one else was in the shop.

'Oh wait. You don't mean Amerie, do you?'

'Yes. That's it!'

The man looked at his watch. 'Tell you what, I'll put on her latest album and you can tell me if you recognize any of the tracks.'

That sounded like a plan. 'It will be track one. The first one, definitely.' Michael was pleased to be able to provide something to go on. The man rummaged about under the counter and picked up a CD case, slid out the disk and slipped it into the player. What followed was a strong mix of heavy base and the smooth tones of the singer he'd recently grown to recognize. Problem was, he didn't recognize the song.

'No, this isn't it. No, it's softer than that!' he shouted above the music. 'And you're sure it's track one?' asked Mohican-man.

'Definitely.' He didn't want to ask him to go through each and every track, especially as he was closing up.

'Hang on, she's had three albums you know.'

'Has she?'

'Yes,' Mohican-man nodded. 'Tell you what, I'll put in the first album. Then we'll go with the second. Can't be that hard to find it, then.' He rummaged around in the back and Michael heard him replace the CD with another one.

And then he heard 'Lena's' song.

'That's it!' he said.

'"Why Don't We Fall in Love?" Great tune,' said Mohican-man, bobbing his head in time to the music. Michael wished he was *cool* enough to do the same but wasn't about to risk it.

'Thanks so much,' he said.

'Enjoy, mate.'

Back at home, Michael almost left the door open behind

him, such was his haste to load the CD into the player he hardly used any more. He waited for the soft tones of 'Why Don't We Fall in Love?' to flood into the room.

A stab of recognition immediately hit him as well as a clear image of Lena as he allowed every note and each beat to sink into him, absorb him, and take him to another place.

Listening to the words in isolation from the music was something he'd never done before with a song. The chorus, yes, but the rest of the song? No way. Wasn't that what women did? The stuff about falling in love was obvious. But there were other things in the song, *about tomorrow not being promised.* He wasn't sure how long Lena had been with Justin, or if he came before the song, but he suspected that the words meant something special to her. He realized he could sit and hypothesize all night, but it probably made sense to think about what the words meant to *him.*

Now, his first reaction would be to say 'hot girl singing about love.' But now he'd really had a chance to think about it he could say . . . hot girl singing about not waiting for things to happen. Not waiting another minute. The 'love' was just something slotted in to sell records. It was enchanting, haunting, sweet and hopeful all at once. Fast. Slow. Urgent. Questioning. It was like Lena was talking to him. Letting him know about how she felt about her own life. Telling him not to make the same mistakes that he was about to.

So, he wasn't going to let her down. No, more importantly, he wasn't going to let *himself down.*

Not any more.

The cold air felt refreshing as it worked its way into his lungs. Michael was doing something he'd never thought of before – he was jogging. He jogged past the shops on Lordship Lane and managed to make it all the way to the bottom of Sydenham

Hill, ignoring the slight ache in his knees and the stitch in his side. His aim was to get to the top of the hill and he would – even though his legs were on the verge of buckling and he felt on the verge of throwing up his breakfast. His T-shirt was stuck to his chest with sweat and he could hardly hear Amerie's silky tones through his headphones any more – but he was determined not to stop until he reached the top.

This was personal.

Michael doubled over, clutching his knees. He'd done it. It was a victory. Small to some, but massive to him. The start of something new. He felt absolutely invigorated by the adrenaline coursing through his body as he took in the scene before him. A couple were strolling hand in hand, a man was walking two unruly Great Danes, a woman peered into a shop window, and two women were laughing together over a magazine. Michael was ready to be part of all this again. To live again. He wasn't about to carry on waiting for his life to begin. What was the point in looking for this 'something' that wasn't there?` And what was it anyway? A bigger house, a car, a promotion? What happens whilst you wait to get those things? What happens while you are dreaming? Life was too short. Seeing Lena lying in that hospital bed only went to prove that. It could happen to anyone, even him! So he promised himself one thing as he stood at the top of that hill, sweaty, panting and all:

MICHAEL WAS READY TO START LIVING AGAIN.

And it was all thanks to Lena Curtis.

SIXTEEN

'There you go Michael,' said Kitty, handing over the poly-styrene cup of water. This time she was in a burgundy short crop wig, which he thought was a bit 'out there' for someone her age – yet she still managed to carry it off. He only knew it was a wig as she'd quite openly told him. Kitty had also been telling him about all the incredible places she had visited, travelling around the world – Las Vegas, India, Australia. Although she went on a bit, he had to admire her spirit. He was half her age and hadn't gone further than the Costa del Sol, and even that was ten years ago.

'How did you find the money to go to all those places?' he asked.

Kitty squeezed her eyes shut and, for one horrific moment, he thought she was about to burst into tears. Instead she swallowed hard. 'Let's just say, I've done some things without thinking them through.' She moved closer to him. 'Have you ever done something, Michael, that you thought was for the best, to help someone you love, when all it did was make their lives that much harder?'

Kitty was staring intently, making him feel as if a profound and thoughtful answer was needed.

'I'm not sure . . .'

'Never mind. I don't want to bore you . . . You're a good friend to Lena and I'd like to keep it that way!'

Michael nodded silently. All he really wanted right now was to sit with Lena on his own. He realised though that he wasn't family and they needed to be around Lena as much as possible. To be honest, Lena's family had been warm and welcoming towards him so he couldn't really complain. He'd met everyone except Justin, and since buying the Amerie album, had felt so much closer to Lena. He'd even downloaded it onto his mobile phone to listen to on the way in to work.

'I was thinking, Michael, how about you come to the house for dinner?'

Michael almost choked on his water. Kitty was asking him to come to Lena's house. He begun to panic slightly. Wasn't this all happening a bit too soon?

'I won't take no for an answer, you know. I'm going to cook us all a feast. Cara hardly eats these days, so it will be my way of getting some healthy food into her. You'd really be helping me out . . .'

'I'd love to,' he said, suddenly shedding his aprehension.

On the way back from the hospital, Michael was excited about the dinner and he wondered if that made him a saddo. If it did, he certainly didn't feel like one – not like before. As soon as he got in, he immediately changed into his track-suit bottoms, appalled at the thought of spending the evening slumped in front of the telly like he used to – that just seemed like a waste of precious time. Instead he was going for a run again. He also decided that if he was going to carry on with this new fitness regime, he'd have to get some new trainers. His current pair were practically falling apart. So, this gave him the rare urge to shop and purchase those brown suede Pumas he'd had his eye on.

Michael was instantly reminded of why he never went to

Covent Garden, or why as a rule only did a clothes shop once a year. Battling his way through the crowds of strangely animated people getting all excitable over clothes just wasn't him. But he found, much to his surprise that he started to feel a pleasant buzz in buying a new wardrobe. He was feeling brighter than he had in ages. Which was probably why he was currently standing in a branch of Ted Baker holding up a soft caramel leather jacket that had caught his attention.

'Would you like to try it on?' asked the young sales assistant.

'No thanks,' he replied with a smile as he carefully placed the jacket onto the display bench, or whatever it was. This all felt surreal.

'Go on, it's a nice piece.'

Nice price too, luv, he thought. 'It's a bit . . . um . . .'

Michael bit his bottom lip.

'And I think it would look great on you!' she added encouragingly.

Much to the sales assistant's glee, he slid on the leather jacket, which he had to admit felt and looked incredible.

'Looks great,' she said as he unwittingly became part of a corny makeover scene and the store's entertainment for the day.

'Don't you feel great in it?' squealed a voice behind him who seemed to be the store manager.

He glanced at the atrocious price tag as every sensible bone in his body screamed out don't buy it!

But his heart couldn't let go. This jacket represented the *new* Michael.

So, he paid for the jacket and scuttled out of the store, determined never to go back to Covent Garden again to shop for clothes, yet secretly excited that he'd bought an expensive and luxurious piece of clothing for himself without thinking too deeply about the consequences or how it would impact on his future life plans.

Once home, he placed the jacket into the wardrobe, thinking he would keep it 'for best'. But as soon as he thought it, he became annoyed with himself. What did 'for best' actually mean anyway? He could hear his mum's voice in his heard, talking about only bringing out her 'best' China on special occasions. But when would the 'special occasions' be? A year? A month? A decade? And in the meantime, the china set never got used and no one got to experience it until Charlotte kicked a football through the window and straight into the dresser on which his mother's prized crockery was displayed, smashing half of it into tiny pieces. Charlotte got grounded, his mother was upset; but the real sadness was that this tea set had only ever been used once, even though it had been sitting in the cabinet for over ten years!

He saw the same thing happening with the jacket. He'd save it, until one day he'd be too old to wear it and it would no longer fit. No, he was going to wear it *now*. Enjoy it and, yes, suffer the inevitable ribbing from Charlotte sooner rather than later.

SEVENTEEN

A few months ago . . .

It was a Sunday late afternoon. It had been Lena's first afternoon off from Kidzline in weeks and she was exhausted. She'd been pestering Millie and Cara about getting a date in their diaries for weeks. Sometimes Lena and Cara had got together, and other times Millie and Lena. But not all three of them.

Lena felt subdued, distant even, and although this wasn't like her, none of her sisters seemed to notice that day as they sat in Lena's favourite noodle bar in Old Compton Street.

'You know how much I hate it in this cheapo place,' said Cara as she tapped away on her mobile phone.

'The food's good here,' replied Lena and not taking offence at her sister's bluntness.

'But are you even sure the kitchen's hygienic?' said Cara as she inspected the table for dust.

'You're such a snob!' said Millie.

'I suppose this is like going to the Ritz for you!' tutted Cara.

'Girls!' protested Lena as the starters – a huge portion of spring rolls arrived. 'I'm just glad that we could all make it.'

'I can't stay long because I have a date,' said Millie.

'But you just got here!' complained Lena.

'And you were late!' added Cara.

'Sorry, but you know how special he is.'

'Who is it this time?' asked Cara, picking at the spring rolls.

'What are you trying to say?'

'That there's a different man every week!' laughed Cara cattily.

'Why are you such a bitch?' Millie said throwing her spring roll onto her plate.

'Why are you such a slag?'

'Stop it!' shouted Lena. She'd had enough, not just of the bickering but the clear disregard for her feelings. No one had any time for her. No one had any time to listen to her – because if they had, they would know how tired she was of putting in all the hours she could at Kidzline, helping out Cara at the bar, and all her money worries with the house. IF ONLY THEY'D TAKE TIME OUT TO LISTEN.

Cara's phone rang for the third time.

'Oh look, you know what?' said Lena, placing a ten-pound note on to the table and standing up. 'I've had it with you both. I'm leaving.' And with that, she was gone. Leaving both Millie and Cara open-mouthed and amazed at their sister's outburst. Lena didn't do outbursts! And as they both got up to leave – Cara to go to work at her bar and Millie to meet her latest boyfriend – they were left wondering why she'd behaved in such a way, promising themselves they'd call her up and have it out with her. Find out what was wrong.

But the bar was extra busy that night and Rik was just so adorable.

They'd bring it up the next time they saw her.

The next time they saw her was in a room in the Primrose

Ward at Fen Lane Hospital with a naso gastric tube in her nose.

After a particularly tiring shift, and having spent most of the morning at the hospital, Cara couldn't wait to snuggle up to Ade. But when she walked into the flat that night, it was dark and there didn't seem to be any sign that he'd been home. Spending so much time with Lena, she often found herself longing to be home in her cosy flat. Lena's hospital room felt so lonely and cold at times.

She turned on the light and slipped out of her floral stilettos.

'Surprise!' shouted Ade, popping out from nowhere, a dusky rose between his teeth, wearing a smart suit and clutching a bottle of champagne in his hand.

'You almost frightened me to death! Are you insane?' she said with an excited smile. He took the rose from his mouth and handed it to her.

'Happy anniversary, baby.'

'Oh no. I'm so sorry, Ade – I . . . I can't believe this!' Cara had forgotten their ten-year anniversary, the first time such a date had slipped her mind. She remembered thinking about it some time last week, but what with everything it had completely slipped away again.

'No worries. You've had a lot on your plate. We all have. Now you sit down and try and guess what I've bought you.' He leaned over the side of the sofa and retrieved a box.

'A present? For me?' Cara punched him playfully on the arm with glee. The man was amazing and she was the worst girlfriend in the world forgetting their anniversary!

'Open it,' he urged.

She opened the lid of the cream box and took out a most exquisite shoe. It was mint green satin with a large platform heel.

'I hope you like them?' Ade asked nervously.

'They're gorgeous. I LOVE them'. Cara said, planting a big kiss on his lips.

'It's for when we go out . . . you know . . .'

For a moment there, Cara felt a spasm of guilt about daring to think of happy things, about allowing herself to dream of having some fun again.

But, as always, Ade had read her mind. 'It is okay, you know. If anything, Lena would definitely approve. She knows shoes are your thing. And it *is* our anniversary.'

She thought back to their anniversary last year. Ade had booked a table at a lovely little restaurant. It had been so romantic and perfect. Now, here she was a year later, and all she wanted was for Lena to come back. To hell with everything else!

People just don't know how lucky they are.

They ate dinner by candlelight on their tiny balcony and it was wonderful.

He'd made a supreme effort, perhaps more so because of the current circumstances. But as they ate and she reflected on the day, she realized that the only present she had really wanted was to see Lena wake out of that deep sleep with a big smile, high five and a request for a ginger beer. She'd fantasized every night that a call would come through from Fen Lane summoning them to the hospital because Lena was asking for her. But it hadn't.

'To us!' said Ade as their champagne-filled glasses chinked together.

'To Lena,' said Cara.

They were soon interrupted by an unexpected knock at the door and, for a second, Cara wondered if it might be the hospital.

'Who was it?' asked Cara as Ade returned from answering the door.

'Next door – he took a delivery for us whilst we were at work.'

Cara turned around and immediately noticed the bunch of bright purple roses. They were exquisite and must have cost Ade a fortune.

'They're not from me, babe.'

Cara jumped up and took the card from the bunch.

'To My Sister – happy ten year anniversary, I love you.
To Ade – how have you put up with her for so long?
Love and stuff, Lena.
PS – do you know how hard it is to get purple roses? '

EIGHTEEN

Cara gazed happily at the fresh daisies, Michael had quickly replaced the red roses with. It was as if any hint of decay was not allowed in Lena's room. Cara had taken a single purple rose from her anniversary bunch and placed them with the daisies in the vase and she had to admit the display beside Lena's bed looked really good; the CD player was a bright block of pink beside the flowers and the smell of lemongrass wafted in the air as she finished smoothing the oil moisturizer into Lena's scalp. Cara was still dizzy from Lena's wonderful gift. Knowing Lena had planned the delivery in advance had made her almost leap with joy, as it was proof that her sister's thoughts about Cara before the accident had been laden with love and thoughtfulness.

'I did read that familiar sounds can really help,' said Michael as Clara placed Lena's hair back into the pink band. Although she would never complain about coming to the hospital daily, she was glad to have different company in the shape of Michael, who seemed to be coming over quite a bit, which was great as it meant not having to deal with Kitty much, who was thankfully on one of her daily walks around the hospital grounds.

'It's really fascinating, the research . . .'

'I know . . .' she began as her eyes caught Justin standing in the doorway. What she saw shocked her. Justin was usually well dressed and groomed, but in front of her was a bedraggled looking man who looked like he hadn't slept in days, yet she still couldn't conjure up any sympathy for him.

'Cara, how are you?' he asked, either totally ignoring or not noticing the total hunk in a really nice leather jacket sitting by his girlfriend's bed.

'Good thanks. Nice to see you,' she lied. Although she couldn't care if she never saw him again, she was actually pleased he'd come, not least because Michael was around. 'And this is Michael,' she said, a little awkwardly. She watched intently at the expression on Justin's face. She was going to enjoy this.

'Hello,' said Michael. Justin looked towards him, at first confused.

'This is a friend of Lena's, Justin. Michael, meet Justin, Lena's boyfriend.'

As they shook hands, their eyes remained transfixed on one another's. At first Justin looked confused, before switching tack to annoyance. 'Who are you?' he demanded. 'Lena never mentioned you.'

'I'm . . . I'm a friend.'

'You don't sound very sure about that,' Justin said aggressively.

'Leave him alone, Justin!'

'Leave him alone? I just want to know who he is and why he's sitting in *my* girlfriend's hospital room. When I know that, then I'll leave him alone!'

Just then, Nurse Gratten walked in, face like thunder. 'Can you please keep your voices down? I won't have this on my shift!'

'Sorry, Nurse,' said Justin, whilst still gazing towards Michael.

'I'd better be going,' said Michael awkwardly. Cara got up and followed him out of the room, almost skipping.

'Sorry about that,' she said outside the room.

'No. It's all my fault. I shouldn't have come.'

'I'm Lena's family. Me and Millie. And I – well *we* say who comes in here and you are *always* welcome. He's hardly here anyway.'

'Really?'

'It was just a fluke that you met today.' She placed her hand on Michael's elbow.

'Okay.' he replied.

'Just make sure you do. Come back that is. I really think my sister needs to hear a male voice that isn't Ade's or Justin's. She really needs you.'

Cara walked out to the coffee machine, knowing she'd piled it on a bit thick, but what the heck? Michael was good for Lena, she was sure of that. She realised that Justin had hardly looked at Lena once and, come to think of it, on the odd occasions she had seen him by Lena's bed, he hadn't then, either. Perhaps that was just his way. Or perhaps he was at last feeling some of the guilt they all shared. Or was there something else?

As she went back into the room, Justin startled her.

'How long?' he asked.

Cara placed her coffee on the side table and sat down. 'How long, what?'

'How long has Lena been seeing that guy?'

'Are you out of your mind?'

'She tells you things. You'd have known about it . . . so tell me, how long?'

'You heard what the nurse said, keep it down.'

He brushed his hand over his overgrown hair and he suddenly looked a bit deranged. He clearly needed some sleep, perhaps a bath. And he was obviously losing it, thinking Lena would ever have an affair! Wasn't that something he was more likely to do?

'Michael's a mate.'

'A very good-looking mate.'

'What, into men now, are we?'

'Don't make this into a joke. I saw the way he was looking at her.'

'I'm surprised you noticed, considering you never looked at Lena once!'

Silence.

Cara leaned over to retrieve her coffee. By the time she'd bought it to her lips, Justin was heading out again, shoulders slumped and clearly ready to crawl back into the hole he'd just surfaced from.

The showdown with Lena's boyfriend had been a bit embarrassing, Michael reflected. It was all a bit full-on, considering Lena might be able to hear them.

Still, he couldn't help but feel a jab of envy at the lucky git who got to be with Lena, hold her, kiss her, and yet still happened to be a prat! One of those wannabee city types who, no matter how far he got in his job, would still remain an idiot. For reasons unknown to him, Michael decided that Lena's boyfriend Justin (what type of girly name was that anyway?) would forever be his nemesis and that was that.

NINETEEN

At first, Cara had wanted to turn down Kitty's offer of a dinner party at Lena's house. First off, if she, Millie, and Ade were there, who would be sitting with Lena? Who would be looking after the bar? Of course, Ade had come up with weak reassurances that Eliza was capable of the bar part. And, after all, it would only be for a couple of hours. But then when Kitty mentioned inviting Michael *and* Justin – well, the possibility of a face-off between them was just too delicious to ignore. And Cara finally started to look forward to it.

Her sole contribution was to bring dessert so, on the way to the house, she stopped off at the supermarket. Cara hadn't done a proper big food shop since Lena's accident. Ade would get stuff in but, come to think of it, she couldn't actually remember having cooked a full meal in ages. Apart from the anniversary meal, she'd survived on hospital snacks and bar food at A&R. Perhaps a ready meal and a few vegetables wouldn't go amiss, she thought, as she walked down the supermarket aisles. Lena was always lecturing her about eating healthily, and Cara had a distinct memory of her going on about lychees, a fruit that Cara had to admit was quite tasty, even though it had to be one of the messiest and annoying foods around. Who had the time to eat such a fruit anyway? Hardly 'pop it in the mouth' stuff. She placed four lychees into her basket and finally tossed in a chocolate gateau for Kitty's dinner party. She found the shortest-looking till queue where a snotty-nosed child wailed at the top of his voice as his mother looked away.

'I want car!' screamed the child as the mother, clearly hanging onto said car, shook her head vigorously. 'You're not getting it, okay? You've been a naughty little boy!'

'I *want* it!!!!' he squealed and Cara, in a surreal moment, felt like wrestling the mother to the ground, snatching the car and handing it over to the little sod. She'd had a tough day at the bar and the last thing she needed was some screaming kid attacking her earlobes. The boy continued to cry, big heaving sobs. The mother held off defiantly and Cara felt a bit sorry for her. The woman looked exhausted and dressed in a saggy tracksuit and scuffed trainers. Something about her suggested that she hadn't always dressed like this, that 'before' she had cared about how she looked.

As the mother finally gave in and handed over the car, the kid smiled and so did Cara. Peace at last, and a firm acknowledgement that some things she would never be ready for. Ugh!

At the house, Cara shoved the gateau into the fridge and sat down at the huge kitchen table, which had been extended at the sides to accommodate the extra guests. Michael, Ade, Millie, and Kitty were there, with Justin yet to arrive. Kitty had made an effort with the tableware, laying out decorated napkins and Lena's 'best' crystal glasses. It was probably the most effort she'd ever made for any of her daughters' 'parties' and the irony was, Lena wasn't even around to enjoy it.

Cara sat down as her mind recalled another party, some years back . . .

'It's my birthday, I can do what I want!' huffed Cara, close to tears as Lena plaited her second pigtail. Cara's teacher at school had told her what a big girl she was and that big girls don't cry. But it wasn't fair! Lena was saying that she couldn't have a ninth birthday party like all her other friends had.

'But Mummy said no!' said Lena as she wrapped the elastic she'd found in the kitchen round the end of the second plait.

'I hate pigtails! Makes me look like a baby!' said Cara, her bottom lip protruding madly.

'Mummy said you can't have a party and you know we can't ask Dad because he's in America on business. And he would say no, anyway.'

Cara couldn't work out why she couldn't have the party. Mummy would be asleep anyway. She was always asleep these days. In fact, she usually wouldn't come out of her room until around five thirty! Sometimes it was even later now that Dad was away. Which is why having a party was such a good idea. And Cara wondered why nobody except her could see that!

'What are you girls up to?' asked Kitty as she appeared in the kitchen, which now resembled a makeshift hair-dresser's. She was dressed in a headscarf and dressing gown.

'Just finished Cara's hair.' Lena said proudly.

'Well try and keep it down, girls, I don't want you to keep waking me up, okay? Where's Mills?' she said, sitting at the table and stifling a huge yawn.

'She's watching TV,' replied Lena.

'She been fed?'

'Yes, Mummy. I gave her some toast.'

130

'Good,' said Kitty standing up. 'I'm going back to bed. Don't let Millie sit at the TV too long, she's only three!' she said as she disappeared into her room.

The day of Cara's ninth birthday arrived. And, predictably, Kitty was nowhere to be seen for the entire day. But this time she wasn't locked in her room, she was out. Apparently she'd heard about an audition, spruced herself up, and raced to the theatre to wait in line.

Of course, if Cara had known, she'd have told her best friend, Sarah from school, to come over, and maybe a few of the kids from next door too. But instead, Lena bought cupcakes from the corner shop, placed a candle in each one, found a lighter (even though they weren't supposed to play with lighters or matches) and lit them up. It wasn't all bad. Especially when they all sang along to De La Soul and sprayed each other in squirty cream and wore the Christmas hats they'd made at school for Kitty and Donald, which were left untouched in the cupboard under the sink. It ended up being a fun day. Lena had made it fun.

Cara glanced around Lena's kitchen. Above the cooker was a framed stuffed chilli pepper. Daisy-patterned blinds covered the window, and on the windowsill stood an array of house-plants, a wooden tribal face mask and a tiny elephant figurine that Millie had won at the school fete when she was just ten. Lena had kept it all that time.

Millie made herself comfortable next to Michael. She'd only seen him a few times, but each time, he seemed different. Happier. And today, he'd put on some really trendy-looking jacket that must have cost a fortune. It really suited him. He was so caring and the fact that he had spent so much time at the hospital visiting Lena meant he had to be a good bloke, and Millie hadn't met many of those in her life. Plus, those bushy eyebrows were just so cute!

'Great to see you, Michael. And away from the hospital. Well, you know . . .' said Millie.

'I do. And I feel really honoured to have got an invite.'

'Can you pass the bread, Millie? asked Cara. Millie handed her the bread basket as Kitty appeared with a tray of drinks.

Justin arrived looking really rough and sat beside Millie. He seemed to ignore Michael whilst greeting everyone else.

Cara disdainfully passed the bread towards Justin, who took a roll before placing the basket back in the centre of the table with a weak smile. 'This is nice,' he said.

'So, how have you enjoyed being back in London, Kitty?' asked Ade.

Millie's heart skipped a beat. She really wanted to hear this.

Kitty finished chewing the bread, then spoke. 'It's very much how I remembered it, you know?'

'You mean, lively?'

'Oh, Southampton can be lively too. No it's just different. London is different to any place I've ever been to – and I have been to some places!'

Cara stifled a yawn.

'You were in Brazil last. That must have been amazing!' gushed Ade.

'It was. But you're probably bored of me always talking about it!'

'I'd quite like to hear about it,' said Ade, as Millie thought to herself that what she'd quite like to hear would be Kitty mentioning how good it felt to be back amongst her daughters. That, even though it was probably the worst time of her life, the plus side was that she now got to spend time with them again. She just wanted/needed some acknowledgement from her. Anything.

'There's not much to tell.'

'Did you go to Cococabana Beach? What did you see?'

'No, I didn't go there for sightseeing, really.'

'More of a relaxation thing then?' continued Ade.

'Something like that. Oh well, I might as well come clean about why I was there. I'm not ashamed about it . . .'

All eyes turned to Kitty. 'I was there to get a cheap facelift.'

Michael felt more than awkward as he sat at the dinner table. Right up until Justin's appearance he'd enjoyed drinking in the surroundings of Lena's home, seeing where she watched TV, noticing the colourful magnets on the fridge, and the pictures dotted around the place. It made him feel even closer to her. But, as soon as Justin had arrived, he'd really felt like leaving. The man just rubbed him up the wrong way, and his refusal to even say hello – well that was just plain rude.

And now Kitty's little confession.

Kitty bent down and took a large dish out from the oven.

'You need some help with that, Kitty?' asked Michael.

'No way, you're my guest,' she insisted, and Michael caught Justin rolling his eyes.

'Here we are, my speciality and my kids favourite – Chicken Yassa!' She laughed. No one had dared follow up on her mention of the facelift, and Michael was grateful – what she did with her face was . . . well, her own business. Although personally he didn't think she'd needed one.

Michael sipped at his water as Kitty began serving up.

'This smells great,' enthused Ade. 'It's delicious. How do you make it?' asked Michael. 'Well, fresh lime, onions and plenty of black pepper; It's simple really' Kitty said, beaming from all the compliments.

I used to cook this for my girls way back.'

'Funny, I can only remember a couple of occasions when

we all sat down to dinner as a family. As long as Donald was sorted—' began Cara.

'Babe?' said Ade, pleadingly.

Michael too thought Cara was being pretty harsh, but figured Kitty could hold her own. He was used to strong women (you had to be with Charlotte as a sister), but also knew that he wouldn't want to be around when everything exploded – and it would, one day.

The main course went down well, and Millie helped Kitty serve up Cara's chocolate gateau as Michael asked about Lena's progress. It was the first mention of her all evening. It was as if no one had wanted to be the first to bring her name up in the conversation.

'She's still the same you know. No change since you saw her two days ago,' replied Kitty.

'I'm sorry,' he replied, jabbing a fork into the cake.

'You know what I do, when I go into that hospital? I look at Lena, but I don't see the tube, don't hear anything. I just see my girl. My beautiful green-eyed girl. Try it and it won't seem so scary. Just go in and think of her and how she was the last time you saw her.' Kitty was directing that at Justin, Millie could tell.

'I remember a woman from my building who moved in with her husband. When he died, the other residents really couldn't handle it. They'd hardly known him, but the way they acted around that wife of his – criminal. Very bad indeed. At first I thought the other ladies were behaving like that because, well, you know, they were worried that this woman might become some type of fancy widow and start making eyes at their husbands.'

'Blimey, at their age!' said Millie.

'But you know, I don't think it was that. I think it was more about not knowing what to say. And also knowing that one day (and in their case, sooner rather than later) their old

134

asses could be in the same position. No one wants to think about death. Or ageing, for that matter!'

'Hence the facelift,' scoffed Cara quietly, but Kitty heard.

'I didn't get to have the facelift in the end,' Kitty told them, 'because as soon as I heard about my daughter I was on the first plane back.'

'Are we supposed to be grateful?' added Cara.

'Kitty, you don't need to worry about age,' said Ade. But Cara's question hung in the air. Millie felt disappointed: they'd been getting along a lot better lately and she'd hoped that Cara's newfound softness might have extended to Kitty. Clearly not.

'Besides, you look about forty,' said Ade.

'I'd prefer to look thirty!'

'Well, I'm sure you could give any young actress a run for her money!'

'You are sweet, Ade.'

'You must miss it. The stage.'

'Every day. You know, I really thought one of my kids would have followed in my footsteps. Probably Millie; she's got the look. Yes, I definitely thought you might.' She turned to Millie. 'Especially as you were such a brilliant little actress in your school plays!'

Millie scrunched her eyebrows in a 'news to me' expression at Cara.

She only remembered being any good in one school production. And that had been Winton Primary School's production of Joseph and his Technicolour Dreamcoat.

It had been an absolute dream come true. The role everyone wanted and the auditions had served up five contenders for the lead, which included eleven-year-old Millie. But, because the standard was so high, the drama teacher, Mrs Pinkin, had decided that all five girls could sing Joseph's songs with only one lucky girl allowed onto the stage dressed in the actual technicolour dreamcoat.

Millie was selected.

'I got picked out of all those girls!' she enthused.

'But that's so stooppid!' whined Cara.

'Why is it?'

'Coz that means they'll all be singing behind you. Who's gonna hear your rubbish voice anyway!'

'Cara, don't say that, Millie can really sing!' said Lena with a proud smile.

She tenderly scooped Millie into her arms, as she had countless times before. Although Millie was eleven now and a bit too old for it, she savoured these 'secret' cuddles from her big sister.

'You think Mum can make it?' asked Millie.

'Did she say she would?'

'Yeah, but you know . . .'

'Don't worry, she'll be there. She's knows I'm working on my assignment that evening,' said Lena, kissing Millie's forehead softly. 'She'll be there.'

Millie remembered the lights, the sounds, the clapping, her nerves. And the way she stood on that stage and searched for her mother's smiling face. A part of her even expected her father to come, but he had already said he wouldn't and was probably at home reading the paper.

The first act began and ended with no Mummy. By the second act, her mother's seat was finally occupied.

By a beaming, smiling Lena.

Remembering her hurt, even after all this time, Millie could feel her eyes smart and discreetly slid out of her chair to go to the bathroom.

When she returned to the table, Cara seemed to be busy stirring up discord.

136

'I don't know what you're talking about,' said Justin to Cara.

'You remember Lena's thirtieth, right?'

'Of course I do!' he scoffed. Millie started to feel embarrassed that Michael was witnessing this.

'A pity you forgot to turn up to that restaurant in Bloomsbury she'd booked.'

'Were you there?' quizzed Justin. Cara opened her mouth to speak, but nothing whatsoever came out.

'I didn't go either . . . I had things going on! Why are we talking about birthdays anyway?' asked Millie.

'Ask your sister: she brought it up out of nowhere!' said Kitty.

'You weren't there either Kitty!' accused Cara.

'I couldn't make it, no. But I called her,' she replied weakly.

'The next day,' said Cara.

'I was in India with friends and it was hard to make a call,' said Kitty quietly, her eyes flickering.

'And you didn't know you'd be in India when she invited you?'

'I got a cheap deal at the last minute!'

'As usual something more important came up, more likely. So don't any of you tell me I wasn't there for Lena, okay? None of you can talk!' spat Cara.

'Let's all calm down,' said Michael.

'Who exactly are you again?' asked Justin.

But Michael bravely continued regardless. 'I thought we were here for a reason. For Lena. Let's not forget that and . . . and let's keep our arguments for another time. Please. For Lena?'

Eyes darted about, heads bowed, mouths murmured.

'I know you're all hurting in your own way, and no one's taking that away from you. But let's try and band together. Please. For Lena. Please.'

'Michael's right. Do you think Lena would want all this

137

bickering?' said Ade. Millie's expression softened, Kitty closed her mouth, Cara uncurled her fists, and the atmosphere became less tense.

Kitty stood. 'You're right, Michael, we're here for Lena and because of Lena. She bought us all together, in her own way. Me from Southampton – via Brazil – Mills, Cara, Justin, Ade, and you Michael, all of us together.'

Millie smiled with relief.

'I believe in many things. And one of the things I do believe is that my Lena will come back to us. I have to believe.' Kitty's voice seemed to break and Millie wanted to hold her up, and she perhaps would have done if she'd been sitting next to her.

'I just don't think she is ready to come back yet. She's not ready. She's waiting for us to sort out our mess first. And when we do, she'll be back. Of that I am sure.' Kitty slowly sat back down. And that should have been the end of it. A lovely speech to end a not-so-lovely gathering before the coffee was served.

But it wasn't.

As always, Cara had the last word. 'One thing's nagging me,' she began.

'What?' asked Kitty with a sigh.

'If none of us showed up to her thirtieth birthday, and Justin cancelled, then who *was* there?'

'She was all alone?' Kitty ventured to no one in particular. The room fell silent again and, although Millie couldn't be sure what the others were thinking, she could only imagine with horror the sight of Lena, sitting alone at a table for five, wearing her favourite dress, a bit of make-up for once, her corkscrew curls as bouncy as ever it, glancing at her watch every few minutes while waiters eventually moved her to a 'smaller' table. Lena must have felt so hurt, and lonely. After everything she gave to others, nothing, not even a few hours of time, could be given back in return on her birthday.

'I have a suggestion,' said Michael, the only one sitting at that table who did not have a guilty conscience. 'Why don't we just . . . turn back the clock?'

TWENTY

At first it had sounded like the most ridiculous idea ever.

Until Cara really thought about it.

Perhaps it was more for them than Lena, a way of shedding a tiny fraction of the guilt they all shared; but Michael's suggestion to hold a birthday party at the hospital for Lena was a good one. Of course Nurse Gratten whinged a bit and spouted stuff about 'hospital regulations', but when Cara promised they'd be tidy with a maximum of three guests (Justin wasn't invited and Ade and Michael thought it best it was just Cara, Millie and Kitty), she reluctantly agreed.

Cara was about to suggest picking up another one of those delicious gateauxs, before Millie said they should bake a cake.

'Me? Bake a cake?' said Cara. 'Do I look like someone who bakes cakes?'

'Go on! It will be fun!' Millie was clearly very excited and it was rubbing off on Cara.

'Okay, let's do it – on one condition. You don't tell Ade. I don't want him getting any ideas!'

* * *

The baking was a disaster. Cara had bits of flour in her hair and Millie looked as if she'd been bathing in it. Their first attempt resulted in a soggy mess of a sponge that seemed to sink in the middle.

'I'm sure the recipe said four ounces of self-raising flour and four ounces of margarine, right?' asked Millie.

'Right.'

'So what did you put in?'

'I don't know!' cried Cara as they both burst into fits of giggles.

After their third and final attempt, they were ready to give up, but not before each blamed the other for their lack of baking skills!

'Hey, it's not my fault you can't cook as well as you snog boys!' laughed Cara as Millie flopped into the chair and sighed with exaggeration. It had been a good day, even if they did ultimately end up relying on Kitty to prepare Lena's favourite pudding – Chakery, made from couscous pineapple and sour cream. She'd enjoyed spending the afternoon with Cara, too, which was the biggest surprise of all.

The next day, the three of them smuggled their wares into Lena's room: Kitty had two 'Happy Birthday' balloons stuffed into her coat; Millie carried the pudding nestled in a Marks & Spencer carrier bag; and Cara was clutching a huge bottle of ginger beer.

Kitty tied the balloons either side of Lena's bed whilst Cara served up the beers.

'Just like being back at the bar!' commented Cara as she handed Kitty a polystyrene cup. Millie sliced the pudding into three pieces.

They all sang happy birthday, as the three women clinked their cups and smiled bittersweet smiles sprinkled with renewed hope.

Cara returned to her flat in a good mood and, as always,

Ade was waiting for her with a kiss. He was wearing that short-sleeved shirt from French Connection she loved, which revealed a slight hint of his biceps, the arms she'd adored for over ten years. As he held onto her, she just wanted to sink deeply into them.

'How was the party?' he asked.

'She would have loved it. Or I hope she did. You know what I mean!'

'I know you miss Lena.' He smoothed and sniffed her hair. 'Every day.'

'It's okay to talk about it, you know. To not be strong, for once.'

'Okay, Dr Freud, I thought Lena was the only one in the family into all that psychobabble.'

'I'm serious. And I miss her too.'

She swallowed hard. 'I know you do.'

'I'm always here if you need to talk,' he said, as she defiantly swiped at a stray tear careering down her right cheek. She hated it when her feelings betrayed her like that – she was supposed to be in a good mood! But it was as if all the laughter, the high of the past few hours was being followed by a come down that she hadn't expected.

They ate dinner, which included lychees for dessert, and settled on the sofa. The purple roses looked beautiful on their coffee table. 'You want a foot-rub?' asked Ade as he dried up the last of the pots in the kitchen.

'Not tonight, Ade, my feet are fine. Thanks.'

Ade was clearly after something. After ten years together, she knew his every move, and offering a foot-rub *and* washing up the pots in one night? He was good, but not *that* good.

What are you after?' she asked quizzingly as Ade placed his arm protectively around her waist and sat beside her. Ade moved his face against her neck, holding onto her gently, his breath against her ear. In those moments, she felt so protected, so loved. She felt as if nothing could touch her and, unbeknown to Ade, every bad feeling, any loitering sorrow just melted away, to be replaced by something resembling hope and a little less fear. That was the power this man had over her, and yet he had no idea. Just the way she liked it.

'There was something . . .'

'I knew it!' she jumped, wriggling out of his embrace and turning to him with one sceptical eyebrow raised.

'I've never understood how you manage to raise one eyebrow. That is such a skill!'

That's another thing he did – babbled – when something was clearly on his mind that he knew she wouldn't want to hear.

Then came the bottom lip biting. 'Cara . . . I know you might think this is not the right time. And it probably isn't . . . it's just that we were talking about it just before Lena . . . well, I really want to carry on that conversation. Not for anything heavy or anything, because I know the time isn't right. I'd just like to know if . . . you know . . . I don't mind waiting, of course not, I just want to know we have a shot. Well, you know what I mean, right? A shot.'

'What are you talking about?'

'You know?'

Cara rolled her eyes in clear exasperation. 'Not that again Ade. Not that.'

She stood up abruptly.

'Where are you going?'

'Ade, it's been a heck of a long day and a good one at that. Can we please talk about this another time?'

'Of course, I'm sorry. I shouldn't have brought it up. When?'

'When what?'

'When can we talk about it again?'

'Soon. Goodnight, Ade. I'm going to bed.'

She left the man she loved smiling to himself in a hopeful, sweet way that she hated to disappoint. But disappoint she would, because there was no way she was ever going to have a baby.

TWENTY-ONE

Cara rolled a tube of lipstick over her thin lips, instantly reminded that it was Millie that had been blessed with ample ones, while Lena had those eyes. And they were both tall . . . Never mind, she had get-up-and-go and the confidence to take on anything that was thrown her way, except . . .

'Baby?'

'What?' replied Cara, feeling more than a little cranky after Ade's baby bombshell, perhaps not so much of a bombshell considering he'd mentioned it days before Lena's fall.

'We're going to be late for the bar.'

'Fine.' She rolled her eyes then scanned the bedroom for her favourite brown sandals with the ankle tie.

She slipped a tiny foot into the shoe.

'I was thinking last night how nice it would be if Lena woke up to a new niece or nephew?' said Ade. 'I think it would be fantastic.' Ade looked hopeful, a look of happiness spread across his face.

'You can be so insensitive sometimes, Ade!'

He looked puzzled.

'Because,' she said, locating the handbag that matched the shoes, 'you're basically saying that Lena won't be coming

145

around for at least nine months! And that's assuming I agree to start "trying" straight away. And that it happens really quickly. And that I say yes to any of it!' She was feeling slightly hysterical.

'It was just a comment, baby.'

'And there you go again!'

'Please keep such comments to yourself in future. They can be bloody upsetting.' Listening to herself speak, she knew she had absolutely no basis for an argument. In fact she sounded about five years old. But she needed to buy time. She needed to stop him from asking her all those questions again. No more baby talk. She knew it had been a bad idea to get satellite in. She knew he'd been secretly watching the baby channel behind her back and cooing over pictures of Eliza's niece lately. Well, it had to stop.

She couldn't breathe.

She needed Lena.

So an hour later, Cara found herself at the hospital.

'Oh, sis, I really, really need you right now. My life's turning to shit,' she began, once they were gone. 'Ade's asking too many questions about you-know-what and I don't know what to say to him. And I'm scared he'll hate me. I know what you're going to say: that he doesn't hate me; he's just going to be hurt that I keep shutting him out and not letting him in on the real reason why I don't want to try for kids. I'm not even sure *I* know Lena. I just know it just doesn't feel right. Never has.' Cara shook her head slowly, a huge wave of sadness washing over her. 'I mean, could you imagine me . . .? With a brat?'

'Oh, and thanks for the support, sis. Ade enjoyed telling me how much you were up for us "trying" for a baby! Apparently you had a secret talk a few months ago.'

She smoothed down an imaginary crinkle in Lena's top sheet.

'I just can't do it. You know why. I just feel that – anyway,

146

you know how much I love him . . .' The door creaked open and Nurse Gratten appeared.

'Sorry to disturb you again, but I need to—'

'That's okay. You go ahead. Just been prattling on.'

'No, that's good. The more familiar voices, the better. Was she always a good listener?'

'The best. She's a sort of adviser on the telephones for a kids' charity. It's what she does,' replied Cara, realizing that this was probably the longest non-medical conversation she'd ever had with Nurse Gratten.

'Oh, I didn't know she helped kids. How lovely.' Nurse Gratten surveyed the clipboard at the end of Lena's bed as Cara turned away. She really needed to talk this out. 'Maybe just talk about fun things. That party was a really good idea, I must say.'

But life isn't always a party, Cara wanted to say.

She left Lena's room feeling dejected. Lena had always been the one person she'd talked to about her problems, and now she couldn't do that any more.

Half an hour later, Millie arrived at Fen Lane from her early shift at A&R. Cara wasn't as strict about 'Lena Watch' any more; as long as someone was with her every day, she didn't bitch. Millie wasn't sure whether to be relieved or sad about Cara's relaxed attitude. She didn't want to think of the possibility of everything just becoming the norm. She had to keep believing that Lena would soon get out of this.

She'd been sitting with Lena for a few moments when she clocked a figure standing just outside the door. He was wearing a baseball cap and peering through the slightly opened door. He was young, maybe a teenager, and was dressed in a huge baggy sweatshirt and jeans.

'Can I help you?' asked Millie, sharply. She hadn't meant to sound gruff, but she was curious as to what this strange kid was doing hanging around. She stood up and went towards the door, just as he turned and left, his steps gathering pace as she followed him into the corridor; she saw him fleeing to the staircase before disappearing.

She went back to the room, wondering who the strange boy had been and why he'd run off like that. Maybe he'd been in the wrong room.

Or maybe he was one of those opportunist thieves, she thought. She didn't want to appear naive but that thought had been the furthest from her mind as the kid just didn't seem to look like he was hanging around for the odd unattended purse. Nevertheless, it wouldn't hurt to let Nurse Gratten know.

Just in case.

Michael had a satisfied smile on his face. He was wearing new clothes, and had a fresh haircut. He was feeling better than he had in months. Visiting Lena, even though she was asleep, had made him in turn feel alive, vibrant, and more full of life than he'd ever felt. He shared his feelings with Charlotte.

'You weirdo!'

'Thanks, Charl!'

'No, not really. But whatever's going on for you – I love it! And I love the new look by the way. The lack of hair – the cool leather jacket.'

'Does my head look big?'

'No, I would have pointed that out in my own loving and sisterly way. In fact it brings out those lurrvly bushy eyebrows and girly eyelashes!'

'Great,' he said dryly.

'In fact, I didn't realize my brother was such a hunk! Maybe I should introduce you to my friend Jeanette.'

'No thanks,' he replied quickly.

'Just a thought . . .'

His voice broke. 'Just seeing her lying there Charl . . . It makes me think.'

'I'm glad something does.'

'I'm serious. She's still young, about my age. She's got so much more to be getting on with, to be doing – but she can't, you know?'

George ran into the room.

'I thought I told you to go sit in the naughty corner, young man?' chastised Charlotte. George curled his lip and sped back into the corridor. And sure enough, with a quick manoeuvre of the head, Michael spotted his nephew near the bottom of the stairs.

'Poor thing.'

'It works!' she protested. 'Anyway, back to you and this girl.'

'One minute her life was full of endless possibilities, and then one missed step and she's gone.'

'But not exactly. She's still alive, right?'

'Yes, she is, but we don't know if she'll actually pull through.'

'We?'

'Her mum and sisters.'

'You are getting quite chummy with the family, aren't you? Should I be worried?'

'They're great Charl. Nutty, but great. Kitty's sixty-five going on seventeen. Millie's sweet. A bit insecure; a good heart. Then there's Cara, who you wouldn't want to cross. A bit like an angry Smurf. She's with Ade, who's a top bloke; and then there's Lena's boyfriend, who is by all accounts a bit of an arse.'

'Why is he an arse?'

'He just is. I've met him. Plus, he doesn't go and see her much. And, by the sounds of things, has never treated her the way she deserved to be treated'

'Perhaps him not visiting is just his way of coping. We

can't judge others who don't fit into what we think is right, Michael.'

'I know . . .'

'Never mind! But it does sound like you're in love.'

'Don't be silly, Charl. How can I be in love with someone I've only spoken to once? That doesn't make much sense, does it?'

'I meant with her family, Dummy!'

He'd walked right into that one.

'But if there's something else you want to tell me?'

'Of course not,' he replied quickly.

'Actually, now I think about it, the girl with the green eyes that never speaks sounds just like your ideal woman.'

'Don't joke about it, Charl.'

'Sorry, big bro. You're right, it's all really very sad,' said Charlotte, finally getting serious.

'I know that, on the face of it, it is sad. Incredibly sad, the whole situation, but—'

'But you don't know her enough to feel sad for *her*?'

'No. Yes. No. Yes, sadness does comes into it, Charl – a lot. Especially when I think about what she could have achieved. That day I met her she was so . . . vibrant, and so full of life. She was singing along to this song on her MP3 player and she was so funny. None of her clothes matched . . .' He was saying too much. 'I just can't get over the fact that she never realized her potential. Does this make any sense?'

'I think so.'

'And I can still feel really sad for her family and friends, because that's natural. Only when *I* look at her, you know what I see?'

'What do you see, my darling big brother?'

'I see nothing but hope. For everything. For me.'

Michael hadn't expected his usually smarter-than-average

sister to get what was going on in his head. He was just about coming to grips with it himself, really. Perhaps the only person that would understand was Lena, so he felt the best place to be was with her.

Michael felt weird, yet calm, when he arrived at Fen Lane Hospital without the 'nod' from a member of Lena's family. At the beginning, Cara had been his go-between, but now he felt more than ready, more than worthy to take a few steps on his own. Besides, he'd been feeling much stronger after the dinner party outburst, and the women actually taking his advice about Lena's thirtieth birthday party. It was nice to be listened to and he now felt he mattered to them.

He now felt he mattered to Lena.

'Oh, hello,' said a large man sitting by Lena's bed. Michael had been so certain that he would be alone with Lena. Kitty often took a walk at this time and Cara was at the bar with Millie. 'I'm Lena's boss, Andy.'

'At Kidzline?'

'That's right. The one and only!'

Of course, if Michael *really* knew Lena, he'd know about Andy.

'I think the world of this girl. Of course there's a load of advisers at Kidzline. Some with years of experience, degrees even, but Lena, she just had "it".'

'It?'

'Yes, this knack of talking to a child, a teenager, a paranoid parent. She had this ability to calm them down, even if she had never gone through what they had. At the end of the call, it could sometimes be really tough for her, though. Like when one of the kids was getting bullied at school, she knew just what to say to him. And the time that little girl was having trouble at home with her dad. She was, well,

151

you know, a great listener. She really cares about people. You know what I mean?'

Michael could sense that this man cared a great deal about Lena. It was as if everyone she came into contact with was touched by her magic in some way – just as he had been.

'One child called for weeks. Didn't have the courage to tell anyone about what was going on in her life, the stuff she was going through every single day. Our Lena persuaded her to talk and now that girl is in a place of safety. All thanks to Lena. Because she cared. Of course, we're just a referral agency. We put people in touch with support networks, but sometimes, sometimes it's hard not to get involved. But Lena handled it like the professional that she is. But I can tell you, she had a little cry about it in my office.'

'Did she have anyone to talk to about it?'

'Of course, all my staff get debrief sessions.'

Michael was thinking about closer to home, but if her birthday dinner and what he'd heard lately was anything to go by, she probably had no one in her family to turn to. And for that, he felt really, really sorry. Sorry that *he* hadn't been there for this wonderful, special girl.

'Only Lena could trip on the stairs and fall arse over tit. Only our Lena.' Andy looked at his colleague with sadness and Michael knew that this portly man cared for Lena as a daughter perhaps and not just as a work colleague.

'I can go to the coffee machine if you'd like some time alone with Lena,' offered Michael.

'Thanks, I'd best be off anyway' he said, getting up, 'I need to go. Already been here an hour. My wife will think I've got lost. Take care of her, won't you? I'm really sorry this has happened, to you both,' said Andy with another glance at Lena.

Both.

'She's a good girl. But of course you know that, being

152

together as long as you were, I mean, are. Take care, son.' They shook hands as Michael briefly considered letting him know he wasn't in fact Justin. But he decided against it.

And then, finally, as he'd hoped – it was just the two of them.

'Lena,' he said as he replaced the Oasis CD with Amerie and pressed Play.

'Lena. A beautiful name for a beautiful lady.' This sounded like a really bad chat-up line, he thought. So he cleared his throat and started again.

'Lena, I don't know if you can hear me but . . . but I'd just like to say I really enjoyed our chat on the bus.' Now he sounded like a prat. He cleared his throat again, feeling very nervous. It brought back memories of when he asked Becky Anderson out in the third year. No, this was worse. Much, much worse.

And then he remembered Lena's eyes. 'So beautiful, they were. So unusual. I think I did mention that when we spoke, didn't I? I really hope I did. Man, I just wish I could remember everything I said to you that day; the first and last time we spoke on that noisy bus into work. If I'd known then what I know now, I would have made more of an effort to get to know you. I would have worn that expensive aftershave Charlotte bought for my birthday instead of that cheap rubbish from the chemist's. I'd have taken an extra ten minutes preening myself in the mirror. Because, if you're anything like what your family and Andy have described, you are just this . . . just this amazing and unique individual. Just like those eyes. Yes, just like your eyes.' He closed his eyes and imagined them. So green, sparkling. He'd never seen anything like it. She was absolutely magnificent – this sleeping beauty on the bed in front of him. He felt a shudder, so he opened his eyes again. 'I have to admit, I thought they were contacts at first. You know, those fashion ones that those young girls wear with tracksuits and high heels. But then you weren't a young girl – I don't mean you're old, though, I mean, you're only thirty. Thirty's the new twenty, so they say in Charlotte's magazines . . . erm. Oh man, is this going pear-shaped or what?' He laughed, and could imagine her doing the same.

'That day we spoke wasn't the first time I'd seen you, you know. I'd clocked you before, you know on the bus – oh sorry, that didn't come out right!'

He scratched his chin absently-mindedly. Start again. 'After our chat, if I'm honest, I really looked forward to seeing you again on that bus. But when I came back the next day, you were gone! So, what was that about? Your sister said you changed your route. Why? Anyway, then your sister called me. And then I met her at the bar! How weird was that? She refuses to tell me why you changed your route into work. Maybe one day *you'll* tell me?'

'I'm sure we've lots to talk about, when you come round. Lots of questions like why you're with Justin, your favourite colour, why you were in such a rush that you tripped and fell down the stairs. But never mind all that now. I'm not going anywhere. And when you do wake up, if you tell me to piss off, I'll do just that. I don't mind, really. Because at least then I'll know that you and those lovely green eyes are safe again. That's all I want.'

TWENTY-TWO

Michael seemed to permanently smell of that Calvin Klein aftershave that Charlotte had handed over three Christmases ago. He was thriving physically and emotionally and was basically trying to enjoy everything life had to offer. He was even tempted to book a holiday, but still hadn't decided where he'd like to go. Africa, Asia, the Americas; maybe even Rio like Kitty. But not for a facelift. The world was absolutely his oyster, and he intended to start seeing as many places as he could because 'you just didn't know what was round the corner'. But for now, what existed round the corner from him was Dulwich Leisure Centre.

Michael hadn't been to the gym in ages and, looking around him now, he was reminded why. Sets of glistening bodies were attached to large machines, plasma screens showed the hardest way to use a gym ball, and all to blasts of house music. He sat on an exercise bike and took the time to think about the direction *his* life had taken over the last few weeks. The changes. Even people at work had begun to notice. All right, they'd actually started to notice *him* for once, which hadn't been easy before, considering how he usually kept himself to himself. But it was as if he was at last telling the world (well, his work colleagues at least) that he was alive and ready for anything.

And they seemed to be listening.

Michael got off the bike after half the preferred time, stood up, and realized his tracksuit bottoms were sticking to his body. As he passed sets of glistening, bulging biceps attached to various gym posers, he suffered a pang of inadequacy which would normally have lasted for the rest of the day, but this time it disappeared as quickly as it had appeared. Michael swapped arms for the stretching exercise which made him feel a bit of an idiot. When he realized that he was being watched, he felt even worse.

'Hello, there.'

Millie.

'I didn't know you came to the gym?' he said. He wasn't sure how to greet her. A kiss on the cheek? Or was that too personal? After sharing visits with Lena, and getting to know the family gradually, he felt fairly comfortable with them but he didn't want to overstep the mark. It didn't help that Millie was lovely. If he was honest, even the Smurf was attractive; but it was Lena who had captured his interest; it was Lena he'd dreamt of only last night . . .

'I usually use this place for the pool, but when you mentioned to Cara that you were thinking of joining the gym, it kind of shamed me into doing the same,' said Millie.

'Unlike me, you don't actually need it,' he said, quickly averting his eyes away from her Lycra-clad body. That was merely because there was still a red-blooded male tucked away inside him. Nothing else. So as soon as his brain resumed normal service, everything was okay again.

'If there's anything you don't understand, you let me know?' he offered chivalrously – like he knew *anything* about gym stuff.

'Why don't we have a protein shake at A&R later? Before my shift,' suggested Millie.

They both laughed.

After another twenty minutes, Michael knew it was time to finish up. He attempted one last look in the mirror and, turning side on, gazed at his slightly paunchy silhouette. Deep breath in, deep breath out. He felt a few slight pangs of regret and then determination flooded his face. With a healthier eating regime, more jogging and now the gym, he was well on his way to a better physique, even if it killed him (which it probably would). All it would take was hard work and inspiration – and he had that in Lena.

At A&R and with Millie, Michael was dismayed to notice Cara wasn't around. Ade shouted them a free drink, though, which was nice. Clearly a top man, Michael had to wonder how he put up with Cara – the bloke was obviously a masochist.

'This is nice,' said Millie. Her eyes were sharp over the Mojito, as if trying to strip him bare and read what was left. Michael suddenly felt uncomfortable.

'What?' he asked with a nervous smile. He was trying to be a better person, trying hard not to be pulled down to the depths of despair he'd been feeling right up until that moment he'd seen Lena at the hospital. But what if Millie could see right through him? What if she still saw the old Michael?

'Sorry, I'm just looking at you to see what my sister saw in you.'

'Thanks!'

'No, sorry, that came out all wrong. You see, she's not like me, she's the most vert . . . vert . . . Oh, what's that word again?'

'Virtuous?'

'Virtuous, that's it! She's one of them. So honest, so kind. And I just know she would never have cheated on Justin.

Which is why she changed her bus route. It was to get away from you because you made her feel . . .'

'Feel . . .?'

'Stuff.'

'You can't be sure . . .' His heart was racing.

'It had to be that. Cara and I have discussed it. She needed to get away from you so things wouldn't have a chance to get silly, you know? And I suppose I'm just curious about the one bloke who made her see things differently?'

'And am I what you expected?' He was nervous of the answer.

'Definitely. You're kind, smart, good-looking. Cheeky, sort of. Great eyebrows. And you care about people.'

He didn't know what to say.

'And that's another thing! You just have no idea.'

He still didn't know what to say.

'In normal circumstances, I'd fancy you.'

He almost choked on a mint leaf.

'I said in normal circumstances. But this,' she waved her hands around, 'me working here, Lena being asleep, and me talking to a gorgeous bloke like you and not trying to get you into bed – none of it's normal!'

It was official: this family were odd. And he couldn't get enough of them.

'There's no reason why this shouldn't be normal, Millie. Maybe it's the start of something much bigger than any of us could have imagined.'

She smiled shyly and all at once she looked younger than her years. Perhaps she was a less gobby and opinionated version of Charlotte.

'I know it's a cliché but things do happen for a reason,' he said.

'I suppose. I never thought I could be friends with a bloke. I mean, we are friends, right?

158

'Of course!'

Millie's face seemed to relax. 'That could be nice. Weird but nice.'

'I think it's going to be great,' he said confidently.

'It's funny: men finding me attractive is the one gift I know I've got.'

'Who told you that?'

'No one. I just know.'

Now he knew he should say something profound and Oprah-like but, fearing his vocabulary wouldn't stretch quite that far, he decided to play safe.

'What do you think Lena would say after hearing you say that?'

She thought for a moment. 'She'd say: "You have many gifts Millie Jayne Curtis. Know your worth".' Millie smiled and then said. 'Lena was always going on about me being worth so much more than I thought and that someday a man would see that. Someone special. Someone worthy of me.' She paused, then grinned. 'I used to think she was talking out of her arse.'

The more he found out about Lena – how she thought and what she'd said – the more he wished he'd known her, really known her. She was clearly an amazing sister. 'Lena's right. Hold out for him, Millie, it's what you deserve. Nothing less. Okay, this conversation's getting a bit girly; can we talk about football now?'

They both laughed again and Michael realized he'd been laughing a lot lately. And it was good. It felt right.

'What's your passion, Millie?' he then said, out of the blue.

'Not working here,' she whispered. 'But I am grateful to Cara as it's given me a lot of extra cash, and at least Cara can now see I'm not a total waste of space!'

He was only just discovering his own passion for life and it was an experience he wanted everyone else to feel. Especially

159

those close to him. He'd be asking Charlotte the same question later on.

'I know where you're going with this . . . but I just don't think I have one. A passion, that is. Cara has always wanted to start her own business and Lena clearly wants to help people, while me? I just don't know, and maybe that's part of my problem. I have never known what I wanted to do with my life.'

'And that's okay. There's no shame in it. We all have different stages when we accomplish things, that's all. Maybe your "moment" hasn't come yet.'

'I know I don't enjoy being on the dole. It's just that the jobs I go for, if I can be bothered, are a bit naff.'

'There's an opening at my firm for an admin assistant. It's not the most exciting place to work and the pays shite. But if you get it, it's a place for you to earn some money while you think about what you really want to do. No guarantees you'll get it, but I know they are totally desperate for someone and you did say you were finishing here this week,' Michael said encouragingly.

'Thanks for that!' she said jokily.

'Hey, I'd get in there if I were you!'

'Thank you, Michael.'

'No problem. Friend.'

'Can I ask you a question, Friend?'

'Anything.'

'When did you become such a life guru?'

'Hmmm . . . That would probably be the day I met your sister, Lena.'

160

TWENTY-THREE

On her way into A&R, Cara noticed a red sign on the window of one of her favourite local boutique shoe shops: 'We regret to announce that, due to the current bleak economic situation, we have been forced to shut our doors for the very last time. Everything must go and all shoes are 75 per cent off. We thank you for your custom over the years. Kiki P.' Although Cara felt sad that yet another store was closing, she didn't experience her customary feelings of glee at a 75 per cent off sale. She entered the shop anyway, as if on autopilot and was immediately faced with shoeboxes piled high. There were green and lace satin stilettos, orange pumps with circular peep-toe effects and silver beaded ankle ties, dipped in sparkles. The smell was of newness and expense. Her dream shop. Her dream scenario. She ran her fingers over a tartan-patterned kitten heel and stared appreciatively at a wood-heeled platform sandal – but 'it' – that feeling of excitement and joy at the prospect of buying a brand-new gleaming pair of shoes – just wasn't there.

None of this mattered any more.

'It' was just pretty shoes.

She left the store empty handed and headed down to A&R,

161

where her nostrils were quickly assaulted by the smell of aftershave, perfume, cocktails and bar snacks. For a few seconds at least, non-regulars regarded her as nothing more than a potential customer. In the past she'd hated that sensation and generally preferred it when Eliza ran up to her, calling her 'boss'. She liked the idea that everyone would know that the owner had just walked in – that this tiny woman with four-inch heels was the BOSS LADY.

But now, she wished she could stay anonymous for just a little bit longer.

To *not* be the boss.

To *not* be the one in charge.

To *not* be Irene Cara Curtis, whose sister was lying in hospital.

Ade came over and planted a firm kiss on her cheek, which put paid to any ambiguity. She soon made her way around the bar and smiled at a miserable-looking woman with red hair hunched over a cold beer.

'You okay, babe?' Ade asked Cara. Actually, it had been a day of mixed emotions. Like most days. One minute filled with optimism, the next . . .

'I'm good, Ade.' She went to fetch some stock from the back and noticed a leaflet entitled 'Surrogacy – what you need to know' lying there. Before she could register her anger, she was stopped by the sound of an almighty crash.

'Sorry,' said Eliza, biting her bottom lip gormlessly, standing by a shattered crate of alcopops. 'Erm, I don't know what happened.'

As usual, Eliza had happened. Cara had never thought that she'd think this, but she missed Millie, who although did mix cocktails incorrectly from time to time, had never broken anything in the whole two weeks she'd been here. Frankly, Cara missed her little sister.

She set about cleaning up the mess whilst summoning Eliza

162

to a group of rowdy hooray Henrys she just wasn't in the mood to deal with.

'I'll help you clean this lot up,' said Ade. 'I love you, you know,' he said out of nowhere, and for no particular reason (she hoped) as she proceeded to mop up the luminous, sticky liquid. 'I really do, Cara.'

She carried on mopping, focusing on the spillage.

'Did you hear what I said?'

'Yes! And I love you too!' Still, she carried on mopping, stabbing at a particularly stubborn stain that was beginning to set. She knew where this was heading. He wanted answers. About having a kid.

'Anyway, I've –' he actually placed his hand on the mop handle, effectively putting a stop to her frantic mopping – 'been thinking.'

Oh great, she thought. Ade only ever said that when he had indeed been thinking. Long and hard. And she was worried. Thinking he may be about to leave her. She couldn't cope with that. Not that. She was being irrational. She was tired. She was emotional.

'What have you been thinking about Ade? Surrogacy?'

'How did you know?'

'Saw the leaflet, you left it on the counter for all to see.'

'Sorry, I'll take it away. I just thought it was something we could consider if you were scared of the whole birth thing. Or adoption, or anything.'

Looking into the eyes of the man she would always adore, she just wanted to be honest. Instead she said, 'How about next year? We could start trying.'

'You said that last year.'

'Dammit, why are you always going on at me about it? My sister's in a—'

'Don't say it, Cara, please. You know I love Lena. You know I miss her.'

163

She knew that.

'But you know what? If anything, Lena's accident has made me want this even more. It's showed me how short life can be. How we can make loads of plans but in the end it comes to nothing because even one missed step can make it – well, you know what I mean.'

She did.

'She said we'd make lovely parents and she's right. I can just picture it: you, me, our little son or daughter. She'd have your eyes, but certainly my temperament. If it's a boy, I'd teach him to play basketball. It would be amazing. I know we can do it. Together.' Moving towards her he clasped her hand firmly and she didn't move. 'And you won't be alone, I'll be with you every step of the way. We're a team, me and you.'

She suddenly felt cornered, especially when Ade had mentioned Lena. It had thrown her a bit and she needed to get back on form. It was attack or leave. She couldn't breath and felt the air leaving her body like a pricked balloon.

She needed Lena.

Now.

But Lena was lying in a deep sleep in Fen Lane Hospital, and all Cara had was herself. She gazed at Ade again, the only boyfriend she'd ever loved. His face was tired, solemn, and she felt a tinge of sadness at the thought that she had caused some of that. It was time for some honesty though, even though she'd no idea what that was. 'Just speak and let it all come out: your fears, everything,' Lena had once counselled her about most things that she and Ade got angsty about. And she wanted to. Perhaps the stockroom wasn't the best place, but it was all they had at that moment.

'Ade—'

'Cara!' shouted Eliza, knocking on the door.

'What?'

Eliza walked in looking dishevelled and Cara wondered if she'd caught her skirt in the till drawer again.

'I'm really sorry but . . .' She bit her bottom lip in 'that way' again.

'What have you done?' asked Cara wearily, wondering when she would get round to sacking this incompetent idiot.

'This came a couple of days ago and I forgot to give it to you. Sorry.'

Eliza handed over a postcard. Rio. Pictures of a carnival. A beach.

'That took ages to get here,' said Ade.

'What do you expect? Wrong postcode,' said Cara as she scanned the back.

Dear Cara and Ade,
    How is my darling daughter? Having a great time in Brazil!
    Weather's great. Just thought I'd say hi.
    Kitty (Mum).

A dark cloud was now descending.

'Just look at my family, Ade. Kitty doesn't even know my correct postcode. I've got a dad who never rings, happily shacked up with his new family. I don't even have his number! We didn't all have *The Waltons*-type upbringing that you had!

'That doesn't mean we'd be the same.'

'Forget it, Ade, I can't.'

'Can't what?'

'I can't do *this*. I mean, I don't want to!'

'Talk? That's okay, we can just stay and clean up. Talk about it later.'

'No, you don't understand.'

He took her hand. 'What is it?'

165

'This is the deal. We work like dogs, yes, but we're working for ourselves and most nights we actually enjoy it. The credit crunch hasn't buggered us up. We can have great holidays when we want and not just during the school holidays. We have a great unchild-proofed flat. We have lie-ins on a Sunday, just because we want to. We can buy what we want without feeling selfish. And on my day off I can just lounge around the house watching *Desperate Housewives* on Sky Plus! We're not beholden to anybody.'

'So?'

'So? Some people would love to have what we have!'

'I want more.'

'More than all that?'

'Yes.'

'How about selling the business one day and going off on a year-long cruise, then? Doing all the things we've talked about?'

'You hate cruises. Always said they were full of geriatrics.'

'We can stay in different hotels, then! Travel around. We could do anything we wanted!'

'I want more. And I'm not talking about material stuff. We're not talking about a new pair of shoes here.'

'Ade—'

'Cara, I don't understand you. Maybe I never will, but you need to understand me!' Ade began patting his chest like a caveman. 'It's in here, Cara! In here! I'm missing something *here!!*' He was shouting now. Really shouting, and she wondered if this would become a habit. She was scared. Not that he would get even angrier, but that what he really meant was wanting something else. Something that wasn't *her*.

'This can't be all there is. It can't be! I want our child, Cara. I just want our family!'

'I know, but, but . . .' She couldn't think of anything else to say.

'But what?' His eyes were pleading.

'I'd be doing it for you. I'm not ready!'

His response surprised her. 'And why would that be such a bad thing? I've always gone with what *you've* wanted! Throughout our ten years together.'

Cara blinked widely.

Ade went on. 'That's right, you heard correctly! Cara wants to move from a relatively good two-bedroomed flat into a new-build apartment, we do it; I want to get married, but you don't because "marriages just don't work", so I go along with that; Cara wants us to pack our jobs in and start up a business, we do it.'

'I thought you wanted to do all those things!'

'Yes I do, but everything we do is driven by *you!* All I have ever wanted to do was please *you* and make *you* happy. Treat you like a queen, the way you deserve, especially with the childhood you've had. And that has never been a problem for me because I have always loved *you*. I just, for once, want something for *me!* I just want you to go along with something I'd like for a change! Is that so wrong, Cara?'

'Well, I'm not ready for kids. Not now and probably not in a year. How many times have I got to tell you that? I like my life – our life – and I don't need it to change!'

He was angry. She knew by the shape of his eyebrows and his whole body language – tense, silent, angry. She'd only ever seen him this angry once before, about five years ago, when her old boss had copped a feel of her bum at an office leaving-do. Ade had gone on about 'no one disrespecting his woman!' and had promised to 'knock his lights out', a notion Cara had found ridiculous, if only because it was so out of character. Of course she had persuaded him not to carry out his threat, after revealing that she had already punched said boss in the gut.

Ade sat on one of the crates. Anger simmering. Head bowed.

'You just don't want to have a child with *me*.' His voice broke and she felt sorry really, really sorry that the only man she loved was hurting like this. She sat beside him, wanting to take his hand, but instead they lapsed into silence as Cara's head swam with possible words and phrases she could use to rectify the situation without stepping off the elevated position she imagined herself to be.

Yet, silence remained.

'Thanks for telling me all I needed to know,' he said in a voice no longer angry, just fuelled with deep, deep hurt.

He left her there in the stockroom, feeling more alone than she had ever felt in her entire adult life.

And that night Ade slept on the sofa as Cara lay wide awake for the entire night.

The next morning, he'd packed a bag full of clothes and was gone.

TWENTY-FOUR

There he was again.

This time he started running as soon as he clocked Millie turning away from the hospital's drinks machine.

'Hey!' she shouted after him, attempting yet another half-hearted pursuit before realizing she was clutching a hot drink. He spun around his face barely visible in his hooded Avivex sweatshirt. Then he disappeared.

'Bloody cheek!' said Millie.

But a few minutes later, she finally caught up with him.

'Gotcha!' said Millie as she reached out to the young boy grabbing his arm. He jumped back stunned and as he turned away from the door to Lena's room and flicked off his hood, revealed a baseball cap, bob-length hair, eye shadow and a dash of lipstick. He was a 'she'.

'Don't *ever* touch me again, you hear that?' the girl said.

Millie recovered quickly from the shock of seeing the girl. 'No problem. I just want to know why you've been hanging around my sister's room?'

Her expression changed. 'Sister?'

'Who are you?'

'Someone.'

'Yeah, who?' She figured it wasn't that long ago she'd been a teenager and could probably relate to her more than she thought.

'Who are you, five-O or something?' said the girl.

'Five what?'

'*The police!* Are you the police? Asking me all these questions.'

'I only asked your name.'

'Well, you can call me DT then. *All right?*'

Millie thought for a moment. That weird poem Cara had found in Lena's 'Important Stuff' folder had been signed by a DT.

'Do you write poems?'

'I write rhymes. Get it right.'

Nurse Gratten appeared with a worried look. 'What's going on here?'

'What's it to you, gran?' said DT.

Millie wanted to giggle. 'Nothing, Nurse Gratten. We're just going in to see Lena.'

Nurse Gratten looked sceptically towards DT, probably because she'd never seen her before, but more likely because vibes of hostility were radiating from every pore of the kid's body.

The Oasis CD was coming to an end as they entered Lena's room.

'DT?' said Millie, as this mouthy teenager with the bravado of ten warriors suddenly resembled a little girl: she stood by the doorway, rooted to the spot and staring at Lena.

'Sorry, mate, can't do this,' she said firmly. Millie had forgotten 'that look'. The look on a person's face the first time they saw Lena on that bed, looking alive but lifeless, asleep yet awake. Disbelief, surprise, and sadness were etched onto their expressions. A look so expertly rolled into one, so interchangeable. Then there were the usual utterances that

170

would always follow, like 'How long has she been like this?', 'What have the doctors said?' or, in DT's case, 'What the fuck!!??'

'Could you not swear in front of her?' asked Millie as the teenager stood before Lena. 'What, are you scared?' Millie asked boldly. 'I ain't scared of nuttin'!' the girl responded defiantly.

'I've seen you before, right?' asked Millie.

The girl didn't answer, just kept staring at Lena. She looked her age – young – and she was clearly frightened beneath all that show.

And who could really blame her? She was just a kid and Millie had been scared shitless the first time she'd come too. And many times afterwards.

'What's your name?' asked Millie.

'DT. I thought I told you.'

'I need to know your real name because I'll have to let the front desk know so they can buzz you in. You sneaked in here, didn't you?'

'Yep. Behind someone who pressed the buzzer.'

'Name?'

'That again.'

'Could you just answer me, please?'

'Deana Thornton.'

Millie stifled a giggle. 'So, how do you know Lena?'

'Why?'

This was getting tiring. 'It was just a question.'

'Let's just say, she owes me.'

'Owes you what?'

'Your sister owes me money.'

'How much?'

'Twenty. Last time I saw her she was meant to give it to me. Sent her loads of text messages and she didn't call back. I'd like the dough back now, please.'

'I saw the text messages.'

'Exactly. Well?' She turned to Millie, eyebrows raised.

'And that's all you came here for?' This didn't sit right with Millie.

'Just wanted to make sure she wasn't trying to run out on me.'

Millie took her last twenty-pound note out of her bag and handed it to Deana.

'Yeah, thanks,' she said. 'So what do you lot all do here. It's a bit boring.'

'We sometimes talk to Lena. Play music.'

'And that's it?'

'I suppose, yes. It's a waiting game really, Deana,' said Millie sadly.

Along with a complete (he hated the word) *makeover* of his physical self, Michael decided his surroundings were next in line for change. And as he hated his flat, he decided that that was a good place to start.

He had worked out that even if he was to be promoted tomorrow, by the time he got himself a decent car, there'd still be some time before he could add to his paltry savings and afford a place of his own. And, at the risk of sounding like some sandal-wearing do-gooder, there were people with no homes not far from where he'd been sitting navel-gazing for too long. People who had nothing. He at least had a roof, a job; what did they have? What did Lena have stuck in that hospital bed? Oh, and how about living for now and not always only thinking about the future? Michael had made the decision to work with what he *had* instead of what he desired – and what he *had* just happened to be a council flat on Dog Kennel Hill Estate that was in need of a paint job and a few knick-knacks.

After work, he bought some paints hurriedly. In fact, he

hadn't known where to start and probably would have gone for luminous green if Charlotte hadn't stepped in with a lecture about 'neutrals' and 'warm tones'. He wasn't sure if she was talking about paint or her moods, but he decided to trust her judgement.

He didn't need special 'painting dungarees' when he had a bag of clothes now destined for a charity shop (along with anything he hadn't used in six months, like the hand-held vacuum he'd once bought for 'convenience' and that hideous vase Charlotte bought him one Christmas just to wind him up).

Slipping into a pair of 'sensible' grey trousers he'd no intention of ever wearing again, along with a short-sleeved shirt with huge buttons he'd always thought suited him, Michael slipped the Amerie CD into the machine and got to work.

His mood lifted as soon as he appraised his handiwork a few hours later. He'd gone completely mad and painted the living room in two colours. Beige and off-white. And, much to his surprise, it looked okay. The fake fireplace was also a mark of genius, as was the huge phallic candle that promised to reek of jasmine and apple. And so that visitors did not assume he'd turned completely into a woman, the large football trophy – won at the pinnacle of his school career – stood proudly on top of the mantelpiece.

The rest of the flat soon followed. Off came the old wallpaper in the bedroom; it was replaced with a fresh, clean coat of paint – a warm eggshell shade. New toilet seat from Argos. Vinyl in the kitchen. It hadn't cost much and it looked great. So, over the next few days, Michael's labour gave birth to a brand-spanking-new living space. He'd also got rid of bags and sacks of old pictures, bank statements, and a whole collection of rubbish he'd once thought he'd use again, but never would.

The new paint and decluttering created a bright, airy, and

very habitable flat. And, for the first time – like – ever, Michael now looked forward to coming home each and every evening.

Cara was having a confusing day. Because, contrary to what she'd expected, Ade *hadn't* come running back the next morning, apologizing for walking out; holding her, kissing her, and burying his nose in her hair. He'd stayed away, and every minute they were apart Cara felt another stab of pain inside. Cara was good at thinking she never needed anyone, yet here she was, crumbling, without two of the most important people in her life. Well, Ade wasn't around but at least she could see Lena.

She banged on the lift button, consumed with impatience. Ade was gone and she needed to see her sister.

After Deana had left, Millie headed for the hospital canteen but was stopped on the way out by Nurse Gratten.

'That young lady you were with left this note for you.' The nurse handed her an envelope. She opened it up and inside was twenty pounds with a yellow posty note that read, 'Just wanted to see how stupid you were. See you next time! DT.'

Millie was confused for a nano second but then began to smile to herself.

After lunch, she decided to take the stairs back up to Lena's room, after promising Michael she'd take her fitness regime a little more seriously from now on. She was also keen to tell Lena about Michael, and what it felt like to have a male friend. She wanted to let her know she'd been right all along: that it *was* possible to be platonic friends with a man and more importantly, that *she* was capable of not chucking herself at any guy who was nice to her and in turn, he *could* respond the right way. Wow, her sister was teaching her stuff even from her hospital bed she thought, as she caught up with Cara on the way. Cara was heading to Lena's room as well, of course, much to Millie's disappointment, which meant that their private time would definitely have to wait.

Cara opened the door to the room and what they saw at that moment would stay with Millie forever. It would never leave her scariest nightmares and would deliberately torment her during deepest moments of fear and insecurity. This would give her a hint of what it felt like to be totally helpless, bereft, and consumed in a cloud of despair.

For Lena was gone.

TWENTY-FIVE

Once, when Millie was eight, Cara thirteen, and Lena fourteen, Kitty had called from Chester. Nothing strange about that because she'd been checking in daily with them ever since being called to perform in some big production of *Much Ado About Something* – or whatever it was called. Most days, Lena would take the call. And, with one eye on the ironing or the washing, she would run through the day's developments as she sneaked in reports of bad behaviour. But what was special about this call was that Millie was able to get to the ringing phone before Lena, who was busying herself in the kitchen, preparing that night's evening meal of yet another 'magical' feast of sausages, baked beans and eggs. Millie had quickly grown to hate this dish, along with the tap water they had now been forced to drink because Lena said buying fizzy orange was 'a waste of money'.

'When are you coming back?' whispered Millie into the phone as she stood in the hallway. She didn't want Cara to hear – she'd just tease her to tears about it. Or she'd call her a 'wuss' and say horrible things like, 'She doesn't care about you or us!'

'Speak up, Mills, I can't hear you!' said her mother.

Millie peered into the lounge. Cara was glued to a magazine, which had a free cheap lipstick attached to the front cover.
'When are you coming back? Are you coming back soon?' she
continued.

'Yes, Mills . . . Soon.'

'When?'

She could hear the exasperated sigh from Kitty, but she
really needed to know when she was coming home, because
she needed some money for an upcoming school trip to a
museum. And even though Millie ultimately found such trips
a bit boring, she didn't want to be the one left behind because
her parents 'couldn't afford it'. Her mum was a famous actress
(well, sort of), after all!

'I told you, Millie. It all depends, but soon. Maybe even
next week some time. You know how showbiz is.'

'Yes, Mum.'

'This show could become a sell-out, a wild success! You
more than the others know how hard I've worked for it.'

Millie felt pleased to be singled out from the others.

'You want me to be a success, don't you, darling?'

'Yes,' whispered Millie, snaking her fingers around the
telephone cord.

'Exactly.'

'So it's going good, then?'

'Yes, it is, Mills. Very, very good. It's great. Just where I
belong.'

Millie smiled. Her mum was a real actress, just like on
the telly, and she was proud of the fact that she was acting
in a play. In fact she was thrilled.

So her only hope now was to grass up Lena and see if
that yielded any results. 'I need some money for a trip to the
museum with school. But Lena won't give it to me.'

'Why not ask your father?'

'Dad's not here.'

'Oh, right, I forgot – he's away, isn't he?'

'In America on business, Mum. You knew that already!'

'Forgot, that's all.'

'When will you be back?' asked Millie, fearful she would never get the money for the trip. Lena had said something about what money they had left being for food.

'Millie don't whine. I thought you wanted me to do my acting. You just said!'

That night, Lena still wasn't budging.

'Don't start, Millie!' she'd argued as Millie rolled her eyes in mounting anger. She was unable to see the fairness in the whole situation and resented Lena – not her mother or father – for allowing her to be in such a predicament. It was all Lena's fault.

Mille stomped off to her room that night screaming, 'I hate you!' at the top of her voice. As always, Lena remained calm and noncommittal as she picked up the school bag Millie had thrown down in disgust.

Of course as an adult Millie could see the melodramatic response for what it was. But over the years, she'd begun to understand more and more of how hard it must have been for Lena to keep everything together for her and even Cara – when they hadn't been the best of kids. Lena was constantly running after them, making sure they were all right, fed, and clothed, reaching way beyond her duties as a sister. She had picked up the roles that had been assigned to others who, for one reason or another had not taken them up.

But of course she herself had been too young to understand this. She had an excuse. That was Millie's get-out clause. Until now.

Because, even as adults, she and definitely Cara continued to throw their toys out of the pram, never letting Lena know just how much she was appreciated and loved. Lena had definitely been like a mother to them – that couldn't be denied. But Millie hoped that Lena had been aware of the impact she had made on her life especially. Millie hoped she knew how much she loved her.

Having already lost one mother in Kitty, many, many years ago – the thought of losing another one was absolutely, heartbreakingly, unbearable.

TWENTY-SIX

Cara immediately grabbed hold of Millie, still not clear who was holding who up, aware only of the ugly scrunch of her insides as she refused to acknowledge the scene in front of them.

An empty bed.

There was no sign of Lena in or out of the bed that had been her enforced home for over two months. Even the side table was empty – flowers and CD player were gone. It was as if the last few, painful weeks had been a figment of her imagination. If only they had been.

Cara's mind refused to compute the worst of the only two possibilities: that Lena was dead or that she was awake and talking, sipping a chilled can of ginger beer in the canteen.

'No, please no . . . *please!!*' wailed Millie as Cara clutched her sister's hands fiercely. They were holding each other up, being a firm support for one another, united in this weirdly intense and powerful feeling of helplessness and fear.

They rounded on Nurse Gratten as she casually entered the room. As if the end of their world *hadn't* just begun.

'Where's my sister?? *Please!*' barked Cara and Millie in unison.

Nurse Gratten looked momentarily stunned, blinked, and then she spoke.

'What is it?'

'Just tell us! What have you done to her??' barked Cara.

'We've had to move her – she's okay. We had a health and safety concern with this room, that's all . . .'

The girls seemed to tumble into one another, like a melting ice-cream sundae, a mixture of emotions blending into one another as their bodies collapsed with relief.

Cara felt her heart resume beating. 'Then why didn't anyone let us know?'

'I am so, *so* sorry,' said Nurse Gratten.

'Sorry? First you lose her notebook, and now this?'

'Cara, Cara?' Millie soothed her. 'It's okay, she's alive, that's all that matters.'

Cara scrunched her eyebrows in temporary confusion. Millie was right; she had to calm down. Her little sister placed her arms around her and, as she squeezed against her Cara felt both strength and gentleness. This was something she wasn't used to with Millie.

'Let's go and see our sister,' said Millie, as Cara allowed her to lead the way into Lena's new room. Nurse Gratten continued apologising.

That day, the two sisters stayed with Lena. They folded her sheets and made sure her side table was correctly replicated from the previous room: CD player, fresh daises, and a new addition to the table – a picture of the three of them that Kitty must have brought over earlier. What shocked but pleased Cara was that the picture was of the three of them, Millie next to Lionel the dog, Cara and Lena on the end of the line-up. Lena's arm was around her neck while Cara held onto Lena's waist. Their backs were facing the camera. She'd no clue when it was taken, but knew there hadn't been any before or after of all three of them.

When they were kids, Millie was the glamour puss always on hand to pose for a pretty picture, while Cara could 'take or leave' a request to stand in front of a camera lens. Lena's preoccupations with her imperfections ('I'm too tall, my hair's too dry and frizzy') led her to be the one who always shied away from the camera lens. There was never an abundance of photos taken anyway, but those that were taken, usually ended up without Lena. So one day Kitty decided to creep up behind the three of them as they sat on the ledge in front of the house, chewing bubblegum. It was a sneaky shot that had been rubbished at the time but now meant so, so much.

As first planned, Cara decided not to talk about what was going on with Ade. Instead, she and Millie both ended up having a bit of a laugh. They reminisced about the good times they remembered growing up – because there were some. More importantly, growing up had been a time of togetherness, regardless of whether it was 'forced' because they lived together or not. It had still been a magical time that allowed them not to be bothered with the complexities of a world that all too soon would become demanding and consuming. It had been a time when they were still open to new experiences. Fearless, maybe. But also a time when Cara longed to wear high heels, go out to work, and be a woman. Longing to become an adult while never knowing that childhood should have been one of the most precious and cherished times of her life.

Millie poured out three polystyrene cups of ginger beer and more stories followed. Cara was almost wetting herself as Millie recounted the 'wig incident' that had seen them grounded for a week and the time when they had hidden their father's paper and the intense pleasure they had felt when he'd spent all evening looking for it.

Fun times.

Together.

TWENTY-SEVEN

Vulgar, glittery, tinsel-decorated shop windows, along with fake snow and empty cheers of goodwill were everywhere as the world entered the month of November. Cara didn't want to acknowledge the imminent onset of Christmas, mainly because Lena was absent. As for Ade, he'd called and said something about needing more time apart and how he would be staying in North London to help his mother out. Cara and Ade had had their ups and downs over the years but this was the first time he'd ever moved out. Ade loved her and she was confident that, when he realized his place was with her, he'd come home. Of course when she greeted him in the bar, she'd had to fight the urge to beg him to come back – but Cara had *never* begged for anything in her life and wasn't about to start now. At least she still saw Ade every other day as they served customers together, took staff meetings, and gazed momentarily into each other's eyes, unable to ignore the connection of ten years of being together and knowing one another so intricately. At first Cara quite enjoyed having all the bed to herself and complete control of the telly. She could watch a whole marathon of *Desperate Housewives*, she thought excitedly, until she thought about just how much she enjoyed curling up on the sofa with Ade, watching her favourite show and pretending to be annoyed when he kept asking questions about the plot.

Millie loved Christmas, but not as much as Lena, she thought sadly as she stared into the shop window of a department store. This particular one had gone all hip-hop – with a break-dancing Father Christmas and head-bopping reindeers dressed in trainers. The snow and stars made a magical backdrop as passers-by gathered round taking pictures on their mobiles as kids danced about in excitement. Millie could imagine Lena taking out her own phone and snapping away. Perhaps she'd even send a few picture messages to her and Cara too.

Millie had only come into the West End to window-shop and enquire about Christmas store vacancies – because even though she hated shop work, her desire to earn her own money had increased since her stint at A&R and she wasn't entirely sure that Michael would come through for her on that admin job at his firm. But she'd now gone off on a tangent, transfixed by all the Christmas lights – knowing Lena would have loved it all. She was such a kid! And Millie had always loved that side of her sister. It was only as a teenager that she'd realized that it had been Lena who'd left the biscuits and milk out for Father Christmas and Rudolph all those years and who'd imprinted their father's shoe into spilt caster sugar on the floor to look like a footprint.

Millie reached home that night with a couple of application forms and a new lip gloss. She'd considered buying Lena's Christmas present, but figured she could tell her what she wanted herself. One day. Soon.

'Hello darling,' said Kitty, dressed in one of Lena's aprons and a long dark flowing wig. 'Dinner will be ready soon. Your letters are in your room. And something from Michael who was round earlier.'

'Thanks, Kitty.'

'No problemo!' she sang as she returned to the kitchen. It still felt so weird, but nice, to have Kitty around – all baking, all mumsy, thought Millie as she tackled the mail on her bed. A brown envelope without a stamp stood out immediately – it was from Michael who, unlike any other man she'd ever met before had obviously kept his word. He'd dropped round the job details (because she didn't have a computer) as promised and had even written notes on what to include in the 'why should you get this job?' bit. He'd even suggested what to say at the interview! Apparently Mrs Hobbs from HR wears a lovely green necklace: he thought she ought to make a comment about that. Michael had also included a bit of company trivia, which was sure to earn her extra brownie points.

'Above all, be yourself,' he said, in his follow-up call that evening.

'What: lazy, annoying, and irresponsible?'

'Is that how Lena saw you?'

She sighed into the mouthpiece and swallowed hard. Lena would be so proud of her attempts to get a job. She was also secure in the knowledge that she was actually going through all of this for herself. Not for a man, not for Lena, but for herself. And that felt uncharacteristically good.

'Lena would say I should go for it. That I am capable.'

'Exactly! Your sister's right!' he enthused.

'You are so weird!'

'No, just happy. For the first time in ages.'

'Must be all the endorphin thingies you're releasing at the gym and on those runs.'

'Maybe. But there's so much making me smile these days.'

'Like what?' In fact, he was always smiling, like a deranged Cheshire cat with 'issues', she thought affectionately.

'The trees, the sunshine.'

'It's November. There is no sun and the trees are naked!'

'So? It's still great to be around it all. To experience it. To drink it all in. Don't you think?'

'Okay, I'll take your word for it!' Millie laughed. 'Can I shout you a drink at A&R tomorrow after you finish work? To say thank you?'

'I'd better not. I'm off to see Lena before visiting hours are over and then it's an early night again. It's like I've re-discovered sleep!'

Millie wanted some of what Michael was on: the energy, the hope. Whilst she too felt things were changing, she acknowledged that it would take some time for her to get to where Michael was.

A few days later, something strange happened.

'Kitty?' called Millie as she noticed Lena's room door ajar. For a quick second she imagined that Lena was back. But that was silly. Even though, as she peered into the room, she half expected Lena to be there, bouncing on her huge bed and laughing about how much she'd missed it, MP3 earphones stuck to her ears. Instead, it was Kitty who was sitting on the bed, clutching items of clothing, papers, the belt with the loveheart buckle. The contents of Lena's jewellery box, strewn all over the bed and Kitty's face smeared with tears.

'I've tried, Millie. I've tried to be strong. I cook, I clean, I try to keep busy, but I just want to know when she's coming back. I need to know!'

Millie felt a shot of total alarm. She had never seen Kitty like this; almost mad looking. Her eye make-up was smeared about, and it made her look like a deranged panda. Her hunched, five-foot frame was suddenly and obviously tiny and emphasized her vulnerability on that bed. Millie wanted to walk over and scoop her into her arms. Swap roles and become the mum that Lena used to play so well. But how would Kitty react? Would she shrug her away?

Millie took a step forward. 'Kitty, are you okay?'

'I just wanted to feel close to her, but I realized that I don't know much about my own daughter.' She swiped at her eyes. 'So, so I looked around. Found some stuff. She likes magazines, is that true?'

'She likes the celebrity ones, but she'd never admit it.'

'I can also see she likes old stuff like . . .' she looked around frantically. '. . . antique things, oh, and flowers! She got that from me. Daisies. I knew she liked daisies. She always has – since she was a little girl. She picked some for me once. . .'

Kitty had stopped crying and was staring into space. Millie sat on the bed beside her and noticed she was clutching an opened letter.

'What's that?'

'It's nothing, I'm going to put it back into her drawer once I get myself together. All this stuff's going back just as I found it. I'm so sorry.' Normally Kitty never apologized for anything, but Millie had a hunch that she might have been apologizing for something else.

Once Kitty had reapplied her make-up and *Diagnosis Murder* came on, she seemed to get back to being Kitty. They'd put back Lena's things together, and Millie opened the drawer just to make sure everything was neat again. Then she saw the letter Kitty had been clutching. Millie knew it wasn't right, but she couldn't help herself: she took out the letter and immediately wished she hadn't.

September 2006

My Dear Daughter, Lena,

I know you must be disappointed that I didn't turn up at the airport.

I was about to get on the plane here but as you know, I didn't.

In fact I have decided that it is best we don't keep in contact. It is commendable that through the Internet, you managed to track me down. You always were the inquisitive one out of the three. But this has to end now. So much has happened. So much time has passed.

I have decided that the past should be left in the past. This means I won't be calling, writing or visiting England again. That's the way it has to be. It is time for us all to move on. I know you will understand this. Please don't see me as a bad person.

I wish you and your sisters the very best in life.

Take care,

Donald Curtis.

At first Millie felt a strange numbness, then a swirling of anger in her tummy once she'd read the letter a second time. Then sadness, but not just for herself and the fact he hadn't even mentioned her by name in the letter, but mainly for Lena, who'd been the one to carry the burden of knowing that their father, Donald Curtis, never wanted to see the three of them ever again.

The next morning she found out that she had been selected for interview at Michael's firm. Now she had something really positive and concrete to prepare for. Normally, when she was feeling at a real emotional low she would run to Rik or Stewart but getting the interview gave her a proper sense of purpose.

Millie was proud of herself for seeing things from a new perspective and of course the fact she had landed a job interview. So proud, that the first person Millie wanted to tell – of course – was Lena. But Lena was at the hospital and she wanted to share her news with somebody *now*.

'I have news,' she began cautiously, basically because it was only a poxy job interview, hardly a Nobel peace prize. What would Kitty or even Cara care? What would anyone care? Millie thought about what Lena would have said and knew it would be positive, uplifting, and most of all genuine.

'I have a job interview, Kitty!'

'What?'

'I have—'

'No, I heard you!' said Kitty, who then proceeded to dance around the lounge in a sort of country-and-western-style hoedown.

'My Mills has a job!'

'Not yet, Kitty!' But Millie was absolutely thrilled with Kitty's obvious faith in her abilities, especially as she hadn't expected it.

'We need to celebrate this, but I don't have anything. No champagne, *nada*!'

'But Lena has!'

In the kitchen cupboard, behind the glasses and inside a wooden Moroccan square box was Lena's secret Toblerone stash. And laid down behind that was a bottle of white wine.

'Do you think she'll mind?' asked Kitty as Millie poured. She was sure Lena wouldn't. 'A hundred per cent sure. Besides, with my first pay cheque, I'll buy her a whole crate!'

They settled down on the sofa and toasted Millie's job interview. Anyone would have thought she'd just won an Oscar the way Kitty was behaving, but Millie had to admit she liked the attention her mother was lavishing on her.

'You remember the time that me, you, your daddy, and the girls went to the States together? Stayed with your dad's cousin with the small head?'

'Not really.' She wanted to remember, wanted so much to be a part of a shared conversation about the past. Instead, she snuggled into the sofa and took another sip of wine.

'No, you must have been around four then. Lena about ten, Cara nine. Yes, that was a good holiday. 'Course, I had no idea he would move there a few years later with that Creole woman Glenda Martinique. Who knew?'

'Do you miss him?'

'Who, your father? Let me see, do I miss the coldness? The "not speaking to each other for three weeks at a time"? No way, Millie. I'm sorry to say, but your father was a no-good – anyway, at least I got my baby girls. Some women like my friend Eloise never did, unfortunately. Besides, a big strong man was hard to find back then and still is. In Southampton, I'm surrounded by little seven stone weaklings with bad joints! Wouldn't give them the time of day.'

'He was cold, wasn't he. Dad?'

Kitty paused, and Millie wasn't sure whether to push the issue. Especially after Kitty's emotional reaction when she'd been in Lena's room the other day. But the letter . . . she needed to know that Donald Curtis was like that with everyone and not just with his kids . . . with her. It was important.

'Yes, he was. I think that man was just born that way.'

Satisfied with that answer, Millie moved the conversation on. 'Were you really going to have that facelift in Brazil?'

'Just before I got that call from Ade about Lena. Yes.'

'Why?'

'Because I'm tired of waking up in the morning looking like a rhino's backside.'

'That's such an exaggeration!' Millie laughed.

'It's no joke looking in the mirror and seeing your mum.'

'I wouldn't mind.'

'You're so sweet but, luckily for you, you take after your aunty Hortense. Lena is very much like Donald, while Cara is a lot like me. But don't tell her I told you that!'

'So are you still going to have it? The facelift? When Lena gets out?'

'Darling, you know when I go on my walks around the hospital grounds?'

'To stretch your legs after sitting with Lena? Yes.'

'Well, I used to just walk around aimlessly. Looking at everyone. The whole atmosphere of that hospital. Getting a change of scenery, I suppose. There're only so many times you can look up at that ugly painting above her bed and fix the flowers. Anyway, I started getting a bit brave and going into different wards. Sometimes I used to bump into people who were really suffering, and I began to think that me wanting this facelift was a bit . . . was a bit silly. Why put myself under the knife in a major op when people were going through such experiences to actually save their *lives*. It just didn't make sense to me. Can you understand what I mean?'

Millie nodded.

'It started to make less and less sense to go under the knife to try and look twenty-five again or in my case thirty-five! There's a lot of suffering in the world, Mills, and on our own doorstep.'

'So you've finally accepted how great you look and have decided to grow old gracefully?'

'No way! Are you kidding?'

Now Millie felt confused as Kitty reached into her pocket and handed over a clipping.

'Transderm Meso facial,' said Kitty proudly.

'What's that?'

'Something I can do without having an op. It's all about injecting hyaluronic acid without even using a needle! Isn't that great, darling?'

Millie wasn't quite sure what that was but it sounded a bit painful.

'It only scratches a little, apparently. No pain!'

'Well, if you're sure about it.'

'It's not as bad as having an operation and I still get to look young again. I have a consultation tomorrow.'

'What?'

'Don't look so shocked! I just thought I'd find out more about it.'

Millie *was* stunned at first, and then a little put out on Lena's behalf because Kitty seemed to be getting on with her life. But she knew she couldn't talk – she, too, was trying to get on with her life, which by no means meant Lena was becoming less of a priority. Did it?

That night, Millie called Cara and told her about the job interview. Cara was a bit distant, she sounded glum but when she said, 'I know you can do it, sis', she said it with heartfelt sincerity and Millie felt like jumping through the phone to give her sister a big hug.

TWENTY-EIGHT

The clinic was posher than Fen Lane. All clear glass and silver panelling. Even the receptionist, sitting behind a tall silver desk looked glamorous as she spoke into her earpiece.

'May I help you?' she asked. Her teeth were overly white and Millie couldn't work out if she was only twenty-five – or perhaps she was really twice that age. In fact, as they watched people swan past, Millie had started a 'guess the age' game with Kitty.

'I think the receptionist's about a hundred and three,' whispered Kitty as they waited for their turn in the swish waiting room. Copies of *Hello* were dotted about the place, and fresh fruit and water were displayed neatly by a sign that read: With Our Compliments. Millie suspected that she and Kitty might have been wondering the same thing – whether being in a private ward would have made a difference to Lena's well-being, her comfort – anything. But Millie for one knew that, contrary to Cara's concerns about missing notebooks and not being informed of the room change, Nurse Gratten and the medical team at Fen Lane had taken, and were still taking, excellent care of Lena.

'How old do you think she is? Thirty-five?' asked Millie as a nurse strode past the glass-fronted waiting room.

'No way. It's all in the neck, Mills. She'll never see fifty again.'

Millie smiled mischievously as a couple in matching sweatshirts came in and sat opposite them. Millie glanced at the plasma screen, showing the 'new advances in surgery', and bit on her complimentary apple.

'Mrs Curtis?' said a green-coated young woman, who Millie guessed to be about seventy-five but who looked thirty.

'You kept Dad's name?'

'Nothing to do with him, I just think it sounds better than Kitty Badjie!, besides everyone on the circuit knows me as Kitty Curtis. So if any new work came in . . . they'd know who to look for.'

The surgeon was really nice, explaining the whole procedure to them, and the two women ended a lovely day in a little bistro nearby. It might not have been a traditional mother/daughter day out, but Millie had truly enjoyed it.

That evening, at Lena's bedside, Millie felt positive and hopeful as she gave a run-through of Kitty's procedure. The Amerie CD was just ending when a knock sounded at the door. Through the glass Millie recognized Deana immediately, mainly because she didn't know anyone else who wore jeans *that* baggy.

'That song is sick!' said Deana.

'Sick?'

'Cool.'

'Yes, I knew what it means!' Millie was almost twenty-five, not thirty-five.

Deana hovered by the door. 'Sorry 'bout the other day,' she said.

'It's okay, I got the money. Thanks.'

'Just me having a laugh,' she sighed, inching slowly into the room.

'Sit down if you like.'

'I don't need permission, Miss.'

'My name's Millie. And I know it's upsetting to see her like this. So . . . take your time.'

Deana sat on the empty chair. 'I'm fine.'

'Oh, right.'

'So tell me, how can you be like, happy and that?'

'Happy? You've got to understand, Lena's been like this for some time now . . .' She clocked Deana's horrified expression. 'What I mean is, you have good and bad days.'

Deana just shrugged her shoulders.

'So, how do you know my sister?'

'Long story.'

'We have time.'

'I s'pose I can tell you, but you can't be telling people. I don't want her boss at work finding out and she gets the sack. You know, if she gets out of this. I don't want her gettin' into any trouble because of me. That's the last thing I want.'

'Trouble?'

'Yeah. It all started 'bout a year ago. I called up Kidzline because . . . well, my dad was behaving like a twat, innit? And I was about to punch him up. Well, Lena, she helped me.'

Lena, just known to Deana as Advisor L, had taken all her subsequent calls when she demanded she only be put through to Lena. But, unbeknown to Kidzline and totally against the rules, they had begun to meet regularly at a cafe called Giraffe in Muswell Hill, and even more after when Deana started to get into trouble with the police. Lena and Deana would chat about everything: life with her new foster family – who Deana believed made her feel like an outsider – school and boys.

'There were times, right, when I'd feel like there was no

196

one. I'd get so angry and then I just wouldn't know what to do with it. So Lena said when I felt that way, I should just pick up my phone and call her. Any time. So that's what I did. It really helped. *She* helped.'

Lena, she said, made her feel normal, whatever that was. More than just a kid whose dad liked to have a go at her from time to time. It was Lena who was interested in her love of music, poetry, and the TV show *Lost,* and it was Lena who let her know she was worth a lot more than anyone had ever made her feel and that she had the ability to do anything positive she wanted to do in her life.

'I s'pose she cared. At least someone did. I'd never really felt that before. I started to feel like, like she was saving my life. Sounds stoopid,' said Deana as they both stared at Lena again – at this beautiful sleeping beauty lying on a hospital bed. Millie felt moved, fighting her emotion, but still wanting to know one more thing.

'How did you find her?'

'I got suspicious when she didn't show up two Wednesdays in a row and her mobile was going straight to voicemail. Then I remembered she'd given me her house number – for emergencies only.'

Millie widened her eyes in disbelief. It was astonishing how Lena, a stickler for her lists and always doing things by the book, could have risked her job like this. But then Lena was a caring person first and foremost, so none of what Deana was telling her should really have come as a shock.

'So you called her at home?'

'Yep, and some old dear said she was here.'

'That would be Kitty. She must have thought you were one of her friends.'

'Yeah. That was ages ago. Plus the security is tight around here.'

She gently held Lena's hand. 'I've been getting into a little trouble lately, you know, when I thought Lena hadn't showed up because she didn't give a damn. But then I found out.'

Millie's words came naturally as she addressed this young girl with the baggy trousers and swagger, who inside, Millie could see, was just an innocent young girl. Her words were calm, controlled and very, very sincere. 'Lena would hate to think you were getting into trouble, Deana.'

'I know. I know all that. I owe it to her not to be a bum like my dad. I do know, you know!'

'I certainly do,' smiled Millie as she surprised herself by placing a friendly palm onto the girl's shoulder.

The afternoon of Millie's interview, Kitty was tackling Sodoku at the kitchen table while Millie tried to iron her interview suit. Kitty bustled over and took the iron from Millie, then sent her out with a hearty breakfast of scrambled eggs and toast. As Kitty waved her off, Millie wasn't sure, but she thought she noticed pride in her mother's eyes.

She reached her destination in good time and spoke to a receptionist named Moira who directed her to the correct room. She sat down with the other candidates who she thought all looked more knowledgeable, clever, and prettier than she did, but decided to stay positive and picture the look on Lena's face when she awoke to find her little sister in a full-time job.

It was Lena's face that got her through the interview. And it was Lena's voice that kept telling her to be assertive, be herself, and kick ass!

And Lena was the first person she told, the minute she heard, 'We'd like to offer you the job, Millie!'

TWENTY-NINE

Millie often fantasized about what it would feel like to skip into the dole office, sign on, and then just let slip to the snotty assistant that she'd be starting a job in a few weeks. Or what it would feel like to waltz into a nice shop, eye a dress she liked, thinking, 'perhaps I'll be able to afford something like that in a few months.'

And just what did it feel like to look into the mirror and see more than a good figure, wild hair, and nice lips staring back?

Bloody fabulous, that's what!

Which is just one of the few new words Millie was willing to use to describe herself lately.

Fabulous!

And she was proud of the fact that she was able to maintain a platonic friendship with a man like Michael while still thinking of herself as . . . well, fabulous! In fact, she hadn't maintained contact with any man except Michael, lately. Stewart was probably expecting another call, and Rik, (whose watch remained tucked away in her drawer,) hadn't entered in her mind for ages (she was saving it for a 'rainy day' that had yet to arrive). Millie knew that the true test of whether

199

or not she was that same girl any more would have a lot to do with that watch; that simply sending it off in the post with a quick note saying something like, 'Here's your watch, have a nice life,' would be classed as progress. And although she was well aware she wasn't quite ready for that just yet, something told her she was very, very close.

'I am so proud of you!' enthused Michael as he, Millie, and Kitty each sat on an A&R stool. She'd never heard another man say that to her before.

'Thank you, Michael,' she replied earnestly.

'And I know you don't usually put that much in!' said a clearly delighted Michael as Cara poured him almost half a glass of rum for the Mojito.

'Sorry, my mind was elsewhere. Oh, and congratulations on the job, Millie,' she said.

'And that's it?'

'Did you want a fanfare?'

'No, but at least some sarcastic comment about turning up on time, not getting caught with my fingers in the till—'

'You're not the same old Millie so I'll expect nothing of the sort!' said Cara, smiling warmly.

'What's up with you, Cara? You've been so different, lately.'

'You mean more miserable than usual? Everything's fine. I'm just having an off day.'

Kitty quietly sipped her Diet Coke as she gazed around the bar. She'd never been before, but had finally succumbed to Millie's insistence that she join them for celebratory drinks.

'You've done a good job with this place,' said Kitty.

'Thank you,' replied Cara politely, as Millie vowed to find out what was up with Cara and see if she could help in any way. That's what sisters did. They needed to stick together.

*   *   *

'You don't want to roll up in your new job with nails like your father's,' Kitty had insisted, which is why there were currently two girls scraping the dirt from underneath Kitty and Millie's nails and babbling to each other as a TV screen belted out vintage MTV at Monique's Hair and Nail Salon.

'So I told him, right, no way!' said the girl to her friend.

'You kidding?' said the other girl.

Millie looked at Kitty and they both smiled knowingly at one another, sharing in the nonsense of the moment.

'Would you like French or colour?' said one of the girls to Millie.

'Make it a French.'

'Going anywhere nice?' she enquired annoyingly.

'No. Just spending time with my mum and working.' Millie quickly glanced at Kitty for a reaction to the name change. Nothing. So far, so good.

'She can't be your mum. She looks far too young!'

'That's what I keep telling her!' added Kitty.

Millie's smile waned.

'But she is and I'm proud of that fact!'

Millie's smile returned, this time brighter.

Thirty minutes later, both sets of nails were drying under a tiny fan as the girls started on another customer. Kitty's red, gold, and green concoctions gleamed defiantly against the sunlight peering in through the windows as a ping sounded and another customer arrived. That's when they both saw Cara stride up to the counter in killer heels and enquire if there were any slots available for a cut and retouch.

'Cara!' called Kitty.

'Kitty,' replied Cara, clearly not able to match Kitty's enthusiasm. She looked drawn, even worse than before. Something was definitely up with her and Millie was now even more worried. She figured it must have something to do with Ade. Perhaps he'd left. She'd noticed tension at her celebratory drinks, she was sure of that. Millie shuddered at the thought. A few months ago, she'd have been pleased if Ade had taught Cara a lesson, because Millie had been a lot more jealous and self-pitying when it came to both her sister's 'perfect' boyfriends than she'd dare admit. But now the thought of them splitting up was too much to bear, and she felt really bad for her sister.

'Do you have any slots available for a manicure?' asked Cara.

'Cara, of course! We can fit you in, in say ten minutes?' replied one of the hairdresser's.

'Thanks.'

'So you know each other?' she asked nosily.

Kitty turned off the small fan. 'That's my other daughter.'

'Oh, lovely! Well, that's good that all three of you are here together, isn't it?'

'I have another girl. Lena. She's – well, she's poorly at the moment.'

'Oh, I'm sorry' said the hairdresser, before thankfully tending to another customer.

Millie switched off her own fan and glanced at her French manicure, a total contrast to Kitty's flamboyant creation.

'Looking good,' remarked Cara.

'Do me a favour and take out some money from my purse. I don't want to risk getting my nails scraped,' said Millie.

Cara rummaged through Millie's bag and took out thirty pounds.

'No, there should be sixty there. I'm paying for Mum's too.'

Millie waited for a response about the word 'Mum', but nothing came. Cara must really be in a bad way if she hadn't picked up on that, thought Millie.

Contrary to what Cara had hoped, a fresh new hairdo hadn't gone any way towards helping. She still felt like crap.

With her newfound enthusiasm for life, Millie had tried to coax her out of herself, but the emptiness remained. Almost two weeks after he'd left, Ade still hadn't come home. They saw each other at the bar, remained civil, jovial even, but it was as if he was waiting for her to back down while she was at home thinking he should do the same! The flat had never felt so empty. It had only ever been the two of them, but that had never seemed to matter. She missed the sound of Ade's voice as they discussed their day at the bar, what to cook for dinner and Ade tickling her as she tried to watch TV. All the laughter, all the rows, all the joy was nowhere now except in her memory. She sat down on the 'paint-splattered' arty sofa and smiled, remembering the day they'd bought the thing, of how she'd persuaded Ade what a good idea it would be to spend over a thousand pounds on a sofa that wasn't even leather. She'd finally worn him down after putting him through the tried-and-tested ploy of pouting – pushed-out lip, eyes downwards. It worked every time! Regardless of pouts, he'd always put Cara and her needs first.

She thought about phoning him at his mother's. She'd always hated Cara and was probably pleased to have her son back home, so that she could fill his head up with all sorts of crap – like letting him know how much better he could do. She was probably right: perhaps he could do better.

Unfortunately, Ade had rota'd himself off for two night-shifts in a row, but nevertheless she'd been hopeful. The shift was as normal: Eliza was as incompetent as always and Cara refused to serve a bunch of clearly underage teeny-boppers; one of the female toilets was even teetering on the verge of a flood. There were the same old dramas at A&R, but Ade wasn't there to share any of them with, and that made her even more miserable.

Only Michael walking in lifted her spirits temporarily.

'I wish Lena had met you before she met that wanker, Justin.'

There, she'd said it. Out of line? She didn't care. She was in that type of mood. Plus, to be perfectly honest, it was something she'd wanted to say ever since she'd first set eyes on him, because he was absolutely and without doubt perfect for Lena.

Cara had never been one of those nauseating people who saw it as their divine right to set everyone up just because they happened to be in a couple – and never would be. But there was something about Michael. And what had started off as a mere game to wind Justin up had now morphed into something more. He was clearly a good bloke. He went to see Lena on his own without any prompting; he bravely spoke the truth in his outburst at the dire family dinner, and he helped Millie get a job.

After the initial rush of customers, Cara almost dialled Ade's number, just to have a laugh with him about the fake twenty that someone had tried to pass through the till, and about the rep who'd tried to sell them the most foul-smeling plantain crisps she'd ever come across. That was the problem with being with someone for over ten years – every new thing you experienced, you wanted *them* to experience too. Every little joke you heard, you wanted to remember in detail, so you could repeat it back to them. She was still smiling to herself as Eliza approached with a concerned look on her face, and she wondered what the girl had done now. She was clutching a large envelope that Cara hoped was her resignation.

'Erm . . .' began Eliza, biting her bottom lip as always. Cara wasn't sure if Eliza was capable at any time of a conversation that didn't start with *erm*.

'Me and some of the staff have . . . erm . . . put this together.'

She thrust the envelope into Cara hands, which Cara felt

compelled to open, especially as Eliza seemed to be staring at her with total, manic expectancy.

It was a card.

'You can open it up,' said Eliza pointlessly.

Inside, the simply decorated card read, 'Thinking of you,' along with the signature of three members of staff, including Eliza's, complete with smiley face.

'That . . . that's really thoughtful, thanks,' was all Cara could say. Of course, in this situation, Ade would have known what to do, because that's the kind of person he was: the sweetness to her bitterness.

Cara took the card into the back office and placed it on the little makeshift ledge that Ade had 'built' in a rare moment of DIY madness. It was then she caught the front caption and her whole body froze.

In sympathy.

Oh no, they *didn't?*

She opened up the card again and scanned the signatures of her stupid, brainless staff, a mound of fury threatening to engulf her as she set about destroying it.

Sympathy?

Sympathy?

She tore at it, hoping also to tear out the rage she was currently feeling. But the card wouldn't budge; it was clearly one of those expensive ones from higher up on the shop shelf. Damn this, she thought, still struggling to make some type of dent in the card. In the end she had to chuck it forcefully in the direction of the door, just as it opened to reveal Ade staring at her like a moron.

'What *is* it?' he asked, rushing over to her. By now she was hunched over her desk, a film of frustrated sweat clinging to her forehead, breathing deeply and really wanting to spill out the tears, but not wanting her staff (or indeed Ade, considering their current disagreement) to see her 'lose' it.

'I'm fine!'

Ade retrieved the bent white card.

'No you're not, come here,' he said as he wrapped his arms around her, entirely against her will.

'I'm okay. I just came in here to look for something. What are you doing here anyway? I thought you were off.'

Ignoring whatever jumble of words tumbled recklessly from her mouth, Ade buried his face in her, held her so tight, so close, she thought she'd break into tiny little pieces. And that day, she would have, if Ade hadn't been there to hold her up. Just as he had been for the last ten years. She needed him, would always need him. Who had she been trying to kid?

He followed her back to their apartment, soothed her forehead with his kisses, tucked her into bed, and told her everything was going to be okay.

He was with her again, just where he belonged.

———

THIRTY

In just under a week's time, Millie would be starting a new job.

She'd started new jobs before. The doughnut shop a year ago, Pizza Hut the year before that (with the dodgy octopus-handed boss); then there'd been the clothes shop that fancied itself as a boutique in West Dulwich – what a cow that manageress had been. For the most part, she'd stuck at some jobs, got fired from others, and this was enough to tell her that perhaps the nine-to-five shuffle wasn't for her. So what would be different with this one? She would be able to start paying back Lena whilst having some cash in her pocket.

Millie began flicking through a fashion magazine as Nurse Gratten completed Lena's daily wash.

'Did you always know you wanted to be a nurse?'

'Me? Not really. I just knew I wanted to help people. Not sure what you want to do?'

'Pathetic, isn't it? Almost twenty-five and still no clue.'

'Really? You look about seventeen, if that helps.'

'Well, for the first time in my life, I feel my age.'

'What about that magazine you're looking at? You're a pretty girl, you could do some modelling.'

'I doubt it. I'm too old.'

'Crikey! If you're too old, then I must be ancient.'

Throughout her time coming to Fen Lane Hospital to visit her sister, Millie hadn't spoken much to Nurse Gratten, hadn't really looked past the ancient hairstyle and ill-fitting uniform.

'Why don't you look to your sister for advice?'

'Cara? The mood she's been in lately?'

'I meant Lena.'

'She'd usually be the first person I'd go to.'

'Think about it. You think a lot of Lena, don't you? And you admire her too.'

'She's so much to so many people. She's changed lives. Even whilst she's been in here, people are still coming out of the woodwork. Michael, Deana, and probably loads more at the charity where she worked. Then there's me. She's bloody amazing.'

'You know what they say, don't you?'

'No?'

'Imitation being the highest form of flattery, or something like that.'

Millie wasn't quite sure what Nurse Gratten was going on about.

'Look to Lena,' she concluded as she patted down the sheets.

Cara, on more than one occasion, had been told by Lena that Ade was a man in a million, that she was blessed to have found him. That, although very different in personality, they were perfectly matched, destined to be together forever and all that.

So Cara wondered what Lena would say if she could see them now? Ade was sleeping in his mother's spare room over in North London, while she lay restlessly in their bed, feeling the coldness and emptiness of the space beside her.

Because Ade had gone again.

Even after her mini-meltdown the other night, he'd left the next morning before his shift, after fixing her some soup, soothing her to sleep and telling her that everything would be all right. She'd taken that to mean he was coming home. That he'd forgiven her and they could go back to how it used to be. But that was the problem, he'd said – *things had to change, and as he couldn't see that happening in the foreseeable* . . .

So, he was gone again, and she felt more lost than ever, having had a taste of his sweetness, his tenderness, and of his downright blatant and open love for her. In fact, she was feeling more lost than the day her parents announced they were splitting up. More lost than when she heard her father had started a new family. More lost than she could ever, ever have imagined.

She looked into the mirror, her pristine hairdo concealing the fact she felt so messed up inside.

Oh, how she missed him pottering about the kitchen of a morning and complaining about her dirty cup on the windowsill – what an old woman he was! How she wished she could creep up behind him and hold him – her tiny frame pressed against his impressive torso. But none of that was happening right now because he still needed time to think and wanted Cara to do the same. She was under no illusions, she was a child of divorce after all; Ade had gone off to think about whether he could continue with their relationship, knowing that she wasn't able to consider the possibility of having children.

He was thinking about leaving her.

The thought scared her so deeply and she figured a walk, perhaps into Dulwich Park, might clear her head. She hadn't done that in a while and anything was worth a try.

She wasn't sure if it was Michael she saw striding towards

her, because he looked different each time she saw him, but the addition of two kids and a buggy was even more than *she'd* expected.

'Hello there,' said Cara in a higher-than-usual voice, staring at the children in surprise. The fact that she didn't want to procreate didn't stop others from doing so, she supposed. Michael was holding a little girl who had snot dripping into her mouth, while the boy held onto the side of the buggy Michael was pushing. The boy was 'sweet', she supposed, in a munchkin kind of way, but the girl needed to grow a bit more until she evened out.

'Cara, what a surprise! How are you?' he asked.

'Great! And who are these little . . . things?' She put on the 'I am really interested in your kids' voice that she knew was expected of her. Especially when her usual voice was so sharp.

She kissed him chastely on each cheek, hoping that privilege didn't need to extend to the kids, then stood back to 'admire' the scene.

'These are my niece and nephew, George and Serena,' he said, almost thrusting the child in her face. Cara smiled and waved hello awkwardly. She always felt weird around kids. Her friends had started having kids about two years ago. It was a shame that she and many of her girlfriends had drifted apart since then; get-togethers had shrunk to once in a while, and only happened if they could find a babysitter, or if one of the kids wasn't sick. Yes, she could have visited more often, but the thought of having a snotty kid thrust into her hands always made her body turn almost mannequin-like as she stared at the child, and thought: 'What am I supposed to *do with it?*' Cara was used to feeling confident in everything she did: running a business, home, loving her man. But kids? They made her feel uneasy, a side she didn't much care for. Plus, every kid she met seemed to hate her and was inclined to stamp on her beautiful shoes.

So, predictably and thankfully, Michael's niece totally ignored her, while the little boy looked as if he was itching to say something horrible.

'How's Lena? Any change?' asked Michael, thankfully, just as the boy opened his mouth to speak.

It was the first thing Michael always asked, whether he was stopping by at the bar, sending her a text, or just passing in the street, like now. Clearly, the one person who bound them all together wasn't around to see what she'd started. But she would be. Soon. Of that, Cara was sure. 'The same, you know?'

'Okay. Well, me and these two are just off for a nice day out. Going for a run, aren't we?'

The little boy rolled his eyes, clearly not relishing the thought.

'I'm in the middle of a thinking session, so I'll leave you to it.'

'You off tonight?'

'From the bar? Yes.'

'Good for you. I mean, what's it all for anyway?' The girl child wriggled about impatiently in Michael's arms. 'Working yourselves to the bone. I mean, it's fine, if you manage to have a life in the meantime.'

'We have a young business, it takes time to . . .' Cara felt as if she was explaining herself – and she never did that.

'To make a profit, I know. But then, when you do, it's: we must expand the business. So then, there's more work. It can get to the stage where there will always be an excuse to overwork and allow your life to take a back seat.'

'We're not that bad, Michael.' Cara wasn't sure what pill this man had taken, but if it made him happy . . .

'*I'll be happy when* . . . Does that sentence sound familiar?

211

I'll be happy when I get a bigger car. You get the car, then it's, *I'll be happy when I get a better-paying job.* You get the job and then it's something else. Forever dreaming about it and never doing it. What happens in the meantime? What happens *while you were dreaming?*'

'Life.'

'You hope.'

She smiled awkwardly.

'When was the last time you took a walk like this in the park, smelt the trees, breathed in fresh air and listened to the birds, just because?' he asked.

'Because, what?'

'Because. Full stop.'

'The air's full of pollution and the birds crap all over the place.'

'Cara, you know what I mean.'

'Who has time for all that, anyway?'

'I rest my case.'

Cara looked downwards, not sure how she'd got here.

'Okay, I'll leave the hard talk for another time,' he said as the girl began to arch her back and contort her face into something resembling constipated fury.

'But I will ask you this—'

'Uncle Michael, can we go now?' asked the boy.

'In a minute, George. Cara, is there something you've put on a back burner? You know, said, *I'll do it when I've done this, done that*? Maybe something you've been putting off for ages?'

She shook her head, suddenly feeling this was a little too deep for a chat in the middle of the park with two children seconds away from a colossal tantrum.

'No. Not really.'

'Okay. Then you have it sussed then, and I apologize for my mini-rant. I've got to get these two on a swing before

212

they report me to their mum. I'll see you soon? At the hospital?'

'Sure, yes,' she replied.

As she watched them leave, she felt uneasy, as though she'd just lied to Michael. She wasn't sure what about, but yes, she had just lied.

THIRTY-ONE

Alone in the apartment again, Cara tried to concentrate on a DVD, but kept thinking back to Michael's earlier ramblings.

I'll be happy when . . .

Cara had never been one of those people who put things off. When she'd thought about opening a bar, everyone had stood in line to advise her against it, told her to wait until they had more capital, more experience of running a business. When she wanted to buy the flat with Ade, he'd spoken of caution, while she just thought '*Let's do this*' let's buy a swanky apartment they couldn't really afford. *Let's just do it*. When she wanted a pair of shoes she liked, she never even thought about how uncomfortable they'd be – she just bought them because they were great! Unlike her cautious sister, Lena, Cara knew how to live! She'd always known how to live, and if Michael had known her for more than five minutes, he'd have seen that too.

In front of the DVD, the pictures on the screen made no sense as her thoughts continued to dominate. Something deep within was knocking on the door of her defence, not wanting her to discard Michael's words so easily.

So, was there something she was putting on the back burner?

Think.

Think.

The moment she looked up, she felt it.

Hadn't she told – no – been *telling* Ade for ages now that they should wait for a child? That she had so many things to do in life before she could even contemplate such a step? Dammit, she hated moments like this, when she resembled her sister more than she'd like. These were what she termed her 'analysing-to-death moments.' She sat up and scrunched her eyebrows. Okay, first things first, she definitely didn't want kids. No, that wasn't true. She had just never imagined herself *with* a kid. She felt weird around them. They didn't like her – Michael's little ones proved that. She wouldn't know what to do with one. They cried. They required constant feeding. She couldn't trust herself to be good at it. Was that all it was, or was there something else?

Millie was having her own 'analysing-to-death' moment.

If she died, what would she be remembered for?

This question remained tatooed on Millie's brain from the moment she woke up until the time she settled down for the night. Lena had clearly touched a lot of people: Deana and the rest of the kids at Kidzline, her, Cara, Michael, Andy. The list was probably endless. Even while asleep, Lena was still touching people! Amazing.

But what had *she* contributed to the world?

She pondered on this with Kitty.

'Why don't you go to college or something?'

'I don't think so!'

'No, you're like me. No into all that studying. You're more suited to the stage. What about doing an evening course in acting? We could do it together, me and you – it would be great! Actually, I could go and see if they need an acting tutor. I could share my experiences with them . . . Mmmmm.

215

If I'm going to be sticking around for my girls, I'm going to need something to do.'

Although Millie should have been miffed that the conversation had now turned to Kitty, she was more excited at the prospect of Kitty sticking around because, whatever happened, she would always need her mum.

Michael's 'analysing-to-death moments' were a thing of the past. He was a man of action and he was currently beaming with elation because he had just moved into his very own, brand-spanking-new home. Perhaps it didn't look like one of those new-builds he used to lust after down in Lower Sydenham, but the flat he'd lived in for the past five years had undergone something of a makeover. The walls were pristine, the floor spotless, and it glistened with shiny new appliances. Nothing flash, just a trendy new kettle and toaster from Argos and shiny knobs for the kitchen cupboards. Clutter was a thing of the past now, as most of that was packed up downstairs ready for the recycle bin. His space had just become a whole lot more spacious.

What he couldn't help thinking about though, was how all this change was a reflection of his own life now. It was as if the heavy burden of hopelessness and pressure that he had piled on himself every day had just joined the rubbish piled high in the recycling bins.

He felt lighter.

Lifted.

It now felt great to be alive.

Michael peered into his fridge which, instead of being empty, now contained five bottles of water and a selection of various fruits, including lychees. He still hated vegetables, but the vitamins now occupying his cupboard and the disgusting barley grass should help him out on that front. He had also started reading – mainly health books and autobiography of people he admired like Barack Obama. And, best of all, when visiting Charlotte and the kids, he wasn't immediately overwhelmed by a sense of failure at not being able to offer them more. If he really looked at the facts he would have realized that Charlotte had never really judged him, had never even expected him to do what he actually did for them. Thoughts of failure had all been in *his* head, and he could see that now. And while he knew that he'd always try and provide for them, he was now willing to accept his limitations. Instead of moaning about not being able to conduct a dinosaur hunt in his nonexistent garden, he'd take them to Dulwich Park. Instead of a shopping spree in Hamleys, he was sure a trip to a toy stall in East Street would do the trick.

And then there was what Cara had said, about him being perfect for Lena. That had stayed put in his head, almost against his will. He was unable to get it out of his mind and maybe he didn't even want to.

Charlotte came round to inspect his handiwork. The kids were with their father.

'This flat is great! I can't believe it. Really, I can't!' enthused Charlotte.

'That I did it all by myself?'

She looked around her in wonderment. 'Everything. You. Your clothes!'

'And your hair, or lack of. The flat. Even the kids have noticed.'

Michael laughed. 'What, they sat you down and told you what a profound difference they've noticed in my everyday behaviour?'

'Shut up! Although George does say stuff like, "Uncle Michael's not so much of a miserable sod any more" – well, along those lines, anyway.'

'What does Serena say?'

'Much the same, but in baby language.'

She ran a hand over on one of the kitchen cupboards. 'I was really getting worried for a moment.'

Michael looked downwards. 'Really?'

'I thought you were in some type of depression – or were heading that way, Michael, and it scared me sometimes. I was scared for you.'

Michael absorbed her words and allowed himself to go back to that time to just before he met Lena. He used to get in from work, every evening, to his dreary, miserable flat, visit Jen for meaningless sex (okay, that bit was sometimes fun), and generally drifted through a life he didn't actively feel a part of. It was as if he'd been watching someone else take part in his own life.

Until now.

Of course, Michael had no idea how long he had left on this earth – it could be moments, years or decades, but the time he did have, he intended to use very wisely. And, at the risk of sounding like the ending of a sloppy movie, he was going to live, really live his life, and never take a moment for granted ever again.

'You want to know the biggest, most beautiful change in you?' continued Charlotte.

He shook his head, laughed, then nodded truthfully.

'The biggest change in my brother is that he actually gets off his lazy arse and cooks for me when I come over!'

'I'm only going to stick some frozen stuff in the oven! Hardly Gordon Ramsay territory.'

'It's a start.'

'And there will definitely be none of that hummus rubbish!'

He wasn't sure why, but that night Michael dreamed of Lena. It was pretty deep, too, questioning why he hadn't met her years before, before the accident. Then again, if he had met her in a normal context, would she still have had such

218

a huge impact on him? Wouldn't she have become just another 'booty call' like Jen?'

When he woke, he realized that none of that was really relevant because there are some things you just don't have any control over.

It was one of those mornings. One of the ones he used to despise: the sun shone so brightly into the room that it gave the illusion of summer, when in fact it was bloody freezing outside! But, as the fresh November mornings became colder each day, such an illusion was welcome. In fact, Michael felt like singing; so much so that that's what he did as soon as he slotted in the Amerie CD.

He gathered his bag, flung the strap over his shoulders, looked at himself in the newly bought mirror and saw something he wasn't used to seeing. Not just the lack of hair or the broader-than-usual shoulders thanks to regular gym workouts, but there was something even more fundamental staring back at him. Something that warmed him from the tips of his toes right up to the top of his head.

The smile.

At work, he turned to the lift as the door opened and a couple stepped out. He then waved at the elderly security guard.

'Morning,' he said, knowing he sounded a bit high, but not caring. The security guard, unable to actually place him (even though Michael had been working there for two years), gave a cheery but confused reply as the lift door closed. Michael headed towards his office, but not before stopping at the reception desk.

'Hello, Moira,' said Michael.

'Err, hello,' she said.

'I just wanted to say hi,' he said, just as – mercifully – an incoming call came through on her headset. Michael decided he might need to brush up on his conversational skills and offer to buy Moira a coffee at eleven.

Throughout the day, Michael noticed various other colleagues chatted with him on a friendlier level than usual. It was all part of the change in Michael: he was now interacting with colleagues, being a part of the workplace, and was not just a spare part (although it would be a bonus when Millie started too). He knew he wasn't necessarily about to begin joining them for after-work drinks, but it was a positive change that he welcomed, and one that led him into the boss's office.

The boss looked at him sceptically after Michael had said his piece. 'Are you sure about this, Michael?'

'I am. Yes. Definitely.'

The boss scratched at his chin, perhaps never thinking he'd live to see the day. But he had heard right. Michael wanted more responsibility. He was ready for it.

'I am ready, you know, for a project. I can do it.' Michael rarely went in to see the boss because before it had always felt as though he was being hauled up in front of the headmaster at school.

'Okay, Michael. I'll see what projects are available and maybe we can discuss this further?'

Michael was pleased with how the meeting had gone. He wanted to be passionate about everything, and that had to include work – even though he would never let it take over his life, because that too would defeat Michael's new and improved *purpose*.

That smile reappeared again as he almost swaggered back to his desk. He knew he must have looked like a dick, but he just didn't care.

Cara decided that Michael had spoken some sense when they bumped into each other in the park. The bit about *living and not seeing every day merely as an opportunity for more work* had resonated with her strongly.

Of course he hadn't said it in those exact words, but that was how she'd heard them. She had sorted out cover in the bar and asked Ade to meet her in their favourite restaurant. They needed to talk. She was miserable without him, she needed him, and of course, she thought, the same must be true for him too? She hoped so, because she couldn't bear it if he was finding life okay without her. Happy with his mum's cooking as opposed to her constant takeaways (unless he cooked) and burnt attempts (again, unless he cooked), and having his washing done daily as opposed to his white boxers coming out orange. She hoped none of that mattered to Ade, and that he still loved her *because* she was who she was.

She shuddered at the thought of Eliza being in charge of their livelihood, but she figured her relationship was more important than the odd broken glass, or bottle of wine or . . . Cara quickly raced home before she managed to talk herself out of it.

She started with a full-on body scrub and shower. Her nails were pristine as usual, thanks to her weekly nail job at Monique's. Her toes were neat, but she gave them a quick once-over with the nail file and then she toyed between two outfits. The black satin skirt Ade was in lust with, the equally tight grey one she looked good in with the white shirt, or the tight Karen Millen black dress that really shouldn't be worn if she planned on eating considering the lack of flattery around the tummy area. She decided on a blue shiny shift and a pair of killer heels', and applied a coat of her favourite Mac lipgloss. She admired herself in the mirror, knowing she looked pretty good. The concealer nicely covered the bags under her eyes that had recently developed through lack of sleep. She had discovered that she just couldn't sleep in that bed without Ade.

Cara made her way to the train station filled with hope. The car was staying at home, as she intended to have at least one glass of champagne. In celebration, perhaps. She tried to remember their last date outside the flat and bar, but couldn't. Even Valentine's Day, the day on which everyone else in a relationship was guaranteed some treat, had turned into a rushed lunchtime job, as they prepared to serve a bar full of couples who'd forgotten to book ahead.

As the train pulled into the station, she glanced at her watch. The table was booked for eight o'clock and she knew – meticulous stickler that he was – that Ade would be there fifteen minutes early. She headed towards the tube entrance, noting how her little toes were rubbing against the leather of the shoes. As she was about to get onto the escalators, a little girl blocked her way.

'Excuse me,' she said. A quarter of the way down was a woman lugging two huge suitcases, shouting something at the little girl.

'*Va! Monte l'escalator, Solange! Va!*'

The little girl reminded her of someone, perhaps a young Millie. Wild loosely curly hair, mildly tamed by a spotty woolly hat and dressed in a pretty coat and matching scarf, she stood at the top of the escalators like a catatonic statue glued to the floor.

'Solange!' screamed the lady as she slowly disappeared down the escalators. Cara wasn't quite sure what to do until the woman shouted, 'Please, kind lady, take her hand!'

Cara looked around her. Two burly blokes swigging beers were heading towards them. She did what instinct told her to do and proffered her beautifully manicured hand to the child.

'Shall we?' she asked, which with hindsight probably

sounded a bit formal. But hey, she wasn't around kids that often. Well, except Millie.

Surprisingly enough, the child stopped sobbing long enough to place her tiny hand in Cara's, and together they rode down the escalator. Cara never remembered it being so long.

She attempted conversation but struggled to string a sentence together in French. 'So, what's your name then?' Silly considering her mother or guardian had been shrieking *Solange! Va!* for the best part of a minute.

She tried something else. 'Qui?' It was all she could remember from secondary school French classes. But the child remained frozen to the spot and, unlike some kids Cara had encountered (like Michael's nephew), she wasn't being merely insolent. She really couldn't speak because she was gripped by so much fear. This touched Cara; this – and now on closer inspection – very cute little girl with wild hair, long eyelashes, and the smoothest skin was absolutely terrified of the escalator. Her innocence and then total trust in Cara, was actually quite . . . amazing and shocking all at once. A child. Trusting. Her. How could that be when, really, she didn't even trust herself?

Wasn't that something?

They reached the bottom and the child seemed to defrost immediately as she ran into the waiting arms of a rather annoyed mum.

'*Maman!*' sang the child.

'Thank you so much. She is so silly!' the woman said warmly.

'That's okay. I'm glad she's okay.'

'Say thank you to the kind lady.'

'Thank you,' the child smiled shyly, and Cara felt her tummy flip. And no, it wasn't because she'd suddenly fallen in love with the child (which she could see would be highly feasible given the kid's general all-round sweetness), but there was something about her that reminded Cara of someone and perhaps it wasn't Millie after all.

It was herself.

Michael pressed SEND on the computer and felt his tummy contract with excitement.

He'd just spent over £650 on a holiday to Sri Lanka. It was only for a week and he'd been charged the dreaded 'single supplement', but he didn't care. He was off to see a whole new part of the world in just over eight weeks and he couldn't wait.

Nurse Gratten was on her shift and had allowed Cara a few minutes with Lena, even though visiting hours had ended. 'She got me thinking, really thinking. This Solange kid. I was even supposed to be meeting Ade right now, but I had to cancel. I had to come here instead because I needed to talk to you, sis.' She rested her eyes on the pink CD player beside the flowers. 'I'm wearing the shift dress. The blue one, I don't think you've seen it before. I got it just before you . . . well, anyway, it's kind of shapeless, but you know me. The right shoes, the right bag and almost anything can look sexy.'

Cara forced a smile. 'I just couldn't meet Ade today, because I am so confused about everything. What Michael said; you; babies; Solange – *everything*. So I did what I am obviously good at and ran away. Who said I don't take after our parents?'

'I know I need to see Ade and I will. I just need to know what I want first, and I honestly don't know any more. Dammit, if you hadn't slipped into this, none of this would have happened. We'd all be living our lives as normal. I'd never have met Michael, Kitty wouldn't be around, and all these weird feelings wouldn't be surfacing for me. There I go again, selfish little bitch. Ade's probably well shot of me.'

224

She looked towards the clock. 'The restaurant I booked for tonight was our favourite – remember the one I took you to for your twenty-eighth birthday in Covent Garden? My favourite restaurant in the whole wide world . . .' Cara turned back to Lena as the memory hit her. 'Even though you'd told me you were off meat that year, I took you to *my* favourite restaurant which sells steak and lobster.' She took her sister's hand. 'Just how selfish was I? Never enough time, always busy. Never enough time.'

Michael was right; it had all been about work. The bar, the bills, the mortgage. She'd only just had time for Ade, let alone Lena. She'd been putting off aspects of her life, *people* in her life for . . . how long and for what exactly.

Cara buried her head within the sheet covers.

'I'm so sorry, Lena. Really I am.' And then, finally Cara allowed the tears to flow. Each tear representing the hurt, anger, resentment and fear she'd found herself feeling over the last few months. And perhaps even the whole of her life. Who knew? She was certain of only one thing – that the blubbing was well overdue. 'Just come back to us and things will be different. They will be, I promise.' She wiped her eyes. She wanted to beg for some sort of forgiveness from her sister, but she didn't actually know where to start. 'I just want you back. And I can prove to you that things can be different. Promise.' She heard a rustle coming from behind. Composing herself quickly she stood up and was startled to see Kitty standing right in front of her on the other side of the bed.

'Kitty?' she said, totally embarrassed that her mother might have heard her crying.

'I wasn't listening. I came in quietly because I didn't want to disturb your time with Lena.'

Cara gathered her bag. 'It's okay, I'm going now. I have to call Ade. You do know visiting is over and if Nurse Gratten finds you in here—'

'I feel the same way, you know.'

'About what?'

'About taking that child for granted.'

'So, you *were* listening?'

'Just a bit.'

'Great.'

'I want you to know that I feel it too. Doubly so because you are my children and that carries a certain amount of responsibility, I suppose.'

'You *suppose*?' Cara wanted to say that it carried *all* the responsibility in the world. That you can't just have children and then ignore them when it suited you or chuck them away like an unwanted pair of shoes. You had to stick with them through thick and thin. Be there when they needed you and even when they didn't. Be available via phone, visually and emotionally. Surely that was what parenting was all about?

Kitty sat on the chair. 'I don't know when I will be able to make things up to Lena, but there is something I can do now, for my other two girls.'

'And what might that be?' asked Cara, almost as a challenge, but she did actually want to know.

'Millie's almost forgiven me. We are getting on so much better now. So at least I now have . . . I have a chance to make it up to another one of you right now. In this instant.'

It took a few seconds for Cara to register the words and what they meant.

'You don't mean . . . you can't mean *me*?'

'Why not?' She inched closer and Cara almost froze like the little girl on the escalator. 'So, can we try, Cara? Please? I haven't been able to be in a room alone with you long enough to tell you how I'm feeling. For a start, our girl has been here almost three months.'

'I know.'

'And I'm just about losing hope that we will ever speak to our girl again. I can't lose you too, Sugar, I can't. Please. I will do anything to have some type of chance with you.'

Cara scrunched her eyebrows in confusion. Kitty hadn't called her Sugar in years. Kitty was always into nicknames. Millie was Mills, she was Sugar and Lena had been Le Le once upon a time. A very long time ago.

'Please,' she sniffed, tears glistening in Kitty's eyes. This display made Cara feel uneasy. Not because she couldn't deal with emotion. Okay, she was not good at it, but seeing Kitty crying was all a bit too strange and her first instinct was not to cuddle up to her. Besides, this wasn't supposed to happen – Kitty begging her, snivelling. She needed answers and not a tear-fest. She wasn't ready for all of this. Today had already been that much heavier than usual. 'There are some questions I have to . . . Things I need to know. But do we have to do this now? I've had a heavy day and – frankly – I can't deal with all this now.'

'When, then?' Kitty was visibly hurt. Cara could see that.

'At least when Millie's here. The four of us together. I think that would only be fair. It's what Lena would want.' That much she knew. If Kitty was going to answer all the questions that the three of them had amassed but had never asked over the years, Kitty was going to have to tell each of them everything.

They agreed to meet together on Thursday evening after Millie confirmed she'd be there.

By the time she got home, it was too late to call Ade. So, that night, Cara settled down for another night of missing him – but, as well as Ade, she soon became preoccupied with thoughts of another absence.

She remembered reading in some magazine that your 'time of the month' became synchronized with those around you. Indeed, if Lena complained about stomach cramps and

227

Millie about bloatedness and a frenzied need for chocolate, she knew it was only a matter of time before the monthly visit came a-knocking. But Millie had voiced her usual complaints last week, while Cara had felt fine. She checked the calendar again, which confirmed she was late.

She was very, very late.

THIRTY-TWO

Despite any reservations she may have had, Millie had enjoyed her first day's induction into 'Michael's' firm. She was shown how to produce spreadsheets, print labels, and input data and it actually felt new and *sort of* exciting, especially as it beat shop work and snotty customers. But she knew her interest would soon wane. It had happened before.

Perhaps her destiny was to become an Irish Sea Marine Project Manager? (She couldn't swim.) Or a tattooist? (Hated needles.) Or a Biochemist? (Whatever that was.) No, this time though she would stick it out and using the time wisely. Plus, she'd just discovered a delectable sample store a few doors down, where she'd already mentally picked out Christmas presents for Cara, Kitty, and Lena. She'd also made a couple of friends and, after two days, really felt the job was something she could do while she thought about what she'd like to do longterm. What Nurse Gratten had said last week about 'flattery' having something to do with imitating someone, niggled at her. Maybe she'd been trying to tell Millie that she should copy the person she most admired in the world who, of course was Lena.

That was it!

She would help others, like Lena. Hadn't it felt really good to see Deana at the hospital from time to time? In her own colourful way Deana had been keeping her updated on her life: how she was doing at school and in her foster care home. That had given her genuine, real, fantastic satisfaction. That warm feeling in her tummy was something she just wasn't used to.

Her thoughts were interrupted by a call from Cara. Something about coming to a weird family meeting on Thursday. She figured it must be to do with Lena and hoped it wasn't anything major, like selling the house or something. She'd only been in hospital for three months. There was still hope.

She waved affectionately at Mick, the security guard, rushed past him and up in the lift. She'd five minutes to prepare herself, take a pee, blow her nose, and find herself at her desk in time for the beginning of a working day. Her trademark lateness was now a thing of the past. She was determined to be on time always, because she owed it to Lena and herself to make this job work.

She smiled to herself as Michael waved at her from across the room. Her computer desktop beamed out that old picture of Millie, Lena, Cara, and Lionel the dog and she felt so far removed from the child in the picture. She was a woman now, and was ready for all the responsibilities and possibilities that that would bring – or at least she would be once she did one last thing.

Michael pressed the buzzer for the second time.

'What?' spat back the reply. Perhaps he shouldn't have come, but if he didn't do it now, he never would.

'Jen, it's me. Can I come up?'

The familiar scent of her flat welcomed him as she stood at the door, leaning to the side.

'This is a surprise,' she said dryly. Actually, Michael wasn't sure if her tone was dry, angry, or nonchalant. Best not to think about it before he forced out of his mouth everything he needed to say. She led him into the lounge as he recalled the times they used to spend together. Or rather the 'nights'. In fact, he couldn't remember ever taking her out further than the local chinese, or maybe a midnight movie at the cinema. He 'd never introduced her to Charlotte, never rang unless he was returning her call, and never once said he loved her.

'I haven't been very fair to you, Jen.'

She sat down on the sofa and faced him. 'Understatement.' She stifled a yawn, and Michael wasn't sure whether this was put on for his benefit or whether she was really tired. It was only eight-thirty though.

'Jen, I've come to tell you something.'

'Michael, I haven't seen you for almost three months.'

'I know.'

'So why are you here?'

'I just wanted to say . . .'

She rolled her eyes. 'I have an early morning flight to catch tomorrow.'

'Oh. Thing is, I've come to tell you something.'

'What have you come to say, Michael?'

'I just wanted to say I'm sorry.'

It was hard to read her expression, because she just seemed to stop mid-eye-roll. Perhaps she's been expecting some type of confrontation. As it was, this new information rendered her temporarily helpless.

'I'm sorry for treating you badly – and, let's face it, I did – not being there for you and not treating you anything like the way you deserved to be treated. And that's like a princess.'

She smiled. 'You idiot.'

'I know!'

They both laughed and Michael was grateful for the break in tension.

'I was a different person then, you know,' he said.

'And now?' She looked at him clearly, perhaps this time seeing at least the physical changes. 'Nice haircut.'

'Thanks.'

'So what did you do, go to some hippy retreat and hug horses?'

'Not quite. I met someone. A friend,' he added a bit too quickly. Jen raised an eyebrow. 'A friend who taught me about . . . life.'

'Good.'

Michael wasn't sure if this was sarcasm. But it didn't matter; he had said what he'd come to say. Other girlfriends, he'd phoned and apologized to, but realizing that Jen was the one he'd wronged the most, the one who'd really seen a future between them, had meant he needed to see her. And, besides, out of the others, Jen seemed the least likely to send him home with a head gash, so that helped in the decision-making.

She offered him a drink, but he declined. He knew his fifteen minutes was up.

'Are you okay though, Jen? You know, job, life?'

'Don't worry about me, I'm good. In fact I've met somebody, too.'

'Really?' Michael hadn't expected this. Perhaps it was out of male egocentricity but the thought had just not crossed his mind. Of course she'd met someone. Jen was gorgeous, intelligent, independent; it was always going to happen and he was genuinely pleased for her.

'That's good news,' he said sincerely.

'Robert. In fact we're flying off to Morocco in the morning for our first holiday together. He's a great man and I wish

I'd met him ages ago. But with you in my life, that just wouldn't have happened because I wouldn't have allowed anyone like Robert in – I was always thinking about you. Forever thinking, "When Michael gets his act together, we'll be a couple." I'd always compare every man I met to you. So when you did finally leave, as hard as I took it at the time, I now know it was the best thing, because it then allowed me . . . I *allowed myself* to attract a man like Robert, I suppose. Simple really.'

Jen's psychobabble made a lot of sense to Michael. Too much sense, if he applied the same theory to Lena and himself.

By allowing Lena to remain in his life wouldn't HE be preventing himself from moving forward and meeting someone?

It was Thursday tomorrow and he was going to spend the early part of the evening at the hospital with Lena, but Cara had asked him to stay away that day. Apparently there was a family meeting planned. At first he'd felt a bit put out about this, but then accepted that he was a relative stranger to these people. They had let him into their most private space where Lena was concerned when, really, he hardly knew her. She had been in a deep sleep for three months now. Surely things were not looking good as far as her recovery was concerned? Who knew? He was just certain that he should never be in limbo when it came to his life, ever again. Wasn't that what meeting Lena had all been about? Learning to live? So that would be the same for his love life too. He would never wait around in the hope that Lena would wake up or live in the hope that she would actually want *him* if she did. She had Justin, however much of a plank he was, and Michael owed it to *himself* to find someone for himself too. So that's what he would do. He would allow himself to be with someone properly, knowing that would only be possible if he finally let Lena go.

So Friday would be the end of a working week and the day he would finally say goodbye to Lena Rose Curtis, forever.

THIRTY-THREE

With still no sign of her monthly friend, instead of worrying about how it had happened, or if it indeed *had* happened, Cara, immersed herself in thoughts of what she was going to ask Kitty at the hospital. Questions. Answers. She wanted them all. Anything else, she would deal with afterwards.

'You've done a good job today. You go on home,' she said to Eliza.

'Erm, but Ade told me not to leave you to lock up alone.'

Cara raised an eyebrow. 'Did he?'

'Yes, Cara.'

'Don't worry, I can look after myself. You go on home, Eliza,' she said, secretly pleased that Ade still cared.

She set the building alarm, locked up, and headed towards her car. One of the streetlamps had broken. Behind her, she thought she could hear footsteps.

'Eliza?' she called. Her heart began to beat faster. The footsteps drew closer as she searched the inside of her handbag for that mace spray and her car keys – whichever came first. But when neither materialized, her bag tumbled to the ground and as she bent down to pick it up, there he was.

'Who are you? What do you want?' she said, trying to sound confident but fear was spiralling in her stomach.

'Just give me the bag and I won't hurt you!' he demanded. Cara's usual instinct would be to jab him in the eye with her keys, but something unfamiliar took over. A feeling she had never felt before, over anything. A searing panic, but not for herself.

'Give me the bag, you stupid bitch!'

'Take the thing!' she said as she handed over the bag. She placed a hand over her tiny stomach.

'Nice one,' said the assailant, who turned and skipped off as if he'd just won the lottery. She rubbed her tummy and hunched over the car that she would now not be able to open – the idiot obviously hadn't linked the two together. She stood there for a full five minutes, unable to follow anything in her mind except an overwhelming surge of protection towards someone she had never met before – who might not even exist! The feeling had been very surprising, very unexpected and very, very alien.

She found a pay phone and called the police, all the while caressing her stomach gently while she tried to steady her nerves.

At that moment, Millie was attempting to stuff a bulky but small envelope into a postbox. Just one last push and it was in and quickly fell to the bottom. In contrast, she felt a rush of something swoosh out of her. At first, she wasn't sure what it was, but soon she recognized it as relief.

Relief that she *had* indeed changed for the better.

She wasn't that scared little girl any more, looking for someone to bail her out financially or, in this case *emotionally*. She'd just proved that, because she'd just returned Rik's watch without using it as an excuse to call him and beg him to come round and collect it, so that she could try and seduce him into taking her back. Nor had she written a ten-page love letter setting out why she was the perfect woman for him (she *had* done that to a guy once). She'd simply sent it alone and without words that didn't need to be expressed any more.

The final thing she did before heading back to the office was press DELETE on Stewart's number.

THIRTY-FOUR

Cara remembered how she'd felt during and after the mugging: all that had concerned her, consumed her, was the safety of her unborn child. That was all that had mattered and, for the first time in her entire life, she realized she might actually be capable of loving a child of her very own.

As it turned out, though, she wasn't pregnant just very late due to the stress of worry about Lena, working hard, and her relationship crisis with Ade. But something within her had shifted. That much she knew.

And then, all too quickly, it was Thursday evening.

'Millie's not here yet. Late as usual,' said Cara as Kitty approached the bed.

'Hey!' said Millie, five minutes later, planting a kiss on Kitty and Lena's cheek and blowing one across the room for Cara. Cara hadn't got to the stage of kissing Kitty on the cheek – and she might never, regardless of the outcome of this 'meeting'. There were so many questions she hoped would be answered today, and perhaps then she would at least be able to move on and into the next stage in her life with Ade. She'd had to beg him not to come over after she'd told him about the mugging. Cara knew that this meeting had to be over with before she could ever face him again. And for it to be over, it first had to start. She'd also decided not to tell Kitty and Millie about the mugging – for now. It wasn't important. She wasn't hurt and the credit cards had all been cancelled. What was important was what had occurred as a *result* of it.

So Kitty, Millie, Cara, and Lena were together in a hospital room and Cara was first to speak. 'Tell us why you married our father.'

A short pause. And then Kitty began. 'As you know, my father, your grandfather, was a great man, very respected in our village.'

'I remember you telling us that,' said Millie, taking hold of Lena's hand.

Kitty smiled. 'He used to sit me on his knees and tell me the wildest stories about his life. He was a brilliant man and so brave. So, I decided I wanted to marry a man just like my dad. But my mum on the other hand said she'd always wanted me to marry a "proper English gentleman", and that if she hadn't got knocked up with me, she would have done just that!'

Cara couldn't hide her shock.

'Don't be so surprised. That was one of the nicer things my mum said to me. That was just her way and I have no quarrel with her for that.'

Cara smoothed a hand over her short crop.

'I knew back then that I was going to be someone. Something special in my family. I would travel to London and become a huge star, an actress, and perhaps, along the way, meet a real English gentleman who would love me for ever and ever,' she said, looking at Lena.

'So what happened?' asked Cara.

'I became a mum.'

Anger began to rise in Cara and she stood up from beside the bed. 'It didn't take you long to blame us, did it?'

'Cara!' moaned Millie, as if this was all her fault.

She took a deep breath and decided it might be best to keep quiet. She had to keep it together. She knew she needed this from Kitty, in order to move on with Ade, and being all brusque and aggressive wasn't going to help.

'I don't blame you, Cara. Neither of you. Why would I do exactly what my mum did? Never would I ever do that. I never would.'

'So what's all this about not being able to fulfil your dreams. Isn't that typical Kitty rhetoric?'

'I said, I'm not blaming you!'

'So why has it always felt like you have!?!'

Kitty turned her gaze to Millie, who then looked sheepishly at Lena – grand confirmation that all three had felt the same way about their mother for years.

A single tear trickled from Kitty's left eye. 'I chose a man who I thought was like my dad. Donald Curtis: so strong, powerful and commanding. But he turned out to be an arsehole. Basically he left us to fend for ourselves the minute he caught the short hem of that cow, Glenda Martinique. She's been controlling him ever since.'

'You're not the first single mother,' observed Cara.

'But I'm not one of life's copers either. I'm not like you and Lena. Sorry, Millie, but Cara has my sense of style, no matter what she tells you, while you are burdened with the same in ability to cope that I had at your age. I just wasn't capable!' She grabbed Millie's hand. 'Sweetie, you understand, don't you? I've been through some things over the years, before you were even born, that have perhaps made me how I am today. At the same time, I found the whole motherhood thing a struggle. No one prepares you for a little baby coming into your world, and then another not far behind.

I just couldn't do it. I just couldn't. But your father was so persuasive; he said he wanted a big family. Anyway, I was a clumsy-enough Mum when Donald *was* around but, when he started to go on those long "business trips" to America, there was no way I could cope. And, to add to it, the bulk of my family were abroad or all off doing their own thing. They all thought I was coping, because I was always so loud and strong but really, inside . . . I was crumbling.'

Cara could relate to that.

'Is that why you couldn't wait to retire and move away?' asked Millie, still clutching Lena's hand as if for support.

'One of the reasons I left the day after I retired was that you girls all had your own lives to lead. You didn't need me hanging around you any more, and frankly I could do with being around my own siblings and my old friends. I really thought I was doing you girls a favour as well as myself. I truly had no intention of burdening you with a bitter and twisted old gal like me. Always looking in the mirror and thinking how my career could have been.'

'Caught up in yourself,' said Cara.

'I'm an actress, what do you expect?'

That raised a smile with Cara, and then the atmosphere seemed to lighten. They had definitely turned some type of tiny corner.

'Leaving the house with Lena, after remortgaging and taking the cash . . . I know it looks selfish – but I truly thought I was doing her a favour. I just didn't think it would have such an impact on her finances. If I'd known she was in financial difficulties . . . if only, if only, if only,' she sighed heavily.

And then it was Millie's turn to speak again. 'Are you happy?'

Kitty smiled warmly. 'Until Lena's accident, I was very happy for the first time in my life. I was travelling the world

241

and about to have my facelift. I was doing things I had only dreamt of while I was married to your father. So, yes, I really can say that I was happy, even if I had to be alone to realize it. Do you know, your father only ever told me he loved me once?'

'Really?' That was Cara.

'Yes. In front of the vicar marrying us. Donald was a selfish man. Never interested in my thoughts, feelings. I was just a nursemaid to you kids and a body for him to well, you know, take to the bed. We never shared anything except you girls, and at the time we never realized what a privilege that was.'

Cara was listening intently.

'Even without the talking and loving towards me, it was still a kick in the guts when I busted in and caught him in bed with Glenda Martinique.'

A collective gasp.

'They never met in America, they met *here*. They both moved there because it's where she's from. She insisted, apparently.'

And not to get as far away from us as possible, thought Millie and Cara simultaneously.

'And let me tell you this: I NEVER and I mean NEVER want any of my girls to feel the pain of seeing the man they love in bed with another woman. Besides, your father's behind is a sight no one ever needs to see!'

Nervous giggles.

'That's better, Cara.' Kitty placed her hands together in a praying pose. 'If I could go back in time, I would do things so differently from the way I did. I regret so much.'

'Like the way you were with us? Growing up, you were never around—'

'She was around, Cara,' cut in Millie.

'You know what I mean.'

'You're right. I wasn't the best. But, at the time, that *was*

242

my best. And yes, I do. I regret it all. Why do you think I take a walk around the hospital every day?'

'Your joints?' said Millie.

'The main reason was because looking at Lena reminds me of my failings, because she's there, just there, saying so much to me, even though she's asleep. There is no running away from what I have done when I'm in here with her. When it's just her and me. So, when I take those walks, I think about everything. Believe me.'

'So what would you change, if you did have the chance to go back?' Cara swallowed hard.

'For a start, I'd tell my girls that I love them every day, because I do.' She bravely took Cara's tiny hand as she held Millie's, who was still clutching onto Lena's.

Kitty squeezed her eyes, opening them to reveal more tears.

'Would you?' asked Cara, softly, still not sure what her answer would be.

'Yes, I would.'

They sat there, all four of them, holding hands.

'Strangely enough, today has been one of the happiest I can remember since arriving back here,' said Kitty, firmly.

'Thanks, Mum,' said Millie, as Cara attempted to absorb everything Kitty had said. But it was hard. Especially when the only thing she could focus on was the bit about Kitty telling her girls every day that she *loved them*.

She also accepted that, while this wouldn't be a tender *Little House on the Prairie* moment between mother and daughters, at least Kitty had gone some way to giving her the answers she had craved for an entire lifetime. But one last confirmation still remained.

'So, you . . . love us?'

'Of course, Cara! Always have; always will. I may not show it like those earth-mother types – that's just not my way. But that doesn't mean I'm incapable of love, does it?'

243

The moment seemed to stand still for Cara as she thought about what Kitty had just thrown into the pot, but then was punctuated by the arrival of Nurse Gratten, who had an urgent look etched on her face.

'We've found it!' she almost screeched, which was very unlike her. 'We have Lena's notebook.'

THIRTY-FIVE

They'd sat staring at the orange notebook for what seemed like ages. It was a window into Lena's thoughts and feelings, her upcoming plans and perhaps even her hopes and fears. Cara was the one who actually opened the orange notebook eventually. Just as they were about to peer at the words, there was a knock at the door.

'Hello,' said Lena's former lodger, Meg.

'Meg. It's nice to see you at last, but this isn't a good time,' said Millie.

'I know I haven't been in to see Lena before, I just needed to say something . . .' She looked uneasy, which was understandable for someone seeing Lena for the first time; trouble was, she hadn't even glanced at her yet. Perhaps that was understandable, too, but something was niggling away at Cara, especially when Meg held out her hands, revealing a most exquisite silver slipper sandal.

'Can we please go into the waiting room? There is something I need to explain. Its really, really important. Its about Lena.'

Inside the waiting room, Cara was shocked to see Justin

sitting down with his head bowed. He looked better than when she'd last seen him although, not surprisingly, the deep sadness in his eyes, remained.

'I needed to come here, because I needed to tell you this,' said Meg.

'Don't,' pleaded Justin.

'It was me,' continued Meg.

'What was you?' asked Millie.

'It was my shoe. This one.'

On closer inspection, the sandal was really nicely constructed. Sequins, beads, and a huge buckle at the side. And silver. Very good combinations indeed. Focus! Focus! This wasn't the time to indulge in her shoe fetishes. Cara knew something horrendous was unfolding before her eyes.

'It was me. I was sleeping with ... with JUSTIN!' Meg said, her voice breaking with tears as she placed the sandal onto the floor.

'You were sleeping with Justin? Lena's Justin?' Kitty said with disbelief.

'Yes! And there's more.'

'Go on,' urged Cara.

'She fell down the stairs after catching us—'

'Don't!' whined Justin.

'—in bed.'

'I don't believe this!' roared Cara, pacing the room as the truth started to dawn on her.

'Believe it. It all makes sense. It's why they never wanted to come in and see my daughter,' confirmed Kitty as Cara gave in to feelings of disgust.

Tears were now streaming down Meg's face. 'I'm so sorry,' she said, swiping the back of her hand across her crumpled face. Cara was tempted to give her a back-hander of her own, but decided it would be better to wait until there were no witnesses, or swift medical care.

Cara placed her head in her hands, then looked up. 'See, I can believe this, of him – the smug git – but you?' She giggled briefly. 'I always saw you as this quiet little mouse, head always in a book. The clever little student who hardly made any noise. More fool me.' She looked towards Meg with an evil expression, wondering if she should just sock her one anyway. For Lena.

Millie was feeling more confused than enraged.

At the beginning, she'd always seen Justin and Lena as well . . . perfect. The couple she wanted to emulate. They had the relationship she could only ever dream about: stable, solid, faithful. Men had never stuck around Millie for longer than breakfast, while Lena seemed quite capable of holding on to them long term. Even her boyfriend before Justin had lasted a good few years. Justin came along about six months after that had ended. Handsome, with a good job and attentive, he was always taking Lena out. She'd thought Lena was happy, until the relationship started to unravel before Millie's eyes, after Lena had gone to sleep. He hadn't showed up at her birthday dinner, had hardly ever visited the hospital and now they were all hearing about the cheating.

So, Justin and Meg had been responsible for Lena's fall and she, Cara, and Kitty would not be letting them get away with it, that was for sure. But at the same time, Millie wished she too could be angry about it. Instead, she was experiencing an immense sense of disappointment for Lena and aslo, perhaps, for herself – realizing that fairy tales are just that. All an illusion. Just for the books. The only good thing about being let down by all those men in the past was the hope that there did still exist a Prince Charming somewhere and she just hadn't met hers yet. But now Justin had cheated on Lena, and even Cara and Ade were in trouble.

Her thoughts were speared by a sigh from Kitty as she clutched the silver, glass-like slipper in her hands, looking at it as though it was toxic.

THIRTY-SIX

How am I going to do this? Well. . . .

1. Phone Kitty in America and tell (yes, tell Kitty) it's time to get new tenants in or sell house because I'm leaving to downsize! Won't be thrilled about it, but sod it! Have to think of self – just this once!

2. Fill out that form for university AND post off the application form – this time IMMEDIATELY. No more procrastinating year after year. IT IS finally going to happen (Oh and get more advice from Meg and Uni life!).

3. Leave Justin.

Go for it!
Now is the time!!!!
So it's official:
LENA CURTIS HAS FINALLY WOKEN UP!!

Nurse Gratten promised an enquiry as to why the notebook had been mislaid. If they wanted to take action, they could.

But who had the strength? At least they'd found it and had a chance to read some of Lena's thoughts, fears, and dreams. At first reading her most private thoughts had seemed distasteful and Cara had had to fight feelings of betrayal, certain Lena didn't need any more after Justin and Meg's bombshell; but, as they'd continued to read, she knew she had to continue to the very last thing Lena had written before slipping into her sleep.

The three of them sat in total silence around Lena's bed – as they always did, but this time with a lot of extra pain. The madness of the day had been way too much for them to absorb. Knowing Justin was having sex with someone else was one thing, but knowing Lena had witnessed it all, which had then led to her fall when she was tripped up by the sandal, had all been too much for Cara – and clearly for Kitty and Millie, too, who both looked drained with the turmoil of it all. But now that they realized that Lena had been on the verge of something great . . . that was unbearable.

Kitty allowed another tear to fall, and Cara did not hesitate to take her mother's hand and squeeze it gently but firmly. Sometimes, words just aren't needed.

After the emotional seesaw of the day, Cara headed back towards East Dulwich and to the person she needed to be with. She would tell him that she'd never wanted a child before because she had been so scared of making a crap job of it like Kitty and Donald had done; that she was much too selfish a person, just like them and, that no matter how hard she tried, she would be unable to love her child, just like Kitty.

And just how wrong she'd been not to give herself a chance to consider all these things to be false.

Ade was in the middle of explaining something mildly complicated to Eliza when Cara walked up to the bar and said,

'The service here is RUBBISH! Can I have some service, please?'

'Cara?' said Ade, looking very handsome and a little surprised to see her. She dismissed Eliza with a wave and leaned over the bar, beckoning him to her.

She sighed. 'Am I going to get some service, or do I have to go to that nicer bar in West Dulwich with bigger chandeliers?'

Ade decided to play along. 'We can't have that now, madam, can we? What can I get you?' His smile was beautiful, cosy, familiar, and inviting. How she wanted to feel his arms around her and how she wanted to feel his breath on her neck as she sank her body into his.

'How about . . . a kiss?' she asked.

He leaned in close and she thought her heart would catch in her mouth.

'How about a hug?' he whispered. And she smiled. And she waited as he (never one to leap over a bar) walked around to the other side of the bar and reached out to her.

'Feel like a change? Want to help others? How about applying to become a PSO volunteer? Earn your salary while helping others. Read more . . .'

And there it was. A piece of paper stuck onto the staff noticeboard. Apparently it allowed workers to become one of the company's many volunteers overseas, helping communities build and grow while earning their London salary. This way Millie could see a bit of the world and still earn enough to help pay off Lena's debts. She scanned the paper again, allowing soft bubbles to bounce about in her tummy. She would do it. She *could* do it. She wanted this. She needed this. It was too good to be true. She wanted her life to *mean* something.

Her phone signalled a text message. From Deana. 'Tings

goin' gud. Fosta peeps ok. Can't make hospital 2day. Skool work 2 do. DT'

Millie hoped that meant things were moving in the right direction for Deana. She'd felt obliged and certain about keeping in touch with her. For Lena, for Deana, and for herself.

She stared at the paper again and marvelled at how 'too good to be true' it all was, and then noticed the small print – you needed to have been employed by the company for at least a year.

The sky was bright for early December. And it seemed strangely appropriate that he would be doing this at such a time. Ready to start the following year off with a fresh new perspective, new goals, and *without* Lena Curtis – the girl with the beautiful green eyes. The girl who had changed his life forever and to whom he knew he would be eternally grateful.

He nodded to Nurse Gratten as he placed his hand on the door to Lena's room, knowing this would be the very last time.

There she was, lying in the bed as usual, perhaps oblivious to the world around her and what had been going on over the last three months. Or perhaps not. He switched on the CD player and pressed REPEAT for the only song he wanted to hear at that precise moment. 'Their song'.

'Why Don't We Fall in Love?'

He turned the volume down low, sat down and gazed at her.

A sleeping beauty.

His dream girl.

He kissed the top of his right hand, then placed it on her forehead.

Their first kiss.

'Before I met you, Lena, I was asleep in my own life.

Meeting you has been one of the best things that's ever happened to me. You literally, and without doubt, saved my life. Because of you I started to look at each day as if it was something new, fresh, and exciting – something I wanted to experience and not just *tolerate*. I'll always be thankful to you for that, my sleeping angel, and I'll never regret meeting you on the bus all those months ago. I just wish, well, you know what I wish.'

'There's just so much that I know about you now, that I love about you. For a start . . .' He moved in closer and whispered.

'I love it that you wear clothes that don't match. I love it that you cried for a week after you saw a dying bird over in Dulwich Park. I love the fact you enjoy marmalade on white bread. I love it that you would do anything for anyone without expecting anything in return. I love the fact you want it to rain only so you can wear your daisy-patterned lilac wellies. I love it that you don't mind going to the cinema on your own. I love the fact that you care about people.'

Nurse Gratten interrupted the moment. 'You okay there, Michael?'

'Yes, Nurse Gratten. I'm okay . . . I'm just saying goodbye.'

She made an 'oops' face then headed out of the door again. Michael turned back to Lena and clutched her hand, tightly. 'I hope you get out of this. I really do and, well, if you want to find me, then don't hesitate. Cara has my details.' He looked around the room, as if for a hidden camera, and whispered, 'We could perhaps go out for a drink together? Dinner? Catch a movie. Go to a concert. Maybe that Amerie girl might be in town. I like her music and have bought all of her albums now, thanks to you.' Michael swallowed hard and dispensed with the whispering. 'Oh, Lena, I'd do anything to make sure your eyes continue to shine. Every day. Forever.'

He gazed at Lena for what seemed like the longest time,

253

desperate to drink in all of her and retain her in his memory, because soon he'd have to leave and go back to the life he now adored, cherished, and was just so excited about. The song sprang into action again, silky tones filling the room. In another life, the words so very apt. He took a deep breath and a newsreel of the last three months filled his head as he smiled. It had all began with that one meeting on the bus, when, he'd felt a need to protect this stunning girl with the bad singing voice. Charlotte had once remarked that he was a 'rescuer' and maybe if he looked back at his past relationships, that was the role that had been assigned to him. Ironically though, Lena had ended up rescuing *him*.

But now it was time to move on, he thought as he attempted to remove his hand from hers, while at the same time not wanting to. But, strangely, that need wasn't what prevented him from doing so.

Lena was moving.

Eyebrows twitching, eyelids slightly shaking, a definite grip to her hand.

His heart caught in his mouth and he could hardly say her name. 'Le-Lena?' He didn't want to move. Couldn't move. Was he imagining this movement? Was this actually real? Was it some type of reflex? Was he wishful *dreaming*?

'Lena? Please, is that you? Can you hear me?'

She moved again. Her eyes . . .

Millie, Kitty, and Cara returned from the Fen Lane Hospital canteen with a full heart as well as full stomachs. There'd be no group hugs as of yet, but they were working on it. And, having lunch together without bad feeling or sarky comments and with a genuinely open outlook was something Millie had relished. They had made a start.

Millie pushed open the door to the room, and saw the top of Lena's bed obscured by Michael's frame, Nurse Gratten, and a couple of doctors. Her heart sank as she wondered if Lena had taken a turn for the worse.

'Michael, what is it?' *Please, no.*

He didn't answer, but merely stood up and gazed at her with this silly grin on his face.

Must be okay, then.

The grin got wider as he seemed to cry out in abandon, 'She's back!'

Millie's mind didn't dare decipher this as meaning anything more than the return of, say, Nurse Gratten, or something just as uninteresting. But the wail from behind caused her to turn back just in time to see Kitty, hand on chest, warble, 'Oh dear God!' as Cara became catatonic.

'Mum!' cried Millie as she tended to Kitty, and as Cara made a noise, a kind of shrill moan she had never heard from her sister's mouth before and a sound she would never, ever forget.

Nurse Gratten was now surrounded by more doctors around the bed, some Millie had never seen before, but in all the chaos all she could really focus on was the image of Lena, on the bed, green eyes sparkling and lighting up the room like priceless crystals.

Her sister was back.

EPILOGUE

I wasn't ready to look at my world through the eyes of an infant. Looking into the faces of those gathered around my bed and wondering where I was and how I'd got there. But that wasn't the case. I was lucky, blessed, honoured that that wasn't to be my story. As every face, every memory – every part of me quickly began to form into coherent and familiar shapes that represented my life before I'd gone to sleep.

I was back.

Lena Curtis.

My first words were 'Ginger beer' as opposed to 'Dada', and I didn't instantly recognize the total HOTTIE sitting beside me, either. He was holding my hand and talking as I tried to focus. He felt familiar and warm and something deep inside of me felt wholly connected to him.

It was as if I'd known him my entire life.

As the pandemonium around me developed, I was able to zone out and feel myself smile at what was happening. You see, not everyone gets the chance to be 'reborn', to start over and to have that opportunity to do things differently. And, looking around me, it seemed I wouldn't be the only one.

But as for me, I couldn't wait to have another go at living.

I mean, really living.

Because for so long I had been drifting along in a life that in so many ways was unsatisfactory to *me*. Like a flat glass of ginger beer. Like an out of date Toblerone. You get my drift.

I've never had dreams that could be considered massive in other people's eyes. I never wanted to be a singer, an actress, to climb Mount Everest, and I'd never had thoughts of changing the world – I simply wanted to help children. And while I was doing that day-to-day, it was only to a level that still allowed me to feel unfulfilled. I admit it was easy to allow others to virtually keep me under a pillow and keep pressing down. They were suffocating me, not letting me out. But the person who kept me down the most?

Well, that had to be *me*. Always ready with the excuses, the practical reasons, the fear; basically, I was content to keep on *dreaming* about it and not actually *do* it. I kept thinking I had all the time in the world to get my bum in gear.

So here I am with that second chance, and I'm going to run, run, run with it!

SIX MONTHS LATER

Kindness of a Stranger Saves Sleeping Beauty
Her Magazine, June Edition

In part two of our 'Fairytale Endings' series, we take a look at 30 year old Lena Curtis who made headlines last year after emerging from a three month deep sleep.

Lena lapsed into unconsciousness after tripping over a glass slipper at the home of her now ex-boyfriend. As she lay in her hospital bed, her family kept a daily vigil.

However, one day, Michael Johns, 31, who had met her for the first time just weeks before, by chance, on a bus, actually showed up in her hospital room! He visited Lena several times a week, building up close friendships with her Mother Kitty, 65, and sisters Cara, 29, and Millie, 24 and joined them in their regular vigil at Lena's hospital bedside. He was willing her to wake up.

Doctors are hailing her recovery as nothing short of a miracle.

Awake for six months now, Lena's piercing green eyes light up as she speaks. 'I came out of the sleep pretty much the same person, but it was my family who had changed the most. My sisters and my mother. I still can't believe it!'

And not forgetting Michael.

'It was amazing,' says Lena as she clutches Michael's hand. I woke up and there he was, just sitting there, holding my hand and mumbling stuff!'

'I told her I loved her, straight away,' says Michael with a kiss on her forehead.

'It was like a fairy tale. A moment that I'll never, ever forget,' says Lena.

Indeed, Michael, her prince, agrees. 'It was amazing. She's amazing, really. Even though we'd only met once, I was able to find out over the course of those months that Lena is one of the strongest, most caring, most beautiful women I have ever met.'

Asked what the future held for her, Lena replies, 'Anything I am willing to work at. "Maybe", "perhaps" and "can't" will not be part of my vocabulary any more. I've been accepted into university, I'm happy. My sisters are doing well. Millie's off to help out at a community project in Peru next year; Cara's doing brilliantly, and Mum's a joy. Life's about living and I'm really enjoying my journey, really I am. I just can't explain how positive I'm feeling right now. You couldn't make this up!'

Indeed, this story does almost resemble a popular tale from the past. The glass slipper; two (not ugly at all) sisters; a wicked (in a nice way) mother; and Lena Rose Curtis who, having fallen asleep, awoke in the arms of her prince. It did indeed end like a fairy tale for them . . .

The End

The Love of Her Life

Harriet Evans

'Where's all the passion, romance and comedy we love gone?
Enter Harriet Evans and not before time'   *Heat*

Kate Miller is no longer the geeky teenager who preferred curling up with an ancient copy of *Little Women* and pouring over
vintage issues of *Vogue* to going out and getting drunk. Now she
not only has her dream job – working for a glossy magazine, but
a gorgeous fiancée to match.

Then one day, it all falls apart – spectacularly, painfully and
forever.

Ever since, Kate has hidden in New York. But when her father
becomes ill, she has to come home and face everything she left
behind including her friends – Zoe, Francesca and Mac – the
friends who are bound with her forever, as a result of one day
when life changed for all of them.

Like every woman, Kate often thought she'd never meet the love
of her life. But she did – and now she's back, he can't stand to
be in the same room as her. What really happened before Kate
left London? And can she pick up the pieces and allow herself
to love her own life again?

'A lovely, funny heart-warmer…Evans' heightened comic style
and loveable characters make it effortlessly readable'
                                                    Marie Claire

ISBN: 978 0 00 724382 2

A Place Called Here

Cecelia Ahern

Published in June 2007

Since Sandy Shortt's childhood classmate disappeared twenty years ago, Sandy's been obsessed with missing things. Finding becomes her goal – whether it's the sock that vanished in the washing, the car keys she misplaced or the graver issue of finding the people who vanish from their lives. Sandy dedicates her life to finding these missing people, offering devastated families a flicker of hope.

Jack Ruttle is one of those desperate people. It's been a year since his brother Donal vanished into thin air. Thinking Sandy Shortt could well be the answer to his prayers, he embarks on a quest to find her.

But when Sandy goes missing too, she stumbles upon the place – and people – she's been looking for all her life. A world away from her loved ones and the home she ran from for so long. Sandy soon resorts to her old habit again – searching. Though this time, she is desperately trying to find her way home…

Praise for Cecelia Ahern:

'Brilliantly written, you'll laugh and cry.' *Heat*

'Guaranteed to tug on your heartstrings.' *Glamour*

'A heart warming, completely absorbing tale of love and friend-ship.' *Company*

ISBN: 978-0-00-719891-7

What's next?

Tell us the name of an author you love

| Lola Jaye | Go ▶ |

and we'll find your next great book.